Seeing The Life

Sophie Dawson

May your life be a story in faithful living.

Scripture verses used are from the NET.

This is a work of fiction. Names, characters, businesses, places, events and incidents are either the products of the author's imagination or used in a fictitious manner. Any resemblance to actual persons, living or dead, or actual events is purely coincidental.

Copyright © 2014 Sophie Dawson
All rights reserved.
ISBN-13: 978-0-9912293-6-9

This work is dedicated to Pastor Cajun Pauley, whose chronology of the life of Yeshua the Messiah I used and whose teaching and leadership I have followed for many years.

It is also dedicated to Pastor George McVey who has helped me with my writing since the beginning and who has become like a brother to me.

Books By Sophie Dawson

Cottonwood Series
Healing Love
Lord's Love
Giving Love
Redeeming Love (With George McVey)

Stones Creek Series
Leah's Peace
Chasing Norie

Seeing The Life

A Growing Collection

Author's Notes

This is, of course, a fictional work based on the life of Jesus the Christ. I have kept faithful to the Scriptures as much as possible. Events, people and relationships which are not recorded in the Bible. I hope these portray Jesus in a way consistent with his message.

I have chosen to use the Yeshua, Hebrew name for Jesus, for several reasons. Jesus is the Greek transliteration for Yeshua. Since the Jews knew the Messiah or a prophet would be born that year many baby boys were named Yeshua.

Much research was done to portray life in ancient Israel in as authentic a manner as possible. I am not a scholar of ancient times. I am a fiction writer. I hope you will forgive any errors.

The family of Joseph and Mary we know from Scripture contained other children. Yeshua's brothers were James, Joses, Simon, and Judas. There were also sisters. No names or the number of sisters is mentioned other than as plural. I have chosen to have three girls live through childhood.

As with Yeshua, because of the people with the same name, I've chosen to use the Hebrew transliteration spellings for the siblings where needed.

James - Ya'aqov
Elizabeth - Elisabet
Simon - Shim'on
Judas - Yehuda
Hannah - Channah

Joses and Deborah are spelled the same in Hebrew transliteration.

The Hebrew transliteration of Mary is Miriam. I am using Miriam in place of Miriam to avoid confusion.

I have chosen to portray Joseph of Arimethea as a man in his early thirties when he comes to Bethlehem. My research revealed contradictions concerning his birth year, death year, and age at death in my research. This allowed me to set his age wherever I wanted.

The chronology of Yeshua's life used was compiled by Pastor Cajun Pauley. You can find this at http://www.themasterslife.com/

Hebrew Words

Tanakh - The complete Jewish Bible
Torah - Genesis, Exodus, Leviticus, Numbers, and Deuteronomy
Pesach - Passover
Shabbat - Sabbath
Sukkot - Feast of the tabernacles, 15 days after Yom Kippur
Hannukkah - The Festival of Lights

Abba - Daddy
Ima - Mommy
Sabba - Grandfather
Softa - Grandmother
Doda - Aunt
Dod - Uncle
Shushan Gate - Eastern or Golden Gate
Sea of Kinneret - Sea of Galilee

<u>Names of God</u>
Adonai - Lord
Adonai Adonim - Lord of lords
Adonai Eloheikhem - the Lord your God
Adonai Elohai - the Lord my God
Attiq Yomin - Ancient One
Ehyeh asher Ehyeh - I will be because I will be
El De'a - God of Knowledge
El Gadol Gibor Yare - Great, Mighty, Awesome God
El Roi - God who sees
El Selich'ah - God of Forgiveness

Sophie Dawson

El Shaddai - God Almighty
El Shamayim - God of the Heavens
Elah Shemaya - God of Heaven
El-Elyon - God Most High
Elohay Elohim - God of gods
Elohay Mishpat - God of Justice
Elohim - GodRuach Ha-Melitz - Spirit of Comfort
HaShem - the Name
Melek Kabodh - King of Glory
Ruach HaKodesh - Spirit of God
Yahweh - LORD
Yahweh Tzidkenu - God our Righteousness
Yahweh Yerushalem - God of Jerusalem
Yahweh Yireh - God will provide
Yahweh Yisrael - God of Israel

Old Testament Verses Use Within Text

Isaiah 7:14
Therefore the Lord himself will give you a sign. Behold, the virgin will conceive, and bear a son, and shall call his name Immanuel.

Luke 2:14
Glory to God in the highest, and on Earth peace for those with whom God is pleased.

Micah 5:2
You Bethlehem, land of Judah, Are in no way least among the princes of Judah: For out of you shall come forth a governor, Who shall shepherd my people, Israel.
*Many versions use Bethlehem Ephrathah rather than You Bethlehem, land of Judah.

Jeremiah 31:15
A voice was heard in Ramah, a lament with bitter weeping—Rachel weeping for her children, refusing to be comforted for her children because they are no more.

2 Samuel 12:23
But now that he is dead, why should I fast? Can I bring him back again? I'll go to him, but he will never return to me.

Jeremiah 29:11
I have plans for him. Plans for his welfare, for his good, for his future.

Micah 4:12

But they do not know what YHWH is planning; they do not understand his strategy.

Genesis 1:31-2:3
And the evening and the morning were the sixth day. Thus the heavens and the earth were finished, and all the host of them. And on the seventh day Yahweh ended his work which he had made; and he rested on the seventh day from all his work which he had made. And Yahweh blessed the seventh day, and sanctified it: because that in it he had rested from all his work which Yahweh created and made.

Exodus 20:4
You shall not make any graven image to worship.

Isaiah 11:1-5
A shoot will grow out of Jesse's root stock,
a bud will sprout from his roots.
 The Lord's spirit will rest on him —
a spirit that gives extraordinary wisdom,
a spirit that provides the ability to execute plans,
a spirit that produces absolute loyalty to the Lord.
 He will take delight in obeying the Lord.
He will not judge by mere appearances,
or make decisions on the basis of hearsay.
 He will treat the poor fairly,
and make right decisions for the downtrodden of the earth.
He will strike the earth with the rod of his mouth,
and order the wicked to be executed.
 Justice will be like a belt around his waist,
integrity will be like a belt around his hips.

Seeing The Life

Psalm 138:6
Though the LORD is exalted, he takes note of the humble, and recognizes the proud from far away.

Daniel 10:12
From the first day that you purposed to understand and to humble yourself before your Adonai, your prayers were heard.

Deut. 9:6
You are a stubborn and stiff-necked people
There are many verses in the Old Testament in which Hashem uses this phrase. Not only did it characterize the Israelites in ancient times, but it often describes us today.

Isaiah 1:11-14
What are the multitude of your sacrifices to me? says Yahweh.
I have had enough of the burnt offerings of rams,
And the fat of fed animals.
I don't delight in the blood of bulls,
Or of lambs,
Or of male goats.
When you come to appear before me,
Who has required this at your hand, to trample my courts?
Bring no more vain offerings.
Incense is an abomination to me;
New moons, Sabbaths, and convocations:
I can't bear with evil assemblies.
My soul hates your New Moons and your appointed feasts;
They are a burden to me.
I am weary of bearing them.

Sophie Dawson

Hosea 11:1
When Israel was a young man, I loved him like a son, and I summoned my son out of Egypt.

Judges 13:5
You will conceive a son and he will be called a Nazarene.

Isaiah 9:1
Galilee of the Gentiles who are in the darkness will see a great light.

Psalm 94:14-16
Certainly Yahweh does not forsake his people; he does not abandon the nation that belongs to him. For justice will prevail, and all the morally upright will be vindicated. Who will rise up to defend me against the wicked? Who will stand up for me against the evildoers?

Isaiah 41:10
Do not fear, for I am with you; do not be afraid, for I am your God. I will strengthen you; I will help you; I will hold on to you with My righteous right hand.

Deuteronomy 6:5
Love the Lord your God with all your heart, all your soul, all your strength, and all your mind.

Leviticus 19:18
Love your neighbor as yourself.

Psalm 37:31
The law of their God controls their thinking; their feet do not slip.

Seeing The Life

Psalm 119:11
In my heart I store up your words, so I might not sin against you.

Psalm 119:118
You despise all who stray from your statutes, for they are deceptive and unreliable.

Psalm 40:8
I want to do what pleases you, my God. Your law dominates my thoughts.

Zechariah 9:9
Tell the people of Israel, Don't be afraid, people of Jerusalem. Look, your King is coming to you. He is humble, riding on a donkey—riding on a donkey's colt

Psalm 34:20
He protects all his bones; not one of them is broken.

Psalm 14:3
Everyone rejects God; they are all morally corrupt. None of them does what is right, not even one!

Isaiah 55:9
For as heaven is higher than earth, so My ways are higher than your ways, and My thoughts than your thoughts.

Job 38:4
Where were you when I laid the foundation of the earth?'

Chapter 1

"Dassa, Dassa," Miriam called as she entered the back door of the inn, which led to the kitchen and general workroom.

Dassa looked up from her chore of chopping leeks for stew. "Yes, Ima?"

"I need you to go fetch Midwife Tabitha. The couple your abba put in the stable... The woman is in labor. She's in the early stages, but I think you should leave now before it gets any later. Too many strangers in Bethlehem to delay."

"Yes, Ima." Dassa scooped up the chopped leeks and tossed them into the stew pot. She dipped her hands in water for a rinse and went to grab her cloak hanging by the door.

"Take your abba's. The darker color will hide you better. Keep to the shadows. Go straight to her house and back. The darkness conceals those who seek to do evil."

With a nod, Dassa covered her face with her veil, drew her father's black cloak around her, and slipped into the night. She hurried down the narrow alley to the not-much-wider street. A dog sniffing through a pile of rotting garbage growled at her as she passed as far from him as the meager roadway would allow.

Dassa scanned both directions. She did not want to be seen by Roman guards or any others who may be out at night. As a young woman alone, there was great danger. Her eyebrows knotted in confused thought. Something wasn't right. Not seeing anyone, she turned down the street, rushing past the buildings that housed both businesses and homes. Few lights glowed in the windows and on rooftops.

The evening had progressed into night. The inn, during this busy time, stayed active long after the rest of Bethlehem slept. Those who had come to town for the census register seemed to stay up eating and drinking until the last watches before dawn. Then they complained if the noises of a busy day interrupted their sleep.

Dassa didn't think highly of most of the travelers. They were a loud, demanding group as a whole. Sometimes one or two would be polite but... Dassa just tried to avoid them as much as possible. This posed challenges, as some slept in the inn's main room. It was a small inn. Nestled deep within the town, it had a reputation of good food, decent wine, adequate beds, and a fair price. The inn had become a regular spot along the route for a goodly number of traveling merchants. Its lack of a courtyard and only a tiny stable tended to keep the Romans away.

By now Dassa had walked several blocks from the inn. Nervously she slipped into a dark doorway. Something was different. She tried to figure out what. The brightness of the night. It was more luminesce than it should be. The glow quivered, almost like the flame of an oil lamp. No, that wasn't quiet right. She didn't have the proper word. She gazed at the wall across from her. There seemed to be a light that shone separately from the moonlight. She tilted her head back, seeing neither the moon nor whatever created this strange glimmer.

She moved out of the doorway, hurrying faster. The unusual illumination was making her not only nervous but also afraid. The shadows were odd. They seemed to be almost doubled. She wanted to get to the midwife's house and back home as fast as possible.

Dassa stepped out of the narrow street into the town square. She walked quickly. As she passed the well, Dassa looked up. More of the sky was visible. She stopped and stared.

The moon, nearly full, shone brightly. This was not what held her attention, though. A star, brighter than any other, pulsed with a luminosity Dassa had never seen before. There was a strange shifting of the shadows, which seemed as if they were being chased away by the starlight.

A dog's bark and hobnailed shoes sounding on the cobbled street brought her focus back to her errand. Dassa ran across the square into the shadows on the other side. If a soldier found her, she would never be home again. She paused, listening. The clank of the soldiers' boots faded. With a silent release of the breath she'd been holding, Dassa left the sheltering darkness and slipped around the corner. Only two more streets to cross.

Arriving at the midwife's house, Dassa pressed herself into the doorway. The position of the door let the moonlight and the strange starlight illuminate where she stood. Dassa felt as if the moonlight and star's glow outlined her against the wood. She knocked quietly, afraid the sound might carry and alert the guards, hoping someone in the house would hear.

"Who comes in the night?" a male voice called.

"Dassa Bat Eli. We have need of Midwife Tabitha. A guest is in labor."

The door opened and the man's hand reached out and grabbed her arm, pulling Dassa inside.

"What was your father thinking sending you out on this errand? He should have come." Tabitha's husband, David, frowned at her.

"He could not. We are full to overflowing. The couple having the baby are in the stable. It was the only place with some privacy."

Tabitha came from the back room with a bundle containing what she needed. "Stop scolding the girl, David. She just did as she was told." Tabitha patted Dassa on the cheek, a loving grin on her face. "Praise Yahweh for getting you here safely. David, come, escort us to the inn, please."

"Why is it that babies always choose the middle of the night to be born?" David grumbled as he wrapped his wife in her cloak and grabbed his own.

Dassa and Tabitha entered the stable behind the inn. David had gone to the main building saying he would let Miriam and Eli know she was safely home. The journey back had gone faster; they didn't have to keep to the shadows since David was with them. They still kept to the lesser traveled streets and alleys, not wanting to meet any Roman guards. Both the midwife and her husband had commented on the strangeness of the light from the sky. The star, brighter than before, chased more of the shadows away.

"Joseph," Dassa whispered from the dark entryway, "I've brought Midwife Tabitha."

"Praise Yahweh. Will you help my wife? She is young, and we are both scared." Joseph's fear was palpable.

"Peace, Joseph. I'll do what I can. Yahweh Yireh is the one who brings forth the miracle," Tabitha said, approaching the young woman lying on clean straw in an empty stall. "I am Midwife Tabitha. Your husband is very nervous. He did not tell me your name." She shot Joseph an amused glance. He smiled sheepishly.

"I am Mary." As she said the words, a contraction rippled down her body, causing the mother to stiffen in pain.

Tabitha counted until the contraction ended. Kneeling beside Mary, she asked questions. Some the girl answered, others brought confused looks to the faces of the young couple. "Dassa, please get me some water. I have most of what else I need."

"Yes, ma'am." Dassa left the stable again, noticing the starlight shining brighter still. It seemed to pulse like the beat of a heart. Hurrying to the kitchen, she gathered several water bags. Her mother came from the front room and kissed her cheek.

"How is the young ima?" Miriam asked.

"Scared. So is her husband. I'm to bring water."

"You stay near Tabitha. She may need you to get things that are normally in the house. The stable isn't where I'd want to give birth, but it's the best we could offer."

"Yes, ma'am. Ima, have you seen the star that's shining so brightly?" Dassa put the straps of the bags over her shoulders and picked up a large bowl.

"Earlier. Is it still shining?" Miriam stirred the kettle and ladled out the stew into bowls.

"Even brighter. If you can spare a moment, come and look." Dassa held the door open as she and her mother stepped outside. Miriam's mouth dropped open. The moon appeared pale in comparison.

"Oh my, I have never seen anything like it." The women stared up at the sky as light from the single star eclipsed all others.

"I must get back to Tabitha," Dassa said, leaving her mother wide-eyed with wonder.

As she entered the stable, Tabitha and Joseph stood near the entrance talking quietly. Tabitha kept looking at Mary resting in the straw.

"It is not possible, I tell you. I have never encountered this in all my years as a midwife."

"It is so. The angel said she would bear a child as a virgin, and so she is." Joseph's face was serene.

"But how?" Tabitha asked.

Seeing The Life

"By the power of the Most High and the Holy Spirit. An angel came to Mary and told her. When I found out about her pregnancy, I was going to divorce her, but the angel assured me to marry her."

Dassa stood quietly listening. The words of the prophet Isaiah spoke in her mind: *Therefore the Lord himself will give you a sign. Behold, the virgin will conceive, and bear a son, and shall call his name Immanuel.* Her betrothed, Micah, had read them to her just last week. Immanuel, God with us. Was this the sign? Was the prophecy being fulfilled? Here in their stable? How could that be possible? The Messiah was to be a king. He was to free their people. Kings weren't born in cattle stalls.

"Dassa, Dassa." Tabitha's stern call brought her back to the present. Her questions would have to wait until Micah came. "Bring me the water and then go get your mother. Hurry, there's no time to lose."

As she approached the stall where Tabitha now stood waiting, she slipped the bags off her shoulders. Dassa looked at Mary's sweat-drenched face. She held onto Joseph's hand as another contraction pressed down. Dassa handed the bowl and bags to Tabitha and ran back to the kitchen.

"Ima, Ima, Tabitha needs you, come quickly," Dassa said as she found her setting more bowls of stew before hungry men and women in the front room of the inn.

"Coming."

Dassa saw her mother's lips move in prayer as she threaded her way through the crowd. "Is something wrong?"

"I am not sure." Dassa kept silent until they had left the house. "Tabitha and Joseph, Mary's husband, were talking when I came in. They were saying something about Mary being a virgin."

"Impossible," Miriam scoffed.

"It is in Isaiah: *Therefore the Lord himself will give you a sign. Behold, the virgin will conceive, and bear a son, and shall call his name Immanuel.*"

In silence they entered the stable. Tabitha signaled them to come near.

"You must check this girl, Miriam. See if you find the same as I."

"So what Dassa heard you say is true?" Miriam's jaw dropped in shock.

"You examine her. Dassa, you pay attention. I want you to check her too. Are there any women in the inn who could also be a witness? We must hurry. It will tear soon."

Dassa watched as her mother checked the girl. Mary's embarrassment was evident. She turned her face into Joseph's hand, which she gripped.

Miriam sat back on her heals. "*And a virgin shall conceive...* I'll go get some of the wives and Abigail. She and Micah arrived a short while ago to help." Quickly rising, she nearly ran from the stable.

"Dassa, now I want you to check." Tabitha instructed as to how to proceed and what she should feel for. Dassa went red with embarrassment. She looked at Tabitha, who nodded.

Slowly Dassa knelt between Mary's knees and did as Tabitha had said. She found the bit of tissue proclaiming

Mary's virginity. Dassa pulled her hand away and stared at the pregnant young woman. She was about the same age as Dassa. God with us. This woman was giving birth to the Son of God right now, in their stable.

Chapter 2

"I was so nervous, Micah. To be asked to do something like that to a stranger. How embarrassed Mary must be." Dassa was slicing cheese in the kitchen. After she and Micah's sister had confirmed the virginity of the young mother to be, Dassa had been sent from the small mud hut that served as the stable for the family. Travelers needed to leave their donkeys and horses at a public stable.

"You truly think this baby is the one of the prophecies?" Micah snatched one of the slices of cheese and was rewarded with a light slap on the hand and a teasingly stern look from his betrothed. He was leaning against the wall near where Dassa worked.

"You are the expert in the Tanahk. You tell me. Just last week you read from Isaiah that the virgin will bear a son..."

"I know, but now? Here?"

"Where is it said He is to be born?"

Micah thought for just a second. "Bethlehem."

Dassa looked at him. "A virgin giving birth in Bethlehem."

"I'll think it more likely if the baby is a boy. Maybe the entire thing is just a made-up story to get people stirred up against the Romans. Lots of people know the Messiah is to be born here." Micah filched another piece of cheese.

"Are you hungry?" Dassa asked. Micah filched another piece of cheese, and Dassa slapped his hand, harder this time. "Are you hungry?" she asked. "I'll serve you a bowl of stew if you are."

Micah grinned. "I like annoying you in little ways. You're so cute when you're angry." He leaned forward and kissed her on the nose. "Yes, I am hungry and your stew smells wonderful."

"Now you're trying to get on my good side with compliments." Dassa took a bowl from the freshly cleaned stack and ladled the rich stew into it.

"Is it working?" Micah looked at her with innocence pasted on his face.

She laughed. "No, you fool. Here, eat this. Maybe I can get this cheese sliced and out to the men who will pay for it."

Dassa handed the bowl and bread to Micah, who bowed his head, thanking God for the food as she placed the last slices of cheese on the platter. The common room was crowded with men and the few women still awake when she carried the platter to the group of men who had ordered it.

"Hey there, sweet thing. How about you and me finding a corner?" A man with oily hair and foul breath grabbed Dassa by the arm.

She jerked her arm away and scurried back to the kitchen. "I'm not going out there again. I don't care if they are paying customers. I don't want to be pawed one more time."

"Someone touched you?" Micah stood swiftly, looking at the doorway Dassa had come through.

"I'm fine. He's drunk and I got away." Dassa was shaken but didn't want Micah to know. Every time she had ventured into the common room that evening, some man approached her, some more subtly than others. "I can't wait until we're married. I've never liked serving in there. I get so nervous."

Micah wrapped his arms around her. "It won't be much longer. I've almost gotten the house complete. If there had been room at my father's house, we would already be married."

"I know. That's part of being a younger son. No room for the bride." Dassa laid her head on Micah's chest. Sounds coming from outside the building caused them to jump apart, blushing.

Miriam came in through the back door. "Well, the baby's been born and the mother is doing well. Tabitha should be in soon and will be hungry I'm sure. So will the new father and mother." Miriam began laying bowls and bread on a tray.

"Well, what did she have?" Dassa asked.

"A beautiful boy. He started crying as soon as his mouth and nose were wiped out. Healthy and strong."

Dassa's hand shook as she fumbled to find Micah's. His was trembling slightly too. "The Son of God," she whispered.

"Ima Miriam," Micah said. "Let us carry those out to the stable for you. I'm sure you would like to sit for a moment."

Just then Dassa's father, Eli, came into the kitchen. "I'm locking the door. No one else can fit even for a bite to eat. Miriam, has the young woman had her baby yet?"

As her mother explained about the birth, Dassa and Micah filled a bowl on the tray with stew. A loaf of bread and two cups were added as Micah picked it up to carry. Dassa grabbed another bag of watered wine and opened the door, holding it for her fiancé as he went through. They passed Tabitha, who was heading to the kitchen as they went to the stable.

The stable was dark with only one oil lamp burning in the stall where Mary lay. Joseph sat near, stroking the fuzz-covered head of the swaddled infant.

"Here is some stew, bread, and wine. I'm sure you are hungry." Micah set the tray on the floor.

After helping Mary into a sitting position, Joseph looked around for a place to put the infant. Dassa was pouring wine into the cups Micah held. Mary got on her knees and spread a small blanket into the feeding trough.

"It's just the right size for him. Lay him here, Joseph." Carefully the baby was placed in the manger and the blanket wrapped over him.

"I wish we had something besides a feed trough," Dassa said. "It's not right he should sleep there."

"I'm just thankful God provided this for him," Mary said, smiling at her sleeping son.

The young parents ate in silence while Dassa and Micah settled against the gate. Micah placed his arm around Dassa's shoulder.

"You two betrothed?" Joseph asked, grinning.

"Yes. I'm trying to get my house finished so we can marry."

"Do you need help? I'm a carpenter." Joseph dipped a piece of bread into the stew then ate it.

"I could use some help. I am not a carpenter." Micah smiled. "Also, I need a scribe box made. I'm a scribe. The one I've been using is old and falling apart. It was my sabba's."

While Micah and Joseph discussed construction, Dassa scooted close to Mary so she could speak with her. "Mary, are you tired? I could take these two away so you can sleep."

Mary smiled. "A little. I'd like some company for a while. When Joseph gets talking about his work, he can forget I'm even around."

Dassa chuckled softly. "I know just what you mean. Micah can get talking parchment, lambskins, styluses, and inks until I'm cross-eyed with boredom."

"I want to thank you for all you did. Midwife Tabitha said you had come to get her."

"You're welcome. Were you very embarrassed when we...well, you know?"

Mary blushed. "Yes, but at least more now know I was a virgin when he was born."

"Have you decided on a name?"

"Yeshua. Joseph was told by the angel to call him Yeshua."

   📖 📖 📖

The couples continued talking, getting to know each other. Joseph had decided they would stay for a while in Bethlehem since Micah had told him of several carpentry jobs as well as hiring him to build the scribe's box and help with the small house he was building. Dassa was planning on searching for a house or room the couple could live in. If nothing could be found, Joseph and Mary were invited to live for a while with Micah and her once they were married.

Sounds came into the small hut from the alleyway between the inn and the next building. Men's voices shouted excitedly. Eli, Dassa's father, could be heard yelling at them to leave. That they couldn't go into the stable. When the drape over the entry was pulled aside, it was evident his orders had been ignored. A group of ragged shepherds pushed in. They smelled of sheep and unwashed bodies. Joseph and Micah stood, blocking the entrance to the stall where Mary and the baby, as well as Dassa, were.

"What are you doing here? Why have you come?" Joseph's words were fierce, a father and husband protecting his family.

"Peace, peace. We mean you no harm," said the oldest of the men, his grey bearded head bowed and his weathered hand outstretched. "We were tending our sheep out in the hills. The sky was bright with that star. We were talking about it, the star, when there was a flash in the sky and an angel of the Lord was in the air in front of us."

"We all fell on our faces sure we would be dead in a moment," another man said.

"Then the angel told us not to be afraid. How can you not be afraid when an angel appears?" the first man said. "My name is Rueben Ben David. Please forgive me for not telling you sooner. We are rattled by what has happened." He went on to state the names of the other four men. "The angel said he came with good news, great joy for all men. He said the Messiah had been born. The Savior had been born in Bethlehem." Rueben became more excited as he spoke. The others nodded and murmured in agreement.

"Then, then," a youth named Daniel broke in. "Then there were thousands of angels filling the sky. They were singing *'Glory to God in the highest, and on Earth peace for those with whom God is pleased'*."

"We stood as statues until they faded back into heaven. Then we came here to Bethlehem to find the babe. A couple was walking through the street talking about a newly born boy."

"It was a midwife and her husband going home from the birth. We begged the location of the baby." This time a tall, thin man named Caleb spoke. "They told us here."

"Quiet," Rueben said. "We will wake the child." He spoke softly, reverently. "We have come to worship the Savior born this night." Falling on his knees, Rueben bent and touched his forehead to the dirt floor. "Please may we see him?"

The other men followed Rueben's example. Stunned, Micah looked at Joseph, who was kneeling at Mary's side, speaking to her in a hushed tone. Then he stood and lifted the sleeping infant in his arms and walked to stand in front of the men.

Eli was standing behind the shepherds. It was as if a lamp had been lit within him. He had heard from his wife, the midwife, and Dassa about the couple and especially the young virgin giving birth in his hovel of a stable. The Messiah, born here. The King of kings not born in a palace but in a goat stall. With the shepherds, men shunned by all because of their profession, Eli knelt and silently praised Yahweh for the fulfillment of prophecy.

The watch called. The night was passing. Before the shepherds went back to their hills and herds, they were given bowls of stew and wine. They had left small gifts, all they could afford: soft wool from the recent shearing; a smooth, carved spindle; a lambskin. Each expressed their gratitude to Joseph and Mary for the honor of seeing their son. Eli waved off the few coins they offered for their meal. He could well afford to give them the meal. It wouldn't be right to profit off these men. Elohim had given them most wondrous news, and he had profited from it in a way worth more than mere money.

Dassa and Micah stood in the kitchen speaking softly. Eli and Miriam sat at the table. It was late, and Micah needed to return home. The innkeeper and his family needed to sleep. Morning would come all too soon with its hungry guests.

"We need to remember this, Micah," Dassa said.

"Yes, I will get some sheepskin pieces and write it down. We can keep it always. When Yeshua comes into his kingdom, we can let people know. For now Joseph has asked that we not spread the news of his son."

"Why? He's the son of Yahweh."

"That is why. Joseph is concerned about Herod. You know what that madman has done. All the death and destruction he's caused. Joseph fears he would come for Yeshua if he thought the child was threatening his kingdom."

"All right. I will tell my parents and try to get to Midwife Tabitha in the morning to tell her."

"I must go. Good night, my Dassa. Sleep well."

"You also, my husband."

Chapter 3

Finally the house was finished. The marriage contracts and dowry were settled. Micah stood in his house with Perez, his father, who had watched Micah prepare the house as well as the wedding chamber in the courtyard of the family home.

"I am proud of you, my son. You have prepared the wedding chamber well for your bride as well as the house you have built. I wish there was more to give you but..." Perez let the statement fade. Like all in Bethlehem, the family had little. Although Perez had done well, he had four sons and three daughters. Micah was one of the younger ones. As each son married, Perez had helped them prepare, giving what he could.

"Thank you, Abba. Your approval means much to me." He was now prepared to go and get his bride. Excitement filled his being. Fear also. Suddenly the responsibility of a wife descended. Perez placed a hand on his shoulder.

"You will do fine. By centering your marriage on Elohay Elohim, he will bless you. At the least he will get you through the tough times. Here, this is the shofar, which I used, as well as your brothers. My abba and his before him also. It has been in our family for generations."

Excitement filled Micah's being as he took the instrument he would blow as he went to take his bride. He was very much looking forward to the seven days he and Dassa would spend in the temporary chamber at his father's house, not leaving and no one bothering them. At the end of the seven days, they would emerge and the wedding feast would commence.

📖 📖 📖

"It will be soon that Micah will come for me." Dassa's belongings were wrapped into two bundles. The only things she had left out were the things she needed daily, her wedding clothes, and the cosmetics she had purchased.

"Joseph told me Micah's abba was pleased to declare the wedding chamber good enough for you." Mary giggled at the thought. Yeshua was six weeks old now and smiling at those he was familiar with. Micah had helped Joseph repair a small, abandoned house not far from the one he was building.

With his good carpentry skills, Joseph had gained work enough to support his family. The scandal of Mary being pregnant before they completed their marriage made, neither of them was anxious to return to Nazareth. Mary and Dassa had become good friends and Dassa hoped she would have a son as sweet as Yeshua soon.

"Are there any who will wait with you each night?" Mary asked. Usually sisters stayed with the bride, each with a trimmed lamp burning to help the bride be ready for her groom when he came to steal her away. Dassa had no living sisters or brothers. She was the only child who had survived to adulthood.

"Yes, Lydia will come after the evening meal. She is my cousin, the daughter of my mother's sister, and a year younger." Dassa was applying the henna to her eyes and lashes. Dipping her fingers into a small clay bowl, she dabbed the dregs of wine onto her cheeks and across her lips, giving them a soft pink color.

"Do you think he will come tonight?" Mary shifted Yeshua to her shoulder, patting his back.

"I do not know, but I want to be ready just in case. Ima says to be ready so I am beautiful if he comes. I do not have to help serve the evening meal anymore. I have been working extra hard during the day to make their load easier. In a way I feel guilty leaving them, but it is for the man to leave his abba and ima and become one with his wife. I will be with my husband. Where he goes, I will go."

"Yes, it is the way El Roi commanded it."

"Mary." Miriam's voice came up the stairs. "Joseph is here for you."

"Thank you. I am coming." Mary collected her bag with Yeshua's linens. "I hope it is tonight." She hugged Dassa then picked up her son.

"Me too. Lydia will be here soon. Say hello to Joseph for me."

While she waited for Lydia, Dassa picked up her drop spindle and spent the evening spinning flax into linen thread. It was something she loved but hadn't time to do since she worked in the kitchen with her mother. She planned to do more spinning once she was living with Micah.

"Dassa, shall I bring up supper, or have you eaten?" Lydia yelled from the bottom of the stairs.

Dassa went to the top and called down. "Yes, please, I waited for you."

"I will be right up."

Going back to her small room, Dassa packed her spindle and flax into her bag again. She was getting tired of living out of it. It was getting old waiting for Micah to come for her. Knowing his father had to give his approval of the marriage chamber tempered her peak somewhat, but she wanted to be with him.

Hearing Lydia climbing the steep steps, Dassa went to the landing and took the tray from her. It was heavy, and Dassa wanted to share the load.

"I have something to tell you." Lydia's voice was a whisper.

With the loud noises coming from the common room below, Dassa wondered why. "Sit. You can tell me while we eat."

The girls sat on the woven mat, blessed the food, and began to eat.

"So what do you want to tell me?"

"Eat some more. I do not think you will want to after I tell you what I heard."

"Something about Micah?" Dassa's eyes widened.

Seeing The Life

Lydia nodded, her smile wide.

"He is coming tonight?" The bread in her hand dropped into the bowl of stew.

"I am not sure, but I heard his abba when I walked past the house say he was proud of Micah and that he had prepared the wedding chamber well. Nothing now bars the way for him coming for you." Lydia giggled.

Dassa sat still. Fear and panic warred with joy and excitement. "What if I disappoint him? What if he does not like living with me? What if..."

Lydia pressed her fingers to Dassa's lips. "No, Micah loves you. He has for years. He was just waiting for you to get old enough. You will be the best wife you know how to be."

Dassa's shoulders slumped. "You are right. I am being foolish. I have been taught well. I am ready. Well, I think I am."

"Are you scared of the first night?"

Heat shot up Dassa's neck and across her cheeks. "Um, well, I do not know. Ima told me about it. How it would hurt the first time. How the cloth would be used to confirm my virginity."

Lydia's eyes were both curious and tense.

Dassa giggled. "She also told me it was wonderful and would bring Micah and I closer than ever before."

"Well, that is certainly true," Lydia deadpanned. Both girls fell laughing on the mat.

From a distance the sound of a horn could be heard. They jumped into each other's arms.

"A shofar." Dassa clung to Lydia. "Micah comes."

Giving her a hug, Dassa's cousin pushed her gently away. "Here, eat this," she said, grabbing a piece of honey cake and putting it in Dassa's hand.

Obeying without thought, the young bride stood, watching Lydia gather the few items not packed in the bag. After shoving them in and tying it securely, she handed it to Dassa.

"Your groom gets closer. Let me arrange your veil."

"Dassa." Miriam stood just inside the small room, crowded with the three of them. "Micah comes."

"I know."

"Do not look so scared. You do not want him to think you are unwilling." Miriam picked up the cup of wine dregs. "You are too pale." She wiped some dregs on Dassa's cheeks.

Between Lydia and Miriam, they brightened Dassa's cheeks and lips and arranged her veil across her face. Lydia hugged her cousin then stepped aside.

Miriam wrapped her arms around Dassa. "I bless you, my daughter, asking Elah Shemaya to help you be a good wife as it is said in Proverbs. Thank you for being such a wonderful daughter. I love you. Enjoy the next seven days. Make many joyous memories with your husband." Miriam kissed Dassa's forehead.

"Thank you, Ima, for being such a good ima and teacher. I go to my husband prepared to be a good wife. I love you too."

They heard the shofar just outside the inn. All noise from the common room had ceased. Then the door opened.

"Micah, come in. I see you are finally ready to claim your wife." It was Eli welcoming him into the inn. "Perez, my friend, come in. Have you eaten? Shall we sup until Dassa is ready?"

"I will gladly eat your wife's wonderful cooking. Being a widower is hard on the stomach, Eli."

"Should I go down or wait until Micah calls?" Dassa asked.

Almost before the words left her mouth, Micah's voice rose from below. "Dassa, my wife, come to me. Our year of waiting has ended. It is time to celebrate our marriage."

Dassa looked at her mother, who smiled and escorted her to the stairs. Micah stood at the bottom, a wide smile on his face. The smile eased every bit of fear from Dassa. All she saw was the love he had for her.

As she walked down to him, she said, "I come, my husband. I am more than ready to be your wife in truth as well as name."

When Dassa was within reach, Micah grabbed her by the waist and pulled her into his arms, her bag dropping to the floor forgotten when his mouth met hers in a passionate kiss. As it went on, those in the room began to cheer. Micah swung her down the last few steps.

"My friends, my wife and I will leave you to your supper. We will see you in seven days."

"Oh no, you are not getting rid of us so fast, Micah."

Dassa looked around for the speaker, recognizing his voice. Joseph stood next to Mary, who held Yeshua. "Myself and your other friends will escort you to the house of Perez Ben Caleb."

The rest of the people laughed. The friends would celebrate with food and drink in the house while the marriage was consummated, awaiting the cloth of proof.

Soon family and friends crowded around the couple as they made their way to Perez's house.

"If you need help, Micah. I'm willing." That and other ribald jokes filled the air.

Within Micah's sheltering embrace, Dassa was embarrassed but laughed a little so as not to show it. Several times he whispered his love in her ear. Each time her heart beat faster and her excitement grew. She couldn't wait until they arrived, left the crowd, and were alone.

Someone blew the shofar as they entered the house. It sounded right by Dassa's ear, causing her to flinch further into Micah's side even as she laughed.

"Come, my wife. Let us remove ourselves from this reprehensible company," Micah said with mirth and aggrandizement. Laughter met his remark.

As Micah guided Dassa into the courtyard, Perez, Eli, and Joseph blocked anyone from following. Someone had taken Dassa's bag from her back at the inn. It was sitting by the door to the wedding chamber. Micah picked it up as he opened the drape, allowing Dassa to enter first.

"It is lovely, Micah. Thank you." Flowers decorated the poles of the tent. The sides and roof were dyed lambskin and would be taken to their home when the week was up.

Micah slipped his arms around her from the back, pulling her against his chest as they surveyed the small chamber. There was no fire, only braziers for heat. Food and water would be brought to the door and left for them. Several lengths of colored wool and linen draped the ceiling and walls. Dassa knew these were for her to make clothing. It was a gift from her father-in-law, she knew. Perez had asked about her favorite colors, and they were all here. She would make him a garment as thanks.

The pallet on the floor was thick. It would be comfortable for them to sleep on. When Micah's hands began moving over her body, Dassa knew they wouldn't be sleeping for a while.

Micah turned her to face him. Reaching up, he released the veil, kissing first her lips, then each eye, cheeks, and forehead. Then slowly, Dassa's wedding clothes drifted to the floor.

Chapter 4

Eleven Months Later

"Push," Tabitha commanded.

Dassa squeezed Mary's hand and did. "Auuugghh!"

The baby slipped from her body, and she rested against her friend as sweat dripped into her eyes, stinging them into blindness. A damp cloth was wiped across her forehead. It was her mother's hand.

"It is a boy, Dassa. Healthy and loud," Miriam said as cries filled the room.

The new mother felt her mother take the baby from the midwife. Dassa knew the new softa would wash the baby and rub him with salt then swaddle him before giving Dassa more than a brief look. Miriam held up the squalling infant so Dassa could see him.

"He is squashed. Will he be all right?" The tightness in Dassa's body had nothing to do with the contraction beginning in her abdomen.

"Yes, he is fine," Tabitha said with a slight chuckle. "His head will round out in a day or two. It is a tight fit. Part of the curse come down to us from Eve."

Dassa reached her hand up to Mary's face. "Thank you for being here. You are a good friend."

"You have been here for me. At the birth and when Yeshua had the croup. I feel we shall be friends for a long time, Dassa. I hope our sons grow up strong together."

"I do too."

Eight Days Later

Perez held the baby boy on his lap as the sun rose, bringing with it an orange glow. All of his family was there in the courtyard of his house. It was a large gathering for such an early time of the day. He looked at Micah and Dassa chatting with his sons and daughters and their spouses. Soon the ceremony would begin. When it was finished, they would eat the food that was being announced by the aromas coming from the kitchen.

"It is a beautiful grandson we have, eh, Perez?"

He looked up as Eli laid a hand on his shoulder. "Yes, he is a healthy baby. I just hope he does not follow in his abba's footsteps this day." At Eli's puzzled look, Perez continued. "You do not remember how Micah screamed the entire day after his circumcision?"

Eli laughed. "No, we left after the ceremony. I had to get back to the inn and fix breakfast for our guests."

"Of course. Will you leave as soon as this is finished?"

"No, Nathaniel is going to handle everything. He and Rebecca are learning very well. When Miriam and I are ready, we will sell the inn to them. It is good for them and for us." Eli went on to comment that Dassa marrying had led to the hiring of the young couple. Nathaniel was the younger son of an innkeeper in a nearby village. He wanted to continue in the trade but didn't have an opportunity in his hometown.

"Ah," said Perez. "Here comes Rabbi Benjamin now."

Everyone gathered around. Perez, holding the baby, sat in one chair. Another was left empty.

"We have this chair in remembrance of Elijah, who rebuked the nation of Israel for not upholding the command of Elohay Elohim for the circumcision of all boys on the eighth day. Micah, Dassa, I commend you for your obedience," Rabbi Benjamin intoned to the family members and friends.

The rabbi stepped aside. Micah stepped up to his father and picked up his son. "Blessed are You, Adonai, Ruler of the Universe, who has sanctified us with your commandments and commanded us to bring him into the covenant of Abraham, our abba."

"Amen," said everyone. "As he enters the covenant, may he enter into the study of Torah, into marriage, and into the doing of good deeds."

Micah gave the baby back to his father, who unwrapped the boy. The rabbi stepped forward and dropped several drops of wine into the infant's mouth.

Miriam stood nearby with bandages and clean wrappings. Micah wrapped his arm around Dassa.

A scream indicated to all the procedure had been preformed. The crying did not end even when the baby was in his mother's arms.

Perez stood with Eli and Miriam behind the new parents. They faced their family and friends. Micah raised his hands and said, "His name is Perez Ben Micah."

A cheer rose as Perez felt his heart tighten. None of his other children had named a child after him. There had always been others who were honored. He loved all his grandchildren, but this one would always hold a special place in his heart.

📖 📖 📖

"Look, Yeshua's trying to lift Joseph's hammer." Mary pointed to her son, who had his hands wrapped around the handle, attempting to pick up the heavy implement. Losing his balance as the head slid along the floor, he sat down suddenly on his bottom.

Dassa laughed along with Mary. "One day soon he will be able to pick it up." She poured more tea into their bowls then took up her spindle again. Dassa was using flax she had grown and processed herself. Once she had enough thread, her plan was to weave cloth for sale and possibly gain orders for garments. She also hoped to purchase wool so she could spin and weave it.

The sound of infant laughter had them both looking at their sons. Yeshua was covering his eyes then uncovering them over Perez, who lay on his back. Each time the baby giggled, getting more and more delighted as Yeshua continued.

Dassa and Mary joined in the laughter.

📖 📖 📖

"Yeshua is nearly two years now. Joseph has spoken about going back to Nazareth, but I am not encouraging it. I would rather stay here."

Dassa knew why Mary wanted to stay in Bethlehem. She had been the target of much gossip when she became pregnant before her marriage to Joseph was completed. She remembered all about the night Yeshua had been born.

"Well, I want you to stay here too. I want our sons to grow up being good friends." The young mothers smiled at each other. Perez made his presence known and that he was hungry. The seven-month-old had rolled off a floor mat and started to pull himself up using his mother's legs for support. Picking him up, Dassa settled in to nurse her son and continue chatting with her neighbor.

The sun slipped down in the sky until it shown in the small window. The ladies used that as a signal that their husbands would be home soon expecting expect supper, so Mary gathered Yeshua. Dassa put her friend's spindle, wool, and the grain she had ground earlier in a basket to be carried home.

"My house tomorrow?" Mary asked.

"When Micah leaves after lunch. Hopefully Perez will still be awake so I can put him down for a nap at your house."

📖 📖 📖

"Greetings, my wife and son." Micah filled the doorway, his shadow covering the floor to the small oven and fire where Dassa was cooking.

"Greetings, my husband. How was your afternoon? Did you find time to help my abba with the accounts?"

Micah hung his scribe's desk on the peg driven into the wall near the corner of the room. As he took his ink bottle out, he said, "Yes. The inn is almost as busy today as when the census was being taken. There is a caravan of rich men from the East. I could not tell how many, and some of the servants seemed as well dressed as the lords."

Dassa's eyes were wide. "What are they here in Bethlehem for?"

"They are seeking a king. I could not understand much of what they said. They spoke a foreign tongue between themselves. It was not Roman or Greek or Hebrew. They did speak Hebrew but only when necessary."

"There are no kings in Bethlehem."

The lentils, cheese, honey cakes, and bread Dassa placed before him made Micah's mouth water. She certainly was a good cook. Growing up at the inn had made sure of that. "What of Yeshua?"

The bowl of grapes made a *clunk* as Dassa set it down more sharply than Micah thought she had intended to.

"Oh, surely no one outside of town knows of him. He is just a toddler, and his parents are poor."

"You remember the night he was born. What Tabitha, your mother, Abigail, those female guests, and you all found that night was a virgin giving birth. We talked that night about him being the son of HaShem." Micah had blessed the food, and they were eating as they talked.

Seeing The Life

"I know but... He is just a regular baby, Micah. He does everything all babies do."

As Micah dipped his bread into the lentils, he looked pointedly at his wife. "That does not change the fact of what we experienced and know."

The noise of many voices signaled a crowd approaching. Micah and Dassa looked at each other. They rose, Micah picking up Perez, and went to stand in the doorway.

Men dressed in colorful robes, many with costly embroidery, were standing at the crossroads. One signaled to a man not as finely dressed, obviously giving instructions. The servant nodded and ran to Micah and Dassa, who pulled her veil up to cover her face.

"Sir, we are looking for the King of the Jews. We saw his star and followed it here. Do you know where he is?"

"Um...Why do you seek him here? Bethlehem is a small, poor village."

"The prophet Micah stated, *'You Bethlehem, land of Judah, Are in no way least among the princes of Judah: For out of you shall come forth a governor, Who shall shepherd my people, Israel.'* The time of the coming has been fulfilled, and his star filled the sky, leading us here."

Micah looked at Dassa, whose mouth was open in shock. "The one you seek may be in the house down the road at the corner where your masters wait. It is on the left side of the road." Micah pointed, and the servant went back to his group. The young couple watched as the man followed the directions Micah had given.

"Do you think it was wise to tell them where Joseph and Mary live, Micah?"

"The whole village knows where they are. Many know the story of Yeshua's birth. It would not stay hidden long."

"I like it not. It is not good to be proclaiming someone other than Herod as king. I feel frightened for them."

Micah didn't know what to say. He too felt the fear and wrapped his arm around Dassa, holding her and Perez close.

The next day, Dassa left when Micah did after the noon meal to visit and work with Mary. Curiosity made her steps fast, and she dropped her work bag as she went, puffing out a breath as she bent to pick it up. Mary was grinding grain in the sun. Yeshua ran to Dassa, smiling up at her and Perez, who sat on her hip.

"So, what was all that about last evening? One of the servants of the caravan stopped at our house and asked where you lived." Dassa put Perez on the mat Mary had laid out and was sitting on. Spreading out the one she had carried with her, Dassa sat and arranged her work items around her.

"It was so strange. They were mystics from the East. They came to see Yeshua."

"But why?"

"They said they had seen his star. Remember the star on the night Yeshua was born?"

"Yes."

"They said it was his star, and they had come to see him." Mary bowed her head over the grinding stone.

Dassa could tell her friend was keeping something from her. As she thought about the night Mary had given birth to Yeshua, it made sense that the star would be for him. His mother had been a virgin after all. Micah and she thought the baby was the son of Yahweh. It seemed appropriate for him to be honored. It still shown in the sky even though it was dimmer. The star was distinctive from the others.

"Perez, do not put that in your mouth." Mary picked the pebble from the small hand.

"Mary, it seems we are always telling Perez not to do that. I know it is normal for babies, but it never seems you have to tell Yeshua not to do something." Dassa had her spindle in hand and was taking flax from her bag.

"Oh, I do." Mary looked thoughtful. "It seems I only have to tell him once, and he remembers. I know it is unusual. I only hope my next children are as well behaved." Mary laughed.

"Are you with child?"

"No, but Joseph and I have talked about more children once Yeshua is weaned."

"I hope our next one will be even closer in age to yours. It would be wonderful to share the time of expecting with my best friend." Dassa smiled at Mary, who reached out and squeezed her hand.

[Aฺฺ] [Aฺฺ] [Aฺฺ]

A knock at the door woke Micah. It was dark with very little moonlight coming through the window. He rose from the sleeping mat as Dassa stirred beside him.

"Who is it and what do you need?" Micah called as he crossed the room.

A loud whisper followed in reply. "It is Joseph."

"What is the matter? Is Mary or Yeshua ill?" Micah opened the door to allow his friend in.

"No. I have had a dream. Such a vivid one, just like I had when I was told to marry even though Mary was expecting. That the child was Elohim's son."

Micah gasped and heard Dassa's intake of breath behind him.

"This time I was told Yeshua is in danger and we are to flee Bethlehem. We are leaving tonight. I wanted to tell you. I did not want to go without saying goodbye."

"No, please." Dassa reached past Micah toward Joseph. He knew how much Dassa loved the couple and Yeshua. He did too.

"Dassa, if El Roi has warned him and told them to leave, they must obey." He wrapped his arm around her shoulder. "Joseph, where are you going?"

"I am not going to say. I do not want anything to happen to you, and if you know it might be forced from you. You know how Herod is and how the Romans are.

"We can't take much with us. Whatever we leave in the house is yours. Move it here as soon as you can. Leave the house empty and let anyone who needs it move in."

"We will."

"Micah, you have been a true friend and brother. Dassa, Mary and I love you like a sister. If we ever return, we will come to let you know. I must get back to Mary and help prepare to leave."

"Joseph," Dassa pleaded. "Please stop by as you go so I can say goodbye to Mary. Please." Micah could hear the sorrow in his wife's voice and knew tears were streaming down her face. Dassa's friendship with Mary was so very close.

"We will. I must go." Joseph left quickly and Micah shut the door. He was glad no other family lived this far from the well. Others might have heard if there was another house occupied.

"Micah, light a lamp." Dassa was stirring the coals in the fireplace.

"What are you doing?"

"I am going to cook something for them to take. We have raisin and fig cakes and almonds to give them too. I can make flatbread quickly. Oh, and one of the water bags is full. Get it and a wineskin too. They will need those, especially since they will be traveling fast."

Micah did as bid, thinking how wise his wife was. Giving them food and drink to carry was the best way they could help their friends begin their journey.

It was much sooner than Micah and Dassa wanted, but soon they heard the clump of a donkey's hooves on the dirt street. Dassa placed the last of the food into a pouch and tied it closed. Micah picked up the skins of liquid and opened the door.

Mary, with a sleeping Yeshua in her arms and her eyes filled with tears, rushed into Dassa's arms. Joseph held the donkey's lead, not looking any happier.

"Here, Joseph, some wine and water to take with you." Micah hooked them on the donkey's sides. "Dassa has put together a bundle of food. There are raisin and fig cakes and she made some flatbreads fresh."

"Here, I want you to have this." Joseph lifted Micah's hand and place two gold coins in it.

"What is this? No, Joseph, you need this for your travels." Micah tried to press the coins back into Joseph's hand.

"No, Micah. We have what we need. The mystics gave us much. This is the only way I can thank you for all you have done and for the friends you both are to us."

Micah nodded at Joseph, not pleased but accepting, then looked at the women, who were crying. "Dassa, we must let them go. They need to travel as far as they can this night."

"I know. Mary, I love you all. Be safe. Come back to us, Joseph, Elah Yisrael willing." Dassa let Mary go, hugged Joseph, and buried her face in Micah's shoulder. He knew she was crying for the loss of their friends.

"Go with El-Elyon. May he keep you safe and well." Micah placed his hand on Joseph's shoulder as he said the blessing. Then he hugged his wife as they stood outside the house and watched Joseph and Mary leave Bethlehem.

📖 📖 📖

Micah laid down his pen. The words of Jeremiah were burning in his heart. He sat copying the Tanakh as he did in the synagogue every day before he started scribing for the people and businesses of Bethlehem. Normally he loved this time of the day where he could be alone with the Elohim's Word, spending time in prayer and meditation as he carefully placed every jot and tittle so nothing was lost in the copy.

The passage he was copying puzzled him. Right in the middle of Yahweh telling of the return, joy, and

Seeing The Life

prosperity of his people to Israel, there was a sentence that seemed out of place. *A voice was heard in Ramah, a lament with bitter weeping—Rachel weeping for her children, refusing to be comforted for her children because they are no more.*

Why would Yahweh put this in amongst the predictions of the return from exile to Babylonia?

He thought of Dassa and her sadness since Joseph and Mary had fled in the night. They were alone at the edge of town. The house Micah had built wasn't close to any other. Even the small house their friends had lived in was closer, though not much. Maybe he'd made a mistake building there, but no other lot had been available. Hopefully another man would need a house for his bride soon and would choose to build near them. Or maybe someone would move into the one Joseph had left.

It had been three weeks. In the morning, he and Dassa had gone to clear whatever had been left. He had stood holding his wife as she cried while Perez had looked around for Yeshua. It was as if the house itself mourned.

Hoofbeats and screams brought Micah from his thoughts. Romans! What were they doing in Bethlehem?

"Micah! Micah!" It was his father's voice. Micah ran out the door, meeting Perez in the street. "The Romans, they are killing the babies."

Micah turned and ran. Soldiers and horses were in the streets blocking his way. He turned down an alley that was too narrow for a horse. "Abba, no. Please, El Shaddai. Not Perez. Please." Over and over he pled for the life of his son.

Dodging from alley to alley, Micah ran as fast as he could. The dust stirred up by the horses and running people fogged the air. Screams and yelling assaulted his ears. He knew his father followed, but he didn't look back. He had to get to Dassa and his son.

The street was clear when Micah approached his house. The dust was settling. All he could hear was his heart pounding. The door stood open.

Micah ran in, blinded for a moment in the dimness of the room. As his eyes adjusted, his stomach turned. He wanted to wretch. His wife sat in the corner, holding the body of his son. Blood was pooled around her. She was frantically scooping up the blood, trying to put it back into the cavity that had once been Perez's chest.

"The life is in the blood. The life is in the blood." Dassa was saying the concept in Leviticus over and over.

Micah knelt beside her. Tears streamed down his face. "Dassa..."

She looked at him. "I have to put the blood back. The life of the body is in the blood. HaShem said it. It needs to go back in."

"Dassa..." Micah didn't know what to say. His throat clogged with tears. He sat next to her and pulled her into his lap. Drawing her head to his chest, he gave what comfort he could. He knew it wasn't enough. He was mourning too. His firstborn son was dead. His wife wept. Micah did too, praying Ruach Ha-Melitz would comfort them in their loss.

Chapter 5

"Do you want to go to your parents' today?" Micah asked.

Dassa looked at him as if he was insane. She didn't say anything, wondering how long it would take for him to realize how hard it was to see the baby girl of Nathaniel and Rebecca, the couple who helped her parents run the inn.

"I am going to spin some flax today. I have nearly enough for weaving." She didn't look at Micah and instead just kept stirring the pot of grains and raisins they would eat for breakfast.

"Can you not do so at the inn?"

Dassa bit her cheek to stem the tears and to keep from snapping at Micah. He was only trying to help. But it didn't. Nothing did. The emptiness of her arms, the silence of the house, the absence of her son. Their son. Micah was grieving as much as she. Maybe. He hadn't had to deal with the pain of breasts full of milk several times a day. Hadn't had to wash and fold away the wrappings and diapers Perez had used. Hadn't had his entire reason for living been taken away by that devil's spawn, Herod.

Dassa took a deep breath to settle herself. "Micah, I know you are trying to help, and I love you for it. I cannot..." Her breath hitched, and she swallowed to clear her throat of the threatening tears. "It is just too hard to see Rebecca and baby Deborah. I cannot see them yet."

"I hate Herod." Micah's hands balled into hard fists. "I think he did this because the men who came to see Joseph and Mary. The men were looking for the King of the Jews. Herod is so fearful of losing his position he has even killed most of his family. If those men went back to Herod and told him where to find Yeshua, they lead him right here."

"Micah, the prophecy of the king being born in Bethlehem is well known. It would not be hard for Herod to find out even if the men didn't go back to him."

"You are right. Do not blame the men who only came to worship a king. We know they gave valuable gifts. It is what made it possible for Joseph and Mary to flee."

Micah drew her from kneeling by the fire and held her close. "I know. I am sorry. I will not push anymore. I just hate to see you alone all day. It cannot be good to hide away here."

Dassa laid her head on his chest. "I know. I will stay at the well longer than I need. I can visit and see the other mothers with their babies. When it gets too hard to stay, I will come home."

"Good. Do what you can. I know many of the ladies will like to see you. They have been asking about you."

Dassa smiled a little. The people of Bethlehem had been so good to the families who lost their sons. Only boys under the age of two years had been murdered. Meals had been brought in. People had come to convey their sorrow for the losses of the families. Now she needed to move on.

The words of King David came to her. His son from Bathsheba had died too. *'But now that he is dead, why should I fast? Can I bring him back again? I'll go to him, but he will never return to me.'* Dassa believed in what David had said. She would see Perez again. It wouldn't be in her lifetime, but in heaven where he was now. Tears slipped from her eyes and down her cheeks.

The laughter of women and children broke over Dassa as she turned the corner and stopped at the edge of the well square. It was her first trip of the day. Water bags hung limp from each shoulder. She would take her turn filling them then take them home to pour into jars.

Taking a moment to survey the crowd, Dassa saw Rebecca sitting next to Rachel, another mother who had lost her infant son. Rebecca's arm was around Rachel as she lifted a cloth and wiped the tears from her face. Dassa realized she could have given and received comfort from the other grieving women. She thought again about the Psalm of David. She rolled her shoulders back, straightening her body, and strode across the square.

"Greetings Rebecca, Rachel," Dassa said softly when she stood before them. She knelt and took Rachel's hand. "We shall see them again. Though our hearts suffer from their absence, we have King David's words we can believe."

Rachel's dark eyes studied Dassa's face. "What words?"

"*'But now that he is dead, why should I fast? Can I bring him back again? I'll go to him, but he will never return to me.'* He spoke of his son. The boy died, and David knew, he believed, he would go to him once he went to heaven himself. We can have that same faith. It would not be in the Tanakh if they were not true."

"Yes," Rebecca said. "And Ruach Ha-Melitz knows of your loss and is there to comfort you." Dassa felt Rebecca looking at her. Micah had been right; she needed to spend time with others.

The awkwardness was broken, and Dassa, her eyes wet, stepped over to Rebecca, who wrapped the grieving young woman in a tight hug. Soon the other women at the well were crying and hugging, giving and accepting comfort. Rebecca invited any who had time to come to the inn with their handwork. Several agreed to meet there in the afternoon when they had their chores done and the inn was less busy.

As Dassa carried her water bags home, she reflected that she had not been as welcoming to Rebecca and Nathaniel as she might have. The young couple was now living at the inn as partners with her parents. She felt guilty for not spending much time with her parents as well as the couple.

Seeing The Life

Dassa realized she had enjoyed Mary's friendship so much, she hadn't given much thought to the young woman also living in a new town. Then, after the Romans had come through Bethlehem, Dassa hadn't wanted to see Rebecca and the baby daughter she still had in her arms when Dassa's had been empty. It might be a valid reason to stay away, but it wasn't a good excuse.

Micah had urged her several times over the past weeks to go visit her parents. Dassa was ashamed of her waspishness in replying to his suggestion. With softly spoken words as she walked, Dassa poured her guilt out to El Selich'ah. She would go to the inn as soon as her chores were done. Micah wouldn't be home for a meal until evening. She could spend most of the day with her parents, Rebecca, Nathaniel, and their baby, Deborah.

It was time to look forward. Nothing would bring Perez back, and she knew once she was in heaven she would be with him again. Micah was here now and he loved her. She thought about the evening and the ways she could let him know she had come to terms with Perez's death. Dassa smiled to herself as she planned how she would show him that she still loved him.

Four months later

"Dassa, are you all right?" Micah's concern broke through the silence as he saw her lying on their bed pallet. She turned over and looked up at him.

"Micah! Why are you home so early?" She scrambled to rise then put her hand to her forehead, weaving just a bit.

Micah steadied her then pulled her into his arms. "What is wrong? It is my normal time to come home."

"Oh no. I am so sorry. I just lay down for a little while. I must have fallen asleep. How can it be so late?" Dassa tried to pull out of his embrace, but Micah wouldn't release her.

"Are you feeling all right? Are you ill?" Now he was afraid. Illness and death could strike quickly with no warning.

"No, Micah. I am fine, simply tired. Let me see what I can put together for your supper. I was planning to get a little mutton and make a stew, but it is too late for that." She again tried to pull from his arms.

"Stop. Let us go to your parent's inn and eat there. I know you have been seeing them regularly, but I have not seen them lately."

Dassa had recovered from her devastating grief. There was still the aching emptiness, but she was able to look foreword with hope. She now spent several afternoons a week at the inn. She would take her spindle and flax, spinning fine thread. Often her parents would send food home with her since she helped Rebecca with many of the chores. They had become good friends, and the baby, Deborah, squealed in delight when Dassa entered.

Now Dassa smiled at Micah. "I would love that. I only went on Monday. I have been too tired the last couple of days. I know my parents will enjoy seeing you too."

Micah thought about Dassa being so tired as they walked to the inn. She had slept all afternoon. Sleeping a lot was something she had done right after Perez had died. Was she slipping back into the grief? She seemed to be better, but what if Dassa was just hiding it more?

With his arm around her waist, he pulled her closer to his side. "You would tell me if something was the matter, would you not?"

Dassa looked up at him in surprise. "Why do you ask? Nothing is wrong."

"You said you have been very tired. It has me concerned."

"I am fine. Nothing a little time won't cure. I think... Hum, say about six or seven months." Dassa turned her face into his chest. He could feel her smile.

Micah thought for a few moments before he realized what she meant. He stopped, causing her to stop too. "Are you saying what I think you are?" He put his fingers under her chin and tipped her face up so he could see her in the evening light. She nodded, her mouth twitching with delight.

"Yes, Micah. We are going to have a baby. I saw Midwife Tabitha this morning to make sure what I suspected was right."

Micah hugged her to him tightly and spun her around, laughing. "I am so happy I could shout it from the highest hill." He took Dassa's face between his hands and kissed her. "I love you."

"I love you too. I am happy too. More than I can say."

Micah thought about mentioning Perez but decided not to. This baby wasn't going to replace him, but it would restart the growth of their family.

"Let us hurry to the inn. We have people who need to know they are going to be grandparents again."

The inn was crowded with guests, so Dassa and Micah helped serve before the three couples sat down in the kitchen to eat.

"I am so glad you two decided to come this evening," Miriam said as she kissed her daughter on the top of the head before she sat down.

"If I had known there were so many here, I would have planned to come and help, Ima."

"It is nothing we do not deal with often."

They chatted about various things while they ate. Micah enjoyed seeing Dassa relaxed and happy. She did look tired, but he knew the first months of pregnancy were like that. As they finished, he squeezed Dassa's hand, signaling her to tell of their news.

"Abba, Ima, you are going to be grandparents again."

Miriam and Rebecca squealed and jumped up to give Dassa hugs. Eli, grinning from ear to ear, patted Micah on the back, and Nathaniel shook his hand.

"I am so happy, but oh so tired. When Micah came home, I was asleep. That is the real reason we came tonight. I had not fixed any supper."

Everyone laughed, with Eli commenting, "What better place to come than to an inn with good food and family?"

"Yes." Micah chuckled. "And to be put to work for that supper."

Six and a half months later

"Micah," Midwife Tabitha called to the men waiting beside the house in the dark. Eli and Perez were with him. They had spent the night praying as Dassa's labor

Seeing The Life

went on. It seemed to take much longer this time. Many women died in childbirth. Many babies did also. They had heard an infant's cry a while before, but it had stopped. Micah scrambled to his feet, sprinting around to the front of the house.

"It is a fine boy. Dassa is tired but well."

Micah hugged Tabitha and dashed past her into the house. Miriam was there holding his son, swaddled in linen wraps.

"Do you want to hold him?" Miriam asked.

"Just let me see him. I want to see Dassa." Micah looked into the sleeping face of his son. The tiny mouth opened in a huge yawn. "Praise be to the El-Elyon." He touched a finger to the baby's cheek then turned to the pallet in the corner. Dassa was looking at him with tears in her eyes.

"Another son. I am so glad. And he is perfect, Micah."

He knelt beside her, picked up his wife's hand, and kissed it. "All I cared about was that you would be fine and the baby, which ever it was, would be healthy."

"I know. Me too, but a son." This time it was Dassa who yawned.

"You sleep now, my love. We can talk later. You will not be getting much sleep for a while." Micah leaned down to give her a quick kiss, but Dassa had other ideas. She reached around his neck and held his head so the kiss was much longer than he'd intended.

"None of that now, you two," Tabitha teased. "There is a baby in the room."

Dassa let go, and Micah could see her blush. "We will wait until they are all gone. Then we will kiss some more," Micah whispered before he went to get up.

"I heard that." Tabitha slapped him gently on the arm.

Chapter 6

A knock sounded on the door. Startled, Dassa looked around for a place to hide baby Eli. No, she thought. The soldiers hadn't knocked. They just burst in and grabbed Perez out of her arms then stabbed a dagger into his chest. Dassa shuddered at the memory.

Who would knock on her door? She knew everyone in Bethlehem. None would knock. They would call out to her.

"May I help you?" Dassa asked, calling through the door rather than opening it.

"Is this where the scribe Micah Ben Perez lives?"

"Yes."

"My master wants to speak with him."

Dassa cautiously opened the door and looked past the young man standing outside, but didn't see anyone in the street. "Um, he's not here at the moment, but I can locate him."

"Good. We are staying at the inn. When he arrives, have him ask for Joseph the Arimethean."

"I will."

The servant turned and began jogging down the street. Dassa stood for a moment in confusion. What would a man from Arimethea want with Micah? How would he have come to know about Micah?

Something bumped into her leg. Looking down she saw six-month-old Eli looking up and smiling at her. He'd rolled across the floor to her. Dassa bent and picked her son up. "Let us get you changed, and we will go find your abba. Then we will go see Sabba and Softa. That way we can find out what that man wants."

Dassa blew her lips on Eli's tummy while she changed him. His giggles filled the room. Once he was wrapped, she grabbed her shawl, picked Eli up, and they went to find Micah.

Micah worked for several businesses, writing for them and keeping their accounts. Dassa wasn't sure where he would be, so it was a while before she found him at the tanner's shop.

"Micah, there is a man from Arimethea wanting to speak with you. He is at the inn. What could he want with you?" Dassa's wondering had begun to move into fear. All sorts of possible problems and dangers had made their way through her thoughts.

"I have no idea. Samuel," Micah called to the tanner, "I must go to deal with something. I will be back in the morning if I do not get back today." The tanner waved them away and went back to his work.

The couple hurried through the streets. Micah carried Eli, who was cooing and pulling on his father's beard. Dassa prayed for Yahweh's protection for them and especially for Micah. With the Romans in control of Israel, one never knew.

When they entered the inn, Eli shrieked with joy at seeing his sabba. Sabba Eli copied little Eli by holding his arms out to the boy. Micah handed him over and said, "Is there a Joseph from Arimethea here? Dassa said a servant came asking about me."

"He is over there. Must be wealthy. He has a number of servants and mounts." Eli indicated a man of about thirty dressed in finely woven linen dyed a deep blue with embroidery in several colors. His cloak was thick, dark wool. At the moment he was studying a scroll.

"Come with your son and me, Dassa. Your ima and Rebecca are in the kitchen." Eli led the way, leaving Micah standing near the stairs by the inn door.

📖 📖 📖

Micah looked at the man. This Joseph didn't look Roman, but that didn't mean he wasn't paid by them. Micah tried to think of anything he might have done to bring attention to himself. Nothing came to mind. He was simply a scribe in a small Jewish town. Deciding he would find out nothing until he spoke with the man, Micah crossed the room.

"Excuse me. I am Micah Ben Perez. I was told you want to speak with me."

The man looked up then stood and shook hands with Micah. "Yes, please sit down. I am sure you are wondering who I am and how I came to be here in Bethlehem wanting to speak with you. I am Joseph Ben Matthias from Arimethea." They sat down, and Joseph poured wine from a pitcher into a goblet for Micah and himself.

"Yes, I am... well curious as to how you know of me."

"All I can say is that Elah Yisrael has led me here and wants me to get acquainted with you."

Micah felt his jaw drop and quickly closed his mouth. He took a swallow of wine, then another. "Elohim told you to come see me? What for?"

"I'm a dealer in precious metals. I have shops in towns and cities around Israel. I have caravans which travel farther also. Needless to say, there is a lot involved in my business.

"I am also a Pharisee and so must be in Jerusalem often. My main shop is there. Much more traffic than Arimethea. I travel a great deal also. My steward and scribe who has been working for my family many years is old and ready to retire. I'm in need of an honest man with scribe and mathematic skills to replace him."

Micah was dumbstruck. Yes, he had those skills, but he didn't think anyone outside of Bethlehem knew it. "Who told you I was able to do them?"

"I told you before, HaShem," Joseph said with a smile. "Let me explain. I am a man of faith. I go to him with everything, so it was natural for me to pray for guidance and to find the right man for the job. As I was praying one morning, a voice in my head said for me to go to Bethlehem. That the man I needed was there. That he was a faithful, honest man I could trust with my business. Then the voice said, *'I have plans for him. Plans for his welfare, for his good, for his future.'* I knew the Tanakh passage the voice paraphrased. So I obeyed and came to find the scribe in Bethlehem." Joseph paused and looked at Micah. "Are you the man the El-Elyon was referring to?"

"Um, yes. I am a scribe in town. I copy the Tanakh and work for different businesses keeping track of their accounts." Micah didn't know what else to say. Was the man offering him a job?

"I would like to see some of your work. Your copying, that is. I will speak with the men you work for. If I decide to offer you the position as my steward and scribe, it would mean you moving to Jerusalem."

Again Micah's jaw dropped open.

"I know this is a shock, and I want you to pray about what I have told you. Also if it is HaShem's will that you move your family to the city. I saw you come in with those I assume are your wife and child."

Micah smiled. "Yes."

"So you must pray, asking Yahweh Yireh to make clear to you what he wants of you. I will be doing the same. If you will tell me of the men you work for, I can meet with them. When do you do the copying?"

"In the mornings at the synagogue."

"Then I will meet you there tomorrow." When Micah nodded, Joseph said, "Go now and speak with your wife. Spend much time in prayer over the next few days. This is not a decision to be hurried, neither by me nor you."

Micah felt foolish since all he seemed to be able to do was gawk and nod. "Thank you, sir. I shall do as you say. It is very good advice." Then, seeing Joseph nod, he rose and went into the kitchen of the inn.

Dassa hurried to him, placing her hands on his arms. "Is everything all right? You look stunned." The rest of those in the kitchen gathered near.

"I am. He is Joseph, a dealer in precious metals. He said El Shaddai told him to come here to find the scribe. His steward is retiring, and he's looking for a new man to hire."

"You?" Eli said.

"It appears so. He said a voice answered him while he prayed that the man he needed was here and was honest and faithful."

"That does describe you, Micah," Nathaniel said, placing a hand on his shoulder. "You are known for your honesty in the accounting of the businesses you work for. And you know far more of the Tanakh than some rabbis do. Your life demonstrates that you live it also."

"Thank you, my friend. That is high praise I am not sure I can live up to. I fail in my path so often." Micah looked at Dassa. "If I am offered and accept the job, it would mean moving to Jerusalem."

Dassa gasped.

"Joseph gave very good advice which we will follow. He said to pray, seeking HaShem's will. If we can learn that, then we know what we need to do."

"Obey," Dassa said.

"I must get back to work. Will you stay here, Dassa?"

"Yes, I can help with the meal and we can sup here."

Micah looked at her then shifted his gaze to his in-laws and the others. "Please pray that Yahweh Yisra'el makes his will known with no doubts. I will be doing the same. Dassa, I will stop by my abba's on the way back here. Eli, is it all right if I invite him to eat with us?"

"Of course. I was about to suggest that very thing. We will be praying. Don't worry. El-Elyon will make it clear what you should do."

"I know." Micah felt the weight of such a huge change in his and Dassa's lives if he was offered and accepted the job. He leaned down, kissed her, then turned, heading out to return to the tanner's.

Seeing The Life

"Oh my. Leave Bethlehem. Move to Jerusalem. Leave my family and Micah's family." Dassa sat down on a stool, overwhelmed at the thought.

"That is very hard." Rebecca knelt down beside her. Dassa placed her hand on her friend's cheek.

"You have done that same thing. You left home and moved here to Bethlehem. How did you do it?"

"Prayer, faith, love, and knowing it was the best thing for Nathaniel. It was an opportunity we did not have at home. We would have always been the servants. Here we have part of the inn. When your parents retire, we will have it all. Nothing like that would have been possible if we hadn't moved."

Dassa was silent. It would be a wonderful opportunity for Micah. He would never be more than he was now in Bethlehem. But how would she leave her parents and all she knew? There was only one thing to do. Dassa rose and went to a corner, knelt, and began to pray.

"You do very good work. The letters are formed well. How many scrolls have you completed?" Joseph asked as he tied the ribbon around the book of Isaiah he'd been looking at. It was the following morning, and Micah and Joseph were at the synagogue.

"I have all finished except the Twelve Prophets. I am in Obadiah now with eight left after I finish it."

"Do you enjoy the copying?" They began walking to the door of the building. Micah had been copying when Joseph arrived.

"Yes, I read the passage before I start and pray to understand what I am to learn from it. The copying is an act of worship for me." Micah saw Joseph nod and followed him as Joseph walked up the aisle.

Joseph turned and sat on a bench. Micah sat on the bench in front of him. "You employers speak highly of your capabilities."

Micah felt himself blush. It was uncomfortable being so praised. He knew what his failings were.

"So, have you prayed?"

"Yes, it seems like every minute. Dassa is praying too. So are our parents. It is such a huge thing to contemplate."

"Yes, a move from all you know. I have been praying too. I do not want to misread what I think El Shaddai has asked of me. It would be tragic if I caused you to either move or not. I feel the responsibility of your lives and happiness on my shoulders."

The comment surprised Micah. He hadn't thought of Joseph taking on such a burden. This man would be good to work for. He was a caring man. Joseph had not offered him the position yet but it seemed likely.

Dassa and Micah had prayed and talked of nothing but the job offer last night and that morning. He knew Dassa was torn. She didn't want to leave her parents. She had become good friends with Rebecca. He would miss his family and father desperately.

Seeing The Life

So far El Shaddai hadn't made his will clear. Maybe Micah wasn't praying right. His mind filtered passages. One sentence from the book he was named for stood out. *But they do not know what YHWH is planning; they do not understand his strategy.* Micah certainly had no comprehension of what Yahweh was planning. It would take more praying and waiting. Waiting for El Roi to make clear the path to be taken.

"I will be here one more day. I will let you know whether I offer you the job as my steward tomorrow before I leave."

Joseph stood and left the building. Micah watched from where he sat. There was time to copy more before he went to work on accounts. But maybe copying wasn't what he should be doing. He lifted his hand and watched as it trembled. Rather than ruining the sheep's skin with a shaking hand, he lay face down on the stone floor and poured out his doubts, fears, and questions out to the Adonai Elyon.

📖 📖 📖

Joseph from Arimethea did indeed offer Micah the position of chief steward for his Jerusalem headquarters. He also said he would come back in a week to find out if Micah was going to accept the job. That had been on Wednesday. Now it was the following Friday, late afternoon. Shabbat was nearing and with it the thought that Joseph would not be coming back, that the offer had been rescinded. Micah didn't think the man would not notify him of a change, but he really didn't know him at all.

Dassa had been preparing for Shabbat, doing the cooking she needed and fetching water. Micah was setting the table when he heard the knock. Joseph stood before him when he opened the door.

"Joseph. Welcome. Come in, come in." Micah stepped back, allowing the older man to enter.

"Forgive me, Micah, for being so late to get to Bethlehem and to you. My son James was ill, and I stayed until I knew he would be well. I'm sorry if you thought I had forgotten." It was clear Joseph was truly contrite that he hadn't been able to keep his commitment to being there two days ago.

"You are here now. Being there for your son is more important than coming to see me."

"I appreciate your understanding."

Dassa entered carrying her yoke of water bags. Micah took them from her and poured them into the jars at the back of the room. Then he took Dassa's hand. "Joseph, this is my wife, Dassa. She is the daughter of Eli the innkeeper. Dassa, this is Joseph, the man who has offered me the job in Jerusalem."

Dassa bowed and said, "You are welcome in our home. May I wash your feet and offer you some wine?" Micah felt her censure that he hadn't seen to these simple acts of hospitality.

"Thank you, but you must not blame your husband for not doing this. I only just arrived and was telling him of why I was delayed."

Dassa blushed, obviously embarrassed that her look had been observed. She bowed and hurried to the water jar and dipped the ladle, scooping water into a bowl.

Seeing The Life

Micah took the bowl and picked up a clean cloth. He went to where Joseph sat on a stool, knelt, slipped off the man's sandals, and washed the road grime from his feet. Dassa brought a goblet of wine, which Joseph thanked her for with a smile.

When the small welcoming ceremony was complete, Micah said, "It is nearly time for Shabbat. Will you join us? We have plenty."

"I am honored. Thank you."

Dassa quickly laid another place on the reed rug while Micah placed the pitcher of wine and the challah bread. The dishes holding the meal were waiting by the fire. Micah picked Eli up and stood beside Dassa. Joseph stood waiting quietly.

Dassa took a reed to the fire and caught a flame, which she used to light the candles. Waving her hands in welcome to the Shabbat, she covered her eyes and said, "Blessed are You, Adonai our Yahweh, El Shamayim, Who sanctified us with his commandments and commanded us to kindle the Shabbat candles." Uncovering her eyes, she looked at the flames.

Micah held Eli up before him, saying, "May Yahweh make you like Ephraim and Menashe."

After handing Eli to his mother, Micah poured wine into a silver goblet and held it up. "*And the evening and the morning were the sixth day. Thus the heavens and the earth were finished, and all the host of them. And on the seventh day Yahweh ended his work which he had made; and he rested on the seventh day from all his work which he had made. And Yahweh blessed the seventh day, and sanctified it: because that in it he had rested from all his work which Yahweh created and made.*

"Blessed art Thou, Adonai our Elohim, El Shamayim, Who creates the fruit of the vine. Blessed art Thou, Adonai our Elohim, El Shamayim, Who has sanctified us with his commandments and was pleased with us, and his holy Shabbat in love and in favor, he gave us a heritage, a memorial of the work of creation. For it is the day beginning for holy convocations, a memorial of the exodus from Egypt. For you chose us and sanctified us from all the nations. And your holy Shabbat with love and favor you gave us a heritage. Blessed are you, Adonai, who sanctifies the Shabbat."

Pouring wine from the silver goblet into each cup, the three faithful adults each sipped the wine. Dassa picked up a small pitcher of water and handed it to Joseph. He poured some into a cup and rinsed the top and bottom of his right then left hands. Picking up a cloth, he said, "Blessed are you, Adonai, our Elohim, King of the Universe who has sanctified us with his commandments and commanded us concerning washing of hands." Then he dried his hands. Micah, then Dassa, repeated the ritual washing.

Micah uncovered the woven loaves of challah bread. Lifting them high, he said, "Blessed are Thou, Adonai our Elohim, El Shamayim who brings forth bread from the earth."

Each prayed during the silence while Micah broke the bread, passing a piece to Joseph and Dassa. With the Shabbat ritual complete, Dassa rose and brought the dishes of the meal and set them on the mat.

"So," Joseph said as he was served, "have you decided if you will come to Jerusalem and work for me?"

Micah and Dassa exchanged a look. Dassa silently placed food on Micah's plate. "We have prayed and talked. Prayed and talked some more. I have listened for El Shaddai's direction. That above all else was the most important part.

"You said a voice in your head instructed you to come to Bethlehem. I have had a voice in my head all week. It reminded me of Abram when El-Elyon told him to go without knowing where he would end up. Moshe when Yahweh instructed him to go back to Egypt to free his people. Ruth, who left her people to go with her mother-in-law. Person after person went where El-Elyon had told them to go.

"The more I prayed, the more confident I became that Yahweh Yisrael does have a plan for us in Jerusalem. I have no notion of what that might be, but I do know that I and my family will be there for him to do as he bids."

Chapter 7

The move to Jerusalem was accomplished with as little trouble as possible. The sights and smells of the city were overwhelming, even though Micah and Dassa had come regularly for the various festivals and holy days. Joseph gave them temporary housing at an inn of a friend until they found a permanent dwelling. Awed by the vastness of the city, Dassa and Micah spent several days searching through the Lower City before they found a house available.

It was larger than the one-room home they had in Bethlehem. It had four rooms and was two stories with a railing around the roof. It was also close to a well, so Dassa's water trips would be easier.

Leaving Bethlehem had been as hard as Dassa had feared. The morning they moved, she had walked to the hut Mary and Joseph lived in. Micah came up behind her, encircling her in his embrace.

"I miss them too. I wonder often about where they are and if they will come back."

"If they do, we will not be here. They will never know we still miss them and pray for them."

"I am sure they would go to the inn and ask your parents where we are. Then maybe they will come find us in Jerusalem."

Dassa turned in his arms, laying her head on his chest. "I hope so. Maybe someday we will see them at Pesach, though in the crowds I do not suppose it is possible."

"We can hope. Now we need to go get Eli at the inn. It was good that your parents kept him last night. That made it easier for us to finalize our packing."

They turned away and walked hand in hand back to where the donkey cart supplied by Joseph stood waiting in front of the tiny house Micah had built for Dassa. She pulled him into the dimness. "Kiss me here one more time. This is the home you built for me. The home you brought me too. Where our babies were born. I will miss it."

"Are you not wanting to move?"

She smiled softly and caressed his cheek. "No, I have the peace of knowing we are in Elohim's will. He has plans for you in Jerusalem. Good plans, I know. It is just that we were so happy here. At least I was."

"Even with Perez?"

A shadow passed over her face. "Even with Perez. All our days are numbered before we are born. I just wish his number had been larger."

Micah drew her against his chest, resting his chin on the top of her head. "We have Eli and will pray his number is very large. And, Elohim willing, more children who will be born in the shadow of the Temple."

She nodded then pulled away to look up in his face. "I love you. Now we need to leave before I start to cry. I will have far too many when we leave the inn, so I need to save them for later."

Micah laughed and followed her out the door, which he closed and latched. He took Dassa by the hand and with a 'hah' started the donkey moving forward.

📖 📖 📖

"So you are all moved in?" Joseph stepped over the threshold into the room. With him was a young man in his late teens and a boy several years younger. "If you have anything that needs to be moved up the stairs, I brought my sons to carry for you."

"Thank you, Joseph. There are some things that are too bulky for me to carry. How kind of you." Dassa was arranging her dishes in the kitchen. Micah was with the retiring steward learning what his responsibilities were.

"I knew Micah would be busy, and these boys needed something constructive to do. These are Abraham and James." Joseph ruffled the younger boy's hair. James ducked away from his father's hand, scowling just a bit.

"Thank you. It is a pleasure to meet you. Do you see these bundles? They need to go up to the roof. Then that rug and the mat." Dassa instructed the boys in what needed to be taken upstairs, and they went to do her bidding.

"You have found a nice house. I am surprised it was available."

"The owner had died and left no heirs. His brother lives nearby and wanted to sell. We are fortunate. Yahweh Yireh has blessed our obedience."

Joseph smiled. "Yes, he has. My Dinah would have come with us, but with three other children thought it best to meet you another day."

"How many children do you have?" Dassa had filled a bowl with water and was washing Joseph's feet. She had poured a cup of wine, which he held.

"I have a quiver full. Ezra is eighteen and recently married. He is probably with your husband now. Abraham is fifteen, James thirteen, Sarah eleven, James eight. Orli is three, and she a handful."

"You are blessed. We hope to be blessed in that way too."

"You are young yet. It will happen."

The sounds of running feet overhead signaled that the boys were on their way back down. Dassa sliced fruit and bread, placing it on the table. "Here, young men who help get fed."

"What about Abba? He did not help. Why does he get to eat?" Abraham asked as he stuck a piece of fruit in his mouth.

Before Joseph could scold his son, Dassa said, "He has helped us in many ways. He will always be welcome to eat our food. You will too because you are his son." Dassa ruffled his hair and smiled.

"Is there anything else we should carry up for you? Do you have a canopy for the roof?" Ezra asked between bites.

Seeing The Life

Dassa kept them busy for a while, chatting with Joseph as she arranged mats on the floor and put a pot of water over the fire. There was a real fireplace, not simply a ring of stones in the floor.

Joseph told her of the merchants who had the freshest meats and fruits, the ones he knew to avoid, and several he knew were honest. Dassa listened, hoping she would remember when she went shopping.

Eli, who had been sleeping, rolled over and sat up. Picking him up, Dassa quickly removed the wet cloths. When she was done, Joseph held out his arms to the boy, who smiled and nearly leapt out of her arms to go to him.

"Since your parents and Micah's father are in Bethlehem, I thought I could be a substitute sabba to this little man. Dinah will like having more children around too."

"We do not want to impose."

"You are not."

Just then, Micah came into the house. "Dassa, do you know what... Oh, Joseph, welcome. I did not know you were here."

"I brought two of my boys to help finish moving items upstairs. I knew you were working. Besides, they needed something to do to stay out of trouble." Eli was standing on Joseph's legs, holding his beard with both hands. When Dassa tried to pull the pudgy hands away, Joseph laughed. "Pay him no mind. I have been in this position numerous times. Now, Micah, what has you so agitated?"

"Herod has placed a gold eagle on top of the Temple. It is an outrage. It is a blasphemy."

Joseph's demeanor turned instantly serious. "You are right it is. How is the atmosphere of the people?"

"Not good. There are two teachers, I do not know their names, who are speaking out. I fear they will insight a riot." Eli, who had seen his father come in, was leaning over and reaching and was surrendered into his hands.

"Judas Ben Saripheus and Mattbias Ben Margalothus," Joseph said. "They are zealous young rabbis, very eloquent and knowledgeable. They have gathered quite a following. I am not surprised they are speaking against this."

"What will happen?" Dassa asked.

"Unless they want Herod coming against them, they will need to calm down. This could become an issue with Rome if the populous starts causing trouble."

"We will have to pray for reason and patience." Micah bounced Eli over his shoulder. Eli was a mass of giggles.

Ezra and Abraham came down then. "We must go, sons," Joseph said. "I must go to the Temple and see what the mood is. Thank you for your hospitality, Dassa."

"You are most welcome at any time. Thank you for bringing your sons." She gave each boy a hunk of bread.

"I will let you know tomorrow what I find out, Micah. It might be wise to keep close to home."

"We will. May God's protection go with you."

📖 📖 📖

The mood in the city stayed tense, and with each passing day more talk was of the blasphemy of the Roman eagle atop the entrance to the Temple. Several

Seeing The Life

times small riots broke out, but they were quickly squelched by the soldiers.

When Herod left the city for his palace in Jericho, the undercurrent of unrest rose. Dassa stayed at the house unless she needed to go to the market or well. The other women did the same. No one tarried to talk as they filled their water bags. Shopping was done quickly. As a result, Dassa was unable to meet or make friends with anyone. Homesickness ate at her.

Dassa knew they were where Elohim wanted them to be, but she missed her family and friends. She did love her new house, though. As much as she had loved the one Micah built for her, this one was spacious. The roof had usable space was something she never had before at the inn or the house.

Much of her time was spent on the roof. The flax she had brought from Bethlehem was treated and left to dry. She stored the fibers indoors but spent her spinning time on the roof with Eli under the canopy. He was pulling himself up and putting anything he could find in his mouth.

"Hello, hello."

Dassa looked around for the voice. It wasn't Dinah, Joseph's wife, whom Dassa had met within a week of them moving into the house.

"Up here."

Dassa looked up and saw a young woman on the roof across the stepped street that went along the side of the house up the mountain. Getting up, Dassa went to the short stone wall that surrounded the roof. The house the woman stood on was higher, allowing her to look down upon Dassa.

"Hello, I am Uria, wife of Katzir."

"I am Dassa, wife of Micah." The houses were so close, as were all in the lower city, that they did not have to raise their voices.

"You are new here, aren't you?" Uria asked. Dassa could see a swaddled bundle in her arms.

"Yes, we have been here less than two months."

"Forgive me for not meeting you sooner. I was expecting this little one and not doing well. I was kept indoors until today." Uria grinned. "I finally told my mother-in-law I was going onto the roof no matter what she had to say about it."

Dassa didn't know what to say to that. She had no mother-in-law, no family here in Jerusalem. A wave of homesickness flooded over her. Feeling her dress being pulled by the hem, she looked down and saw Eli standing on wobbly legs, gripping the fabric. He grinned, showing two teeth and a chin covered in drool.

Dassa grinned and picked him up. "This is my son, Eli. What is your child's name?"

Uria told of her infant daughter, Nadav, and three-year-old son, Gadi, who was in the house helping Softa make honey cakes. Perez would have been about Gadi's age, and the thought brought Dassa's mood further down.

Uria chattered on about her family. Katzir and his father, Lemuel, were masons working on the Temple. Dassa was impressed. She knew only the very skilled were allowed to shape the stones used. As Uria spoke, Dassa could tell that even though she had made the comment about her mother-in-law, Shifra was well loved by her son's wife.

The baby began to fuss, and Uria said, "She's hungry. Would you like to come visit on the morrow after your morning duties? I would love to learn all about you, and the children could play."

"I will ask my husband. With the troubles he has wanted me to stay here. I do not think he will have a problem with me crossing the street to visit you."

Uria laughed. "If he does, I will send Shifra to speak with him. She will let him know what she thinks. You'll be able to come then."

"Your mother-in-law is that fearsome?"

"She can be. Why do you think Nadav is a month old before I could come on the roof?" Her smile took any criticism from the words.

The baby fussed again, and Uria said goodbye and left the roof. Dassa looked at the angle of the sun in the sky and went down into the house to make supper.

Lamb and lentil stew was simmering on the hearth, and she was nursing Eli when Micah came home. After exchanging greetings, Dassa told of her time with Uria on the roof.

"It was wonderful meeting someone living nearby who is near our age. She wants me to come visit tomorrow. It would be safe enough for me to go there, wouldn't it?"

"With the troubles you've not been able to meet many women, have you?"

Dassa looked down at Eli. "No." She tried to stop the tears of her loneliness and homesickness, but when Micah's fingers lifted her chin, she knew she had failed.

"Why did you not say something?"

"Because there is nothing you could do about it. All the women hurry to and from the well and the market. No one stops to chat, not even good friends, I am sure. Everyone is afraid that the Romans will come to stop the grumbling about the eagle."

"I am afraid of that too. Since Herod is ill and not expected to live, the speeches are getting more passionate to tear the eagle down."

Dassa moved Eli onto her shoulder and began patting his back. "May I go and visit tomorrow?"

"Yes. Just do not go anywhere else. I will go now and introduce myself. I am in need of friends too."

Chapter 8

Uria and Dassa became good friends, spending many hours together. Shifra, Uria's mother-in-law, could be fearsome if she felt a choice was unsafe or foolish but was generally good-natured and loving. She took Dassa under her wing, supplying the mothering Dassa was missing so dreadfully. Katzir and Micah became good friends also with his father, Lemuel, serving as a father/mentor.

Micah had met with the scribes in the Temple and asked if he could do copying there. After showing them several scrolls of his work, they agreed to allow him. Daily, toward the end of the workday, Micah would go to the Temple. Within the walls were small rooms used for many purposes. In one he began where he had left off in Bethlehem. It was his plan to give what he completed to the rabbi of Bethlehem during Pesach. Later he would walk home with Katzir and Lemuel. Sometimes Joseph would be at the Temple and accompany them until he went toward his home in the Upper City.

Micah was engrossed with his copying of Jonah, and it took several minutes for the increasing level of noise coming from the court in front of the Temple entrance to catch his attention. Laying his stylus down away from the lambskin, he went to the room's doorway. From there he could see a large gathering of men shouting and pointing. When he stepped forward, the Temple came into view. Ladders had been leaned against the building, and several men were climbing. More ladders were placed on ledges to continue the assent. On the steps, two men stood taking turns speaking to the crowd, which was growing by the moment.

"This abomination will come down. Just as Samson torn down the temple to false gods, we will tear down the idol that has been placed on the Temple to the one and only Elohay Elohim. Yahweh Yisrael.

"*You shall not make any graven image to worship.* The law is clear, and we will no longer allow this symbol of the Romans who have taken over our land to be seen on the Temple of Adonai Elyon."

The men climbing had reached the high roof, and several had axes. They began chopping at the golden eagle, breaking it into pieces that fell splintering on the steps below.

Micah turned his head at a new sound. It was the distinctive sound of hobnailed souls of the shoes worn by Roman soldiers. Into the Women's Court ran the pagan warriors. Led by a centurion, a hundred men swarmed through. Micah stepped back into the shadows. Men began running in all directions. As some ran near the room Micah occupied, he signaled them to come in. Several ducked in as the soldiers ran through the Court of Israel and on past the altar.

More and more of the eagle crashed to the pavement. Two men stood at the side on the top step watching the rain of wood and gold. Soldiers ran up the steps and grabbed them, pulling them away. Others climbed the ladders, intent on capturing those on the roof. More young men who had not run were captured. Although they did not fight back, the Romans beat them with clubs and tied their arms behind their backs.

Soon about forty men, surrounded by the centurion's troops, were taken from the Court of Israel, through the Women's Court, ignoring those who now ventured from their hiding places to watch the procession.

"We have cleared the abomination from the Temple of Adonai Elyon!" shouted one of the men. Soon all those captured were yelling the chant.

Katzir came running to Micah. "You are safe, praise the Lord. I feared you would be taken." He looked at the Temple. Shattered pieces of the eagle littered the steps leading to the Holy of Holies. "They should have climbed up and chopped it down at night. The Romans wouldn't have known who did it."

"They were faithful to their belief. Their zeal will please Yahweh Yerushalem." Lemuel had arrived. Micah was relieved the older man was safe.

"They were all young men taken. What will the Romans do to them?" Micah asked.

"I am not sure, but whatever it is, it will not be good. Herod will not like that his eagle was torn down." Katzir ran his hand through his hair.

"Come. We must not tarry here. They may return. The Romans have no respect for the house of El Shamayim. Their presence has defiled it. The priests will want to consecrate it again." The others who had taken refuge in Micah's small space left with them.

凸 凸 凸

Dass wrung her hands. The news of the events at the Temple had spread through the city as if on wings. What would she do if Micah was one taken? Would he have been one of the protesters? Climbed the Temple and chopped down the eagle?

Please no she said in silent prayer. Shifra had sent Uria to tell Dassa to stay inside and lock her door. Not to even go out onto the roof.

Now she paced in the dimness. Eli was cruising along the benches hooked to the walls. Dassa envied his innocent belief that all was well.

"Dassa, open the door." Micah's voice brought a sob from her throat as she ran and pulled back the latch.

When he pushed the door open, she flew into his arms. "I was so scared. I thought you might have been taken. They said forty men were taken by the Romans. I heard the Romans running to the Temple. The same sound as when they came to Bethlehem. I hid with Eli under a bench upstairs, and I put bundles of flax above and before us. I can't lose another son to the Romans, Micah. I can't."

Seeing The Life

Micah held Dassa as she sobbed. He understood her fear. He too had heard the sound of hobnails that terrible day in Bethlehem. "It is all right, my love. All is well. We are safe."

"So did the Romans come into the Temple and arrest the men who tore down the eagle?"

"Yes." Micah related all he had seen. "I fear for the men's lives. They were very brave to stand there when the Romans came for them. We shall have to wait for word of them and pray for Yahweh's mercy."

Word did come several days after an eclipse of the moon. The protestors had been taken to Herod in Jericho and burned alive on the very night the eclipse appeared.

There was no true mourning when, three weeks later, word came that Herod was dead. His reign had been that of a madman who not only killed a great many Jews but also many of his own family. There was, however, deep mourning for the young men who had torn down the eagle and were killed by Herod.

Herod's son, Archelaus was to become ruler over Judea. The crowds wailing in the Temple grew, their behavior becoming threatening to Archelaus. He ordered his army into the Temple after midnight. It was said three thousand men died that night. Archelaus also canceled Pesach before sailing to Rome for confirmation by Caesar Augustus as king. Those in Judea feared the continuation of Herod's cruelty by his son.

Unrest continued in the city, keeping Dassa close to home. She was thankful for Shifra, Uria, and her children. The friendships deepened. Leaving the children with Shifra, she and Uria would go together to draw water as well as run daily to the markets. Dassa spun the flax into linen thread and set up her loom. Soon she was weaving fine cloth she hoped to sell to the dealers of fabric. Uria was a basket maker, and the young women laughed and planned how they would spend the vast riches they would earn from the sale of their good.

Chapter 9

Three years later

Dassa watched from the steps of the Woman's Court as Micah handed the lamb to the priest. Both courts were crowded. It was just after on the first day of Pesach, the highest holy day of the year. Thousands flocked to Jerusalem. Dassa's parents weren't coming this year. They had come the previous year, so this time Nathaniel and Rebecca were attending. The couple and their children had visited the night before.

Straightening the sling she carried baby Sarah in, Dassa stepped back, holding tightly to Eli's hand, and descended the steps. She scanned the women and children mingling and chatting, looking for some familiar faces. The sight of a face she hadn't seen in years caused her to sharply intake a breath. "Mary." She kept her eyes on the woman as she tugged on Eli's hand and made her way through the crowd.

"Mary, Mary," she called. A large number of women turned and looked at her.

"Dassa, Dassa." The voice was the same. Mary was moving toward her, several children tailing along.ABigrs were on both faces, and they hugged, pulled apart to see the other's face, only to hug again.

"I cannot believe you are here. I looked for you at each festival but never was able to find you. Where did you go? Why so suddenly?"

"It is so good to see you. I'm so glad we found each other."

"How is Joseph?" Dassa looked at the two boys and a girl who held on to her cloak then at Mary's rounded stomach. "Your family has grown."

"Yours too. But this one is too small to be Perez."

The joy at seeing her friend again was dimmed by the mention of Dassa's first child. "You will come to our home, and we will tell all about the years we have been apart. Micah has already presented the sacrifice. He should be back soon." She turned to look over the Court of Israel, trying to see her husband.

"I have not seen Joseph since he took the lamb and left us here." Mary was several inches shorter than Dassa and could not see through the women and children.

"There is Micah. Oh, and I think that is Joseph with him." Dassa stretched her hand high, waving to catch Micah's attention. "Come, we will go meet up with them." The men, women, and children met with laughter and hugging.

"Dassa, I have invited them to come home with us." Micah's tone was somewhat sheepish.

"I did the same. Are we ready to go?"

Soon they went into the Court of the Gentiles, which was as just as crowded with stalls of lambs, doves, and other offerings for presentation to the priests. Moneychangers were also scattered throughout. Various rabbis taught with few or many listening. The noise was deafening from the animals and people. The smell wasn't much better.

Micah had picked up Eli, and Joseph now held his youngest. "Come, we will leave by the Shalshelt Gate. Stay close, children. We do not want to lose you as we go."

When they arrived at the house, Dassa quickly washed feet as Micah offered wine to Joseph and Mary.

"Let me start a stew we can eat. You all go up to the roof, and I will be up as soon as everything is cooking." Dassa drew more water from the jar, pouring it into the terra-cotta pot in the fire.

"Let me help." Mary moved into the cooking space while the men took the children up the stairs.

Mary began chopping onions and leaks. Dassa poured lentils from a jar into the cooking pot and added barley and coriander. She added raisins then took a platter and filled it with unleaven bread pieces, almonds, figs, raisins, and other nuts and fried fruit.

While they worked, Mary asked what had happened to Perez. The death of a child was not unusual. Many died as infants and toddlers. Dassa paused her chopping and took a deep breath before answering.

"About three weeks after you left, the Romans came to Bethlehem. They rode through the town killing every boy under two years old. Perez died that day."

The knife in Mary's hand dropped to the floor. "No."

"Yes. I struggled for a while. Micah was so patient. I did not realize until later how glad I was that you and Joseph left. You would have lost Yeshua had you stayed. At first I was angry with you. I had lost my son, and yours lived. Then I was so thankful you had gone and he was safe."

Mary wrapped Dassa in her arms and held on tightly. "I am so sorry. Your mother did not say anything when we stopped there. You were already living in Jerusalem."

"They did not say they had seen you when they were here. When did you come? Where did you go when you left Bethlehem?" They went back to preparing the meal.

"We went to Egypt to live. It is where HaShem told us to go. Joseph had a dream saying Herod had died, and we were to come back. We were going to stay in Bethlehem, but when we got there, not only were you gone, but we heard Herod Archelaus was ruling Israel. Joseph did not think it would be safe for us and Yeshua in Israel, so we went on to Galilee, to Nazareth to live. This is the first Pesach we have celebrated in Jerusalem since Yeshua was born."

With the stew needing to cook, they went up to the roof to join their families. The children who had spent the time in the Temple just looking at each other now were playing together while the fathers watched and talked, getting reacquainted.

Micah had told Joseph about the slaughter six years earlier, so nothing more was said on that topic. They had the stew, then Joseph's family had to leave to get back to help with the preparations for the Pesach meal with the family and friends from Nazareth with whom they had traveled. Plans were made to share some meals and daylight hours while Joseph and family were in Jerusalem.

Dassa hugged Mary tightly as they were leaving. She kept the tears from falling by simply silently thanking El Shaddai for keeping her friend and family safe and for finding each other again.

"Yeshua is very mature for his age is he not?" Micah asked as they watched the family walk down the street. The six-year-old boy was holding the hand of his little brother, Ya'aqov. He had not once interrupted the conversation of the adults and had included three-year-old Elizabeth and Eli in all their play.

"He seems to be. Did you speak with Joseph about why they left and where they went?"

"Yes. HaShem told him in a dream to leave because Herod wanted to kill the child. To go to Egypt. You know about his birth just like I do. There's a passage in Hosea. Out of Egypt, I called my son. Do you think Yeshua is Elohim's son?" Micah followed Dassa back into the house. Eli was asleep on a mat, exhausted. Sara fussed, and Dassa sat on the mat next to Eli and began nursing the infant.

"You know the Tanakh better than I. We know Mary was a virgin when Yeshua was born. Only El Shaddai can do such a thing."

"Yes. It is in Isaiah; *Therefore the Lord himself will give you a sign. Behold, the virgin will conceive, and bear a son, and shall call his name Immanuel.*"

"Immanuel, Hashem with us. But Yeshua is just a little boy. How can he be Elohim? El Shamayim is so vast nothing can contain him. Why would he come as a baby born to poor parents?"

"I have not any idea. But God's thoughts are higher than mine. He created the heavens and the earth, and it is his to do with as he pleases. I do not suppose HaShem would just appear out of nothing and become the king."

"I suppose not. I just do not understand any of it. I know what happened the night Yeshua was born with the star and the shepherds, not even taking into consideration Mary being a virgin. Then the wise men coming later to worship him. Then there was..." Dassa didn't go on. They both knew what had happened.

Dassa began making the unleaven bread to be used in that night's meal. Micah put more wood on the fire in preparation for roasting the lamb. He set the small leather pouch with the blood of the lamb on a small shelf high on the wall; he didn't want it to spill. Later it would be smeared on the door frame.

The ceremony of this special Shabbat would take place just as the sun was setting. Elohim had instructed the people Moshe led out of Egypt so many years ago. He told them how to mark their houses so the angel of death, which was going to come over all of Egypt, would kill the first born son of all without the blood of the lamb smeared to identify the Jews.

Seeing The Life

The unleaven bread could be made quickly to nourish the nation as they traveled, which leaven bread could not. It took time for the yeast to cause the bread to rise. Yahweh Yisrael knew his people would have to flee the nation of their enslavement quickly. There would be no time to raise the bread with leavening.

Each year the Israelites celebrated Pesach so they would not forget what the Lord had done for them in Egypt; the blood of the lamb so the angel of death spared their firstborn, the plagues, parting the sea, manna and water in the wilderness.

Eli was still too small to ask the questions of remembrance. Micah would help him repeat the words. He went and looked down at his sleeping son. He prayed that El-Elyon would give his son a heart that would be starving for the knowledge and grace of Yahweh. He then prayed the same for his daughter sleeping at her brother's side.

"Who were the friends with you yesterday?" Uria asked from her rooftop the next morning.

"Oh, Uria, they were friends from Bethlehem who had moved away. We had not seen them in years. I was at the birth of her first son, Yeshua, and she was at my son Perez's birth." Dassa paused as she always did when she thought of her son. "He is gone to be with Adonai."

"Oh, I did not know. I thought Eli was your first."

"No." Dassa lit up with a huge smile as she continued. "Yesterday at the Temple I saw her in the Woman's Court. We were so happy to see each other. Micah had found Joseph, her husband, and we all came back here for a meal. I hope they come and visit sometime this week. I would love for you to meet her."

The slight frown on Uria's face left when Dassa indicated she wanted to include Uria in her time with Mary. She could be a little jealous about Dassa spending time with other women. Knowing this, Dassa tried to include her as often as possible. Uria's need to be central in most of the conversation limited her appeal as a friend.

"How is Levi?" He was Uria's third child and slightly older than Sarah, who was four months.

"His cold is better. Poor little thing. His nose is running all the time. It's so hard for him to sleep, and he seems to want to suckle all the time. I finally propped him sitting between two rolled mats with blankets holding him in place."

It was early in the day, so they made plans to leave the children with Shifra so they could fetch water and go to the market. Dassa wanted to be prepared with enough food if Mary came with her family today.

It wasn't until the following day that Mary and Joseph brought the children to spend some time with Dassa. Micah was working, and although he tried to stay interested in the conversation of the women and help supervise the children, Dassa could tell he was bored. After the midday meal, the younger children were put down for a nap.

"Joseph, would you like to go and do something besides sit and listen to us jabber?" Dassa asked. Yeshua, who was too old to nap, looked at his father, interested in his reply.

Seeing The Life

Joseph looked at the boy who was spinning a top. "Yeshua, would you like to go to the Temple?"

A smile lit up Yeshua's face, whose mouth was missing several teeth and had one front tooth about half way grown in. "Yes, Abba, I would."

"Well, let us go. We can have an afternoon of just you and me. There are many things I am sure you will be interested in there."

Yeshua ran down the stairs to get his sandals on.

"The boy has been asking about the Temple ever since we decided to come this year," Joseph said as he followed his son down the stairs at a more sedate pace.

📖 📖 📖

Dassa and Mary enjoyed each other's company while the children slept. As they woke up, they were given a snack and allowed to play on the roof.

"Dassa," came the call from the neighboring roof.

Smiling, Dassa waved and called back. "Uria, come and bring the children. I would like you to meet my friend. Bring Shifra too if she is available." Once Uria was off the roof, Dassa said, "Uria is my good friend. My first when we moved here. It was not an easy time to come to Jerusalem. There was so much unrest because of Herod. Shifra is her mother-in-law and a wonderful woman. She has taken me on as if I'm a daughter too. It helps since mine is so far away."

"I understand. We were so terribly alone in Egypt. We had planned to move back to Bethlehem, but when we heard about Archelaus we moved on to Galilee. You and

Micah weren't there either. I had so looked forward to seeing you again."

They heard noises on the stairs, and soon Gadi and Nadav's heads peeked from the stairway.

"Come, children. Meet my friend and her family." Dassa urged them forward, and soon Uria, carrying Levi, and Shifra joined them.

Once the introductions were made, Ya'aqov, Elizabeth, and Nadav, all three to four years of age, sat and looking at each other for a few minutes before starting to play together. Sarah and Levi were both around a year old and just looked at each other before going back to chewing on their chicken leg bones and crawling around.

"It is too bad we did not think of it before, Gadi," Dassa said. "You could have gone with Joseph Ben Jacob and Yeshua to the Temple."

"Naw, my abba makes me go with him every week. I would rather play with the little ones than go there again."

📖 📖 📖

"Joseph, Yeshua, what are you doing here?" Micah called when he saw them. He was on his way to his tiny copy room, his last task of the day, when he saw them crossing the court of the Gentiles. His room was in the wall encompassing the entire complex.

"Micah, good to see you today." Joseph patted him on the back, and Micah ruffled Yeshua's hair. "We left the women and younger ones at your home. Yeshua and I

Seeing The Life

came to see the Temple. It is his first time other than yesterday. Much less crowded today."

"So you like the Temple?" Micah addressed his question to the six-year-old.

"Yes, sir. To be where Adonai Elohai dwells is a great honor. Abba has been telling me about all the symbols."

"What is your favorite part?" Micah had knelt down so he could look Yeshua in the eye.

Before answering, Yeshua thought for a moment. "There are two things I like best. The curtain which hides the Holy of Holies and the teachers who will share their learning of the Tanakh with those who want to learn."

"Those are two very good choices." Micah glanced at Joseph. The boy's answers showed great insight for one of his age.

"Someday I would like to be able to see behind the curtain. I know it's impossible, but I would still like to see."

Joseph chuckled. "That is my boy. He always wants ways to be closer to HaShem. When you are older, you can sit by the rabbis and listen. Right now they would probably shoo you away."

"But why, Abba? I would be very quiet and listen."

"I know you would. You go and find Rabbi Caleb whenever you are free. He is very patient and does not mind answering your questions. The rabbis here think they are more important. They would think it beneath their dignity for a child your age to listen to them. That you could not understand what they were teaching."

Micah was impressed with the patience Joseph answered the question. He was probably correct in his thinking about the rabbis who taught in the Temple. Many showed off more than they taught and would denigrate those who came to learn.

"Come, I will show you where I do my copying." Micah led them across the intricate mosaic tile floor to his small room. Unrolling the scroll he was working on, he lifted Yeshua up onto a stool.

"A shoot will grow out of Jesse's root stock, a bud will sprout from his roots. The Lord's spirit will rest on him—a spirit that gives extraordinary wisdom, a spirit that provides the ability to execute plans, a spirit that produces absolute loyalty to the Lord. He will take delight in obeying the Lord. He will not judge by mere appearances, or make decisions on the basis of hearsay. He will treat the poor fairly, and make right decisions for the downtrodden of the earth. He will strike the earth with the rod of his mouth, and order the wicked to be executed. Justice will be like a belt around his waist, integrity will be like a belt around his hips."

Chapter 10

Three years later

Micah came into the house. He grabbed Dassa around the waist, or what would have been her waist but was now round with advanced pregnancy. He kissed her and looked at her in the dim light of the cooking area with a big smile on his face.

"How would you, my love, like to go on a hunt tomorrow?"

"A hunt? No. I do not hunt, and I am way too big to be anything other than the target." Dassa rolled her eyes at him.

"Not that kind of hunt. Something within the new city and which I think you will be very interested in."

"What are you talking about, Micah?"

"I received a letter from your parents today. One of Joseph's caravans came through Bethlehem."

"Oh, Micah. Are they all right? How is everyone?"

"Everyone is fine. I will get it out later and let you read it. The important part is that they are coming to Jerusalem to live. They are selling the inn to Nathaniel and Rebecca. They would like to live with us."

Before he could get another word out, Dassa had jumped into his arms, squealing with joy. "Can they, Micah? Can they live with us?"

"Not here they cannot. Do not look like that." Dassa's smile had vanished. "That is why we need to go hunting. We need to find a bigger house. Something in the Upper City. Not the most expensive part but something bigger than we are in now."

"How can we afford it? We do not have that kind of wealth."

"Your parents sent some money, and I have been saving back. Your father and I talked of this before we moved... How long has it been now?"

"Six years. Why did you not tell me?"

"They did not know how long it would be and did not want you to be discouraged with the length of time it might take."

Dassa looked up at him then smiled. "Okay, I will go hunting with you."

The next day, they left the children with Uria and Shifra. Eli had pouted a bit about being left behind, but the six-year-old stopped at a word from his father. Sarah was now four; Miriam, three; and Perez was two. Dassa and Micah had decided to honor his father by naming this youngest son after him.

"Micah, I have some money from the linen yarns and cloth I have sold. If it will help, you can use it to help pay for a new house." They were walking up the hill toward the second wall past where the houses were more spaced out and larger.

"Only if the houses are more expensive than Joseph thinks they are. He is meeting us at the gate. He knows of several we might be able to afford."

"El-Elyon truly blessed us when he sent Joseph to offer you this job." Dassa glanced up from watching where she was stepping to look at Micah.

"He truly did. Joseph is a great employer and friend. He is much more devout than most of the Pharisees. He gets very frustrated with them. Many either do not know the Tanakh or discard or twist what they say to fit their own views. I know he is wealthy, like most are, but he is so generous with those in need."

"Micah, are we not supposed to fit our views with Tanakh?"

"Yes, many do not, though. I cannot tell you how many times I have heard men say, 'I know Tanakh says that but...' Then they say how they know what is better."

Dassa was silent, causing Micah to look down at her. "Are you all right?"

"Micah, I have done that same thing. Maybe not said the words but thought them and done what I wanted rather than what the Tanakh says HaShem wants us to do." Her voice was small and soft.

"I have too, I am ashamed to say. I watch myself now so I do not fall into that temptation. It was very hard at first to stop and remember what HaShem's Word says. It gets easier."

"Micah, I promise to work on obeying everything and not twisting it to fit what I want. Will you watch me so if you see me doing that, you can tell me to stop?"

"On one condition. You do the same for me."

Dassa smiled up at him. "Okay."

📖 📖 📖

"I cannot believe it," Dassa said. "This house is so wonderful, but can we afford it?" They had spent several hours looking at various homes in the new city. Joseph did indeed know a number of homes for sale. Most were far more expensive than Micah could have possibly afforded, but the ones they looked at they would be able to manage.

The house Dassa had fallen in love with was built in the Roman style of a central courtyard surrounded by rooms with a covered walkway around the courtyard. There would be rooms for the boys and girls as well as one for Micah and Dassa and for her parents. Two more rooms consisted of the cooking area and a room for meals and activities if the weather was inclement. There was also a room for ritual bathing and a small chamber for more personal needs.

It was not a large house compared to many in the new city, nor was it high on the hill. Rather, it was near where the second wall met the city wall on the east.

"I would not have shown it to you if you could not afford it." Joseph patted Dassa's shoulder.

Seeing The Life

"Why is it for sale?" Micah looked around the courtyard they were standing in.

"The owner has built a new, much larger, house up the hill."

"What do you say, Dassa? Is this house the one you want?" Micah looked as though he knew her answer before she spoke.

"Only if you are sure we can afford it."

"Yes, between what your parents sent and have promised and what I have saved, we can."

After that, Joseph took them to his home, which was further up the hill and much larger, where they ate a meal. Micah and Joseph left Dassa with Joseph's wife, Dinah, while they went to meet with the owner and make the deal.

Dinah's gentle soul contrasted greatly with her high-spirited husband. There were seven children so far, with Dinah always either in the mid stages of pregnancy or her body shifting into a matronly silhouette.

Dassa was made to feel quite at ease. She had met the woman before but only sporadically. There would be more opportunities for a friendship to develop now that they were going to be living closer.

As always, Dassa had a bag filled with flax fiber and her spindle. She took it out after the men left and began to spin. They were seated in the courtyard under a large, shady tree. Dinah was embroidering on some blue wool.

"That is beautiful stitching," Dassa said.

"It is for my Abraham. I swear that boy grows out of his clothes each week. He will be interviewed by a rabbi soon. It would be wonderful if he passed and becomes a disciple and studies to become a rabbi himself. I am making this for him. It will be long for him now, but he will grow into it. I will make the hem deep so it can be let down as he grows."

They chatted about their families until Joseph and Micah returned. The smiles on their faces told the story. Micah now owned the house, and they could move in as soon as they wanted.

"Micah," Dassa exclaimed. "We do not have furnishings for such a large house. What are we going to do?"

"Purchase what we need as we can afford it. I know of this carpenter in Nazareth who might be able to make a few pieces for us."

Uria was not pleased that Micah's family was going to be moving to the new city. Some sniping words were tossed at Dassa, who knew it was simple jealousy on Uria's part. There was nothing Dassa could do other than keep being a faithful friend and hold her tongue between her teeth. Even with Uria's faults, Dassa still loved her as well as her family.

At Dassa's urging, they set up a day each week that either Uria, Shifra, and the children would come to the house where Dassa lived, or she and hers would come to see them in the old city. Although Uria didn't think this would continue once Dassa made new friends among the wealthy who lived near her, Dassa decided to make sure she kept coming on the weeks she was supposed to. She thought her mother would enjoy visiting with Shifra also.

Seeing The Life

Micah and Dassa certainly had more to pack and move than when they moved to Jerusalem. Back then it had been what fit in one room. There had also been only one child, the baby Eli who was now six. Three siblings, a new one on the way, and nearly six years increased the amount of what one owned.

Dassa looked at Uria once the wagon was loaded with their belongings and the children. Tears flooded her eyes. "We will be here on the third day of next week. Then you will come the following. Hopefully, we will be settled by then. We will be a little sparse on furnishings, but the courtyard is very welcoming."

Uria laughed with tears on her cheeks. "I have sat on the floor all of my life. It will not be new to me. Now give me a hug and get going. Your oldest son may fall off that thing if you wait around much longer."

Dassa turned to look at Eli. He was hanging off the top of the load holding on to a rope. She shook her head and laughed as Micah scooped him up and sat him on the back of the donkey they had borrowed.

"I will see you next week." Dassa hugged Uria and then Shifra, who also had tears threatening to spill.

"Hep, hep. Move on, beast," Micah slapped a hand on the donkey's rump to get him moving.

With one last hug, Dassa stepped back and followed the wagon to her new home.

Chapter 11

Each year Joseph, Mary, and their family came at Pesach. Many times they would stay at least one night with Micah and Dassa's family, which delighted the children. Each year Joseph would bring at least one piece of furniture he had built over the past year.

This year Yeshua carried a stool he had built as a gift for the family. He was twelve now, studious but also full of youthful energy and laughter. Children seemed to gravitate to him. There was always room for one more in whatever game they were playing.

Yeshua was also one who knew right from wrong and chose the path that would gain approval from the adults. It sometimes caused problems with his siblings.

'You always spoil my fun,' was heard rather often from his brother Ya'aqov, the next child in the family. Just three years younger, Ya'aqov would test the limits of rules set down by their parents. Yeshua would never stop Ya'aqov from doing something wrong unless his safety was in peril; he would simply remind his brother of the rules and give alternate suggestions. Ya'aqov would complain but usually make the proper choice.

Children were running around the courtyard and in the area behind the house. Between Mary's six, Uria's six, and Dassa's five the house was full of laughter as well as skinned knees and jammed fingers.

The men had gone with Katzir, Uria's husband, to their home so they could visit without the commotion of their families. Joseph had allowed Micah the day to visit with his friend from Nazareth. Dassa's father had gone with them.

Eli and Miriam had moved to Jerusalem within three months of the purchase of the house in the new city. Dassa reveled in having her parents living with them. Softa Miriam was a much better cook, at least Dassa thought so. Sabba Eli was enjoying not having to cater to disgruntled patrons and spent many days at the Temple listening to the various rabbis who were teaching.

Some days he would come home shaking his head in disbelief at the way the Pharisees would twist the Tanakh to avoid doing what it said. Years of keeping his tongue between his teeth with know-it-all customers made him a welcome listener by those who honored the Word of Yahweh and those who molded it to suit their purpose. Eli would bend Micah's ear as they walked home at the end of the day about how wise or foolish a particular teacher was.

"It is sad," Mary was saying. "I know Zacharias was old when John was born, but the boy is simply devastated. They were so close."

Seeing The Life

"How old is the boy?" Shifra asked. Each of the women had their chosen handiwork and they would spin, sew, embroider, or basket weave as they visited.

"Just older than Yeshua, who is twelve. John was always a serious child, very dedicated to learning. He and Yeshua are similar in that way. Now, though, it is as if all he wants is to study. He no longer plays with the other boys his age. I worry he will lose these last years of his childhood."

"What of his mother?" This time is was Miriam who spoke.

"She is elderly also and very frail. They live not that far from Nazareth. I went to help Elizabeth when she was expecting John. She is related to me. Zacharias is of the tribe of Levi and was a priest. He was in Jerusalem, and an angel came to tell him that he would have a son by Elizabeth. When he did not believe the angel, he was struck dumb until the babe was born and Elizabeth declared his name was John."

"I would be struck dumb if an angel told me I was going to have a baby too," Uria said. Everyone laughed. Uria was heavy with child. If it lived, she would have five children. There had been three miscarriages in recent years, which brought a sadness to Uria's eyes that Dassa well understood. The loss of a child was an awful thing for a mother to go through.

"Hello, hello." Dinah came into the courtyard with several of her children, daughters-in-law, and grandchildren. "May we join you?"

"Of course." Dassa got to her feet. "You older children head through there." She pointed to a narrow hallway leading from the courtyard to the backyard. "The others are playing outside."

The ladies shifted, allowing the newcomers space to settle themselves and their little ones.

"Well, Uria, you look well, if a little full. Are you due soon?"

"The sooner the better. This one is sitting on my bladder." Murmurs of understanding went through the women. They all knew the issues of pregnancy.

"You let me know when you go into labor. I will pray even more for you than I do now." Dinah squeezed Uria's hand as they sat next to each other. She truly did understand, having birthed several babies before their time.

Several times during the week of Pesach various gatherings of the ladies took place. Joseph took Yeshua to the Temple almost every day for at least a while. Although he never pestered his father, Joseph knew of Yeshua's yearning to be there.

Finally, Pesach was over and the time came for Joseph, Mary, and the family to head back to Nazareth. Just as each time they left, Dassa and Mary hugged and cried. Over the years Dassa had threatened to kidnap Mary and keep her hidden in the house until Joseph gave up looking for her.

After giving each child a kiss and a blessing, the family started off with the large group from Nazareth to walk together back to their home.

[📖] [📖] [📖]

Seeing The Life

"Who is knocking at my door so late?" Micah called through the locked door.

"It is Joseph and Mary."

"What?" Micah unlocked and opened the door to let them in from the darkness.

"Is Yeshua here?" Joseph asked.

"No. What has happened?"

Dassa, Eli, and Miriam now were in the room. Dassa ran to Mary and hugged the crying woman to her.

"I will get wine," Miriam said. "Eli, come get water to wash their feet."

"When we stopped for the night last night, we went looking for Yeshua. We were all traveling together, both family and friends. Those going to Nazareth and other towns. We do it every year. Often the children move between families. When we stopped, Ya'aqov and Elizabeth found us, but Yeshua never came," Mary said.

"We looked everywhere. No one had seen him all day. We finally realized he must not have come with us at all. Mary and I left the children with family and journeyed back to the city. Has he been here? Have you seen him?"

"No," Micah said. "You must be exhausted. Did you journey back during the night?"

"No, we left early this morning, before sunrise."

"Come, sit." Dassa led Mary to a stool. Miriam appeared with wine, and Eli knelt in front of Joseph seated on another stool and began washing his feet.

"We will look tomorrow. I am surprised you were able to get here. Did you see any soldiers once it got dark?"

"No, but that is why we came here. We knew we would be welcome." Joseph lifted his cup and took a long swallow.

"Have you eaten today?" Miriam asked.

The shake of their heads gave the answer. Dassa and Miriam left to heat food for the worried couple.

All the following day they scoured the city. Gadi, Uria's twelve-year-old son, showed them places the boys had gone during the week as they had roamed the city. Mary was frantic by evening. Joseph was not much better.

As they ate their morning meal, Joseph dropped his bread. "What a fool I am. I should have thought of this sooner. I know where he is." He was rising as he spoke.

"Where?" Mary asked.

"The Temple. It is where he always wants to go. Come, Mary. We will find him there."

They hurried from the house with prayers for success in finding Yeshua following them. Mary could barely keep up until Joseph noticed her lagging. "I am sorry. I will slow down."

Into the court of the Gentiles, they crossed straight to the gate leading into the Court of Women and to the steps leading to the Court of Men. There stood their son amongst several of the leading teachers. They were listening to him ask questions few, if any, twelve-year-olds would ever think of.

"Yeshua," Joseph said, "come here."

He did, and Mary rushed to him, hugging him to her as she cried. "My son, why have you treated us so? We have been so worried looking for you everywhere."

The look Yeshua gave them was puzzled. "Why were you looking for me all over? Did you not know I would be in my Abba's house?"

Not knowing how to reply to the question, Joseph said. "Come, we must head back to Micah's house. They are sick with worry too."

"A moment of your time, please?" One of the men who had been speaking with Yeshua now stood beside them.

"Yes?"

"Your son is astounding in his knowledge and understanding. He said he is twelve?"

"Yes."

"Find me next Pesach. I would like to speak with him further. He has the makings of a rabbi. I would like to teach him, but he is too young yet."

"Who are you?"

"No one in particular. My name is Tzofar Ben Judah. I travel around some and enjoy teaching talented young men. My home is in Cana of Galilee. Yeshua tells me you live in Nazareth. That would make it convenient for him to come with me some times during the year."

"Are you going back to Cana soon?" Joseph looked at Mary, then at Yeshua and back to Tzofar.

"Yes. I only stayed here this long to speak with and hear your son."

"If you would like to journey with us as far as Nazareth, you are welcome to. We will be journeying alone since we had to return for some young man." Joseph, now relieved, ruffled Yeshua's hair.

"I would be pleased to join you. I must go and collect my wife and family. Where shall we meet?"

They planned for the return home; then Mary, Joseph, and Yeshua went to Micah's house. Tzofar and family would meet them near midday. They would be able to travel until evening, when they would camp near a town.

Dassa met them at the house. "We were so worried about you. Are you all right? Are you hungry?"

"I am fine, but yes, I am hungry." Yeshua grinned at Dassa. He was almost as tall as she was.

"You are twelve. You are always hungry."

After Dassa had placed a bowl of cooked grains before Yeshua she began to cut bread and goat cheese. "Where did you stay, Yeshua, and why did you not come here at least at night?"

"I slept in Micah's cell. I had my cloak, so I was warm enough. I was safe in the dark there. By the time we finished talking, the rabbis and I, it was dark, and I did not want to get lost in the city trying to come here."

"Did you go without food?"

"No, not really. The priests would give me a little as they left for the day. Vendors gave me some old bread and fruit." Yeshua took a bite of Dassa's bread spread with creamy goat cheese and honey. "It was not as good as yours, though."

"Do not try to make up to me with sweet words." Dassa wagged her finger at him. "You scared your parents terribly."

Seeing The Life

"I know, and I am very sorry for that. I will not do it again. Once I realized I had missed the group when they left, I thought staying at the Temple would be best. I thought they would know to find me there."

"I think if they had thought about it more, they would have. Worry can cause a person to not think clearly."

Mary came in then. "Your father is ready to leave. We must meet Tzofar soon." At Dassa's puzzled look, she continued. "He is a rabbi who stayed these days to speak with Yeshua. He would like to teach him beginning next year. He lives in Cana. We are traveling with him and his family as far as Nazareth. It will give Joseph time to get to know him. I would not want to send Yeshua off with him without knowing the man better."

"Oh my, Yeshua, you are growing up. Possibly going to study under a learned rabbi within a year. Where has the time gone?" Dassa hugged Yeshua, then let him go. She missed the entire family when they were not in Jerusalem but this boy had a special place in her heart.

Chapter 12

Eighteen years later

"Micah, will you come walk with me?" Joseph of Arimethea asked as he came into the office where Micah was tallying accounts.

"Of course." Micah set down his stylus and wax tablet and followed his employer from the building. They walked in silence through the city. The day was overcast but still warm. Micah thought it might rain later.

"Have you heard the young rabbi who is making such a name for himself?"

"The one they call John the Baptist?"

"Yes."

"No, I know he is preaching that the kingdom of Elohim is at hand and we need to repent."

"He certainly is calling for that." Joseph chuckled. "He is preaching repentance for the forgiveness of sin. He does not mince words. He is calling the Pharisees and Sadducees broods of vipers. That we cannot reply on our ancestors for acceptance. That HaShem can raise children of Abraham from stones."

"I am sure he can. He created the heavens and the earth. He made man from the dust of the ground."

Joseph was silent for a while, so Micah kept quiet while they walked. Soon they had wandered to the wall surrounding the Temple. They entered and went to the steps and stood watching the sacrifices and offerings taking place.

"Is not what we do here supposed to take our sins away? I have believed that my entire life," Joseph said.

"I have too, but... as I read and copy the Tanakh, I wonder if there is not something more to the rituals. It is as if there is something that will tie them all together. It seems there should be something which will complete them."

"I understand what you mean. Maybe John the Baptist is that something or someone." Joseph turned away from the entryway to the altar and walked down the steps. Micah went along.

"Joseph, I would like to go and hear this man. I would need some time to do so. A day or two."

"You go and spend the time you need. I have gone and heard him. I want your impression of him. Is he a true messenger for Yahweh or a false prophet?"

📖 📖 📖

Seeing The Life

Micah sat on the hill by the Jordan along with many other people. At the base stood the man they called John the Baptist.

John was a large man with long hair. His clothing was made of camel hair. A leather belt encircled his waist. His hair was long, past his shoulders. It was said he stayed in the wilderness and his food was locusts and honey he gathered from the hives of wild bees.

Zealous was the only word Micah could think of that came close to describing the man. His passion for Yahweh was like fire spreading in all directions.

"Justice and mercy are what Yahweh Tzidkenu wants of us. He wants us to see our sin. He wants us to repent of the way we have been living. He is our righteousness. There is no way but him.

"Repent of your sin. Turn your back on your selfishness, your pride. Are you not dust of the ground? Clay to be molded? Repent, ask forgiveness of your sin, for the Kingdom of Elohim is at hand. Seek righteousness, for only what is holy can approach him.

"Come and wash yourself in the cleansing water that washes away your sin. Then show the change in your life by the fruit of how you live; justice and mercy, compassion, patience, kindness. These are the fruit that will show your righteousness."

Micah could stand it no longer. He had to move. He had to walk down the hill and into the Jordan River. He knew there was no way he could wash the grime of his sins away. Only El Selich'ah could do that.

Not feeling the tears on his cheeks, Micah stood and wove in and out of the people seated on the hillside down to the banks of the river. Others went as well. Micah waited his turn, all the time praying out his regret and listing the sins that were burning in his heart. Jealousy, pride, selfishness, anger, laziness, greed. Each instance he thought about burned his soul.

As he thought about each, one thread linked them all together: pride. Not the pride of a job well done using the talents Elohim had blessed a person with, but pride of self. The feeling that he was better than another person.

Though HaShem is exalted, *he takes note of the humble, and recognizes the proud from far away.* The verse ran through his mind over and over. Micah didn't want to be far away from HaShem. He wanted to be close, under his banner, under his wing, protected by the power of his name.

John finally took Micah by the arm, leading him deeper into the water. Then he wrapped his arm around Micah and looked straight into his eyes. "Come, do you repent of the sin festering in your heart?"

"Yes, for everything."

"Do you want to be baptized for that repentance?"

"Yes."

"In the name of Adonai Elyon, I baptize you with the water of repentance."

John gripped Micah by the arms and laid him back, under the water, then brought him up to standing again. Micah could feel the filth of his sin rinsing away as the water ran down off his body. He was passed on to another man, who helped him back onto the shore.

From the first day that you purposed to understand and to humble yourself before your Adonai, your prayers were heard.

Seeing The Life

The words from Daniel rang in his head now, replacing those that told of pride keeping people from Adonai Elyon.

Micah felt lighter, like a load he was carrying on his back had been removed. He went back up the hillside to sit where he had before. Surely when all those who wanted to be baptized had been, John would speak some more. He wanted to hear whatever this prophet had to say.

After the last person was helped from the river, John stood knee deep in the Jordan and raised his hands. The crowd became silent.

"I baptize you with water, for repentance, but the one coming after me is more powerful than I am—I am not worthy to carry his sandals. He will baptize you with the Holy Spirit and fire. His winnowing fork is in his hand, and he will clean out his threshing floor and will gather his wheat into the storehouse, but the chaff he will burn up with inextinguishable fire.

"Soon... His kingdom is at hand. I have come to prepare for his coming. Watch as the maidens do with the bride, for he is coming."

Micah stumbled as he rose and headed from the hill. He was still somewhat dazed with what had occurred. What was he going to tell Joseph? Dassa? His children? Eli and Miriam? Any of his friends and family? It sounded like John was predicting another powerful prophet. How could there be one more powerful than this one, who could speak with such passion and might?

Micah was humbled by what he'd heard and by the overwhelming grief at how he had failed to live up to

Yahweh Yisrael's law. Not that he openly dishonored any of the commandments, but he had still sinned. The laws he had broken in plain view or been made accountable for he had repented of and worked hard to not repeat them. Those were not the sins he was washed clean of today. But he knew, deep in his heart, where he had broken them in secret, spurred on by his pride. Now they had been washed away. But how did a simple dunking in a river remove his guilt and shame?

Micah thought about John's words as he walked through the city. His clothing had dried in the heat of the day. Instead of going directly home, Micah went to the Temple. He stood on the steps of the inner court looking at the altar where the sacrifices were burned to make a pleasing aroma ascending to heaven. Never had the act of handing the offering to the priest had the power that the words of John and the simple dip in the river had.

Why?

Faith. He had believed without a doubt that El Selich'ah knew he was truly sorry for his sins and was going to turn away from yielding to them in the future.

Faith. Had he ever really believed that killing a lamb, a dove, offering bread or wine was enough to remove his guilt? He well knew what the Talmud said. He gave the offerings as instructed. He obeyed the commands even when he knew he had failed to live up the Law. It was faith that made the difference. Micah knew without a doubt that his sins had been forgiven because he had confessed them to HaShem with true sorrow in his heart.

Leaving the steps, Micah went to his small cell in the wall. A curtain across the doorway indicated it was assigned to someone when he was gone. Today he entered but didn't draw back the curtain to let in the light. Instead he knelt in the small space then prostrated himself on the floor. Again tears came, and Micah did nothing to stop them. These were tears of praise and thanksgiving for the gift El-Elyon had given in the new understanding and stronger faith Micah had in his creator.

Now he had to figure out how to express what had moved him so and make it so his family and friends could understand it. He wanted them to find the peace he now had. It wasn't the trappings of ritual, but faith in El Shaddai; that was the key.

The meanings of the stories of the great men of Israel's past became clear. Abram left all he knew to go somewhere not yet revealed to him. Abraham was willing to tie Isaac to present as a sacrifice. Moses stood at the edge of the Red Sea with all the Israelites behind him, Pharaoh's army ready to attack. Elijah called fire down from heaven. Daniel and the lion; Hananiah, Mishael and Azariah in the fiery furnace. David and Goliath. Event after event of Yahweh's chosen people flashed through his mind. Each of these were based solely on faith in Yahweh Yireh's provision and protection.

Micah thought of the Sadducees and their rejection of the immortality of the soul. If this life was all there was, then what was faith in Yahweh all about? If there were no rewards for obedience or penalties for committing sin, why bother to obey?

The Pharisees claimed to hold the Tanakh and the Oral Torah as equal in authority. It had always bothered

Micah that the Oral Torah laws changed as circumstances changed. There wasn't the certainty of consequence or true justice when the law could be so easily altered. He would need to consider this further before he spoke with Joseph. Right now, he wanted to go home and speak with Dassa and the rest of his family.

"Dassa," Micah called when he entered the house. The years had been good to them. Eight children survived with only two others, besides Perez, having died. They had named another son Perez to honor Micah's father. They had ten grandchildren. Eli and Perez had both built onto the family home when they had married. Having small children in the house again was wonderful, especially when someone else was responsible for them.

Sarah and Miriam were both married and living in Jerusalem. Tabith at fifteen was looking forward to her wedding, which would be in several months. She was to be married to Joseph's son Orli, whose first wife had died in childbirth. Orli was nearly ten years older than Tabith, who would become the mother to Orli's two children. They had decided to wait until Tabith was sixteen before she took on such responsibility.

Benjamin had just become a teenager with the gangliness boys seemed to have at that age. Abigail was nine, and David only six. He had a niece and nephew older than himself.

After David was born, Dassa had said enough was enough. She and Micah had been more careful, and no more pregnancies occurred.

"Dassa," he called again as he went into the courtyard.

"Softa is on the roof working with her flax." It was seven-year-old Joses, Eli's first child. He and David were playing in the water of the fountain, which had been built in the center of the open space.

"And who is watching you two? Are you supposed to be in the fountain when no one is around?" Micah looked sternly at his son and grandson.

"Tabith, but Orli came and they went to the kitchen." David splashed water at Joses, who splashed it back.

Just then the couple came into the courtyard with Orli's two sons Levi and Jude. Each boy had raisins in his hands.

"Abba." Tabith ran over and gave him a kiss on the cheek. "Welcome home. It is early in the day for you to be here. Orli, will you please strip the boys and put them into the fountain?"

Micah watched his future son-in-law as he did as Tabith had asked. *Maybe she doesn't need to wait until she's sixteen. She seemed to be able to order her future husband around well enough.* A grin threatened to appear at the thought, but he was able to contain it.

"Yes. I went to see the man everyone is talking about, John the Baptist. What he says is powerful. I want to talk about it with everyone at supper. Right now I am headed for the roof to speak with your ima."

"We will watch the boys. Tell her I have added to the stew since we have company."

Micah grinned. "Unexpected company?"

"Abba," Tabith said, "Orli has been out of the city. You know that. He just got back today."

Orli came to stand behind Tabith and pulled her against his chest and eyed Micah. "You sent me on that journey. I think just to get me away from this beautiful young woman."

"How right you are." Micah laughed and clapped Orli on the shoulder as he went past on his way to the roof staircase. "I am a father, but I remember being a young man waiting on a wedding."

Dassa was beating the flax with the special smooth stick she kept for this purpose, and heaven help the child who took it to play with. Micah snuck up behind her, knelt, and grabbed her waist to pull her to him. The stick came around and whopped him on the side of the head.

"Ouch. What did you do that for?" Micah fell back onto his seat and rubbed his head.

"Oh, Micah, I am so sorry. You startled me." Dassa dropped the stick and crawled quickly to him. "Let me see." She pulled his hand away from his head and looked for any injury. "The children all learned quickly not to come at me from behind when I was beating flax. You missed that lesson, I see."

"I most certainly did. I need a kiss to make up for the hurt." Micah grabbed her and pulled her to him. When Dassa made to kiss the spot the stick had struck, he quickly turned his head so her lips met his.

"You certainly are in a good mood. And you are home early."

"Joseph wanted me to go hear the Rabbi John the Baptist. I did today instead of going to work." Micah settled himself more with his back against the wall they had built around the roof. He kept his arms around Dassa.

"Is he as powerful a speaker as they say?"

"Even more so. He spoke with such passion and zeal. And his message was so different than what we normally hear from the rabbis. The purpose of his ministry is to get people to repent of their sins and turn to living a righteous life. It is not the righteousness of either the Pharisees or Sadducees but rather the righteousness of HaShem. The forgiveness of sin. That is what John's baptism is. The washing away of sin and putting on HaShem's righteousness. Fleeing the coming wrath and being assured of mercy and grace.

"He spoke of the coming kingdom and that it is near. Someone is coming who is greater than he. Someone who will baptize with Ruach HaKodesh. Someone who existed before him. John is not very old. I would say he has not been a rabbi long."

"So you think around thirty?"

"Not any younger, since a man must be that age before he can become a rabbi. But not much older."

"I would like to hear this man. Would Joseph let you go tomorrow also?" Dassa tipped her head back to look up at his face.

"He told me to take all the time I needed to learn about the man. Joseph has many questions concerning what he believes."

Chapter 13

The following day, Micah, Dassa, Eli, and Perez and their wives, as well as Tabith and Orli and Benjamin, sat on the hill amongst even more people than had been there the day before. The discussion during supper had been lively.

Orli, being the son of a Pharisee, doubted the warning to escape the coming wrath John had preached. He'd been raised without a thought to Yahweh bringing punishment on his people. He lived by the letter of both the Tanakh and the Oral Torah. After all, Orli and his family made sure they purified themselves with ritual baths. They kept the laws set down by Moshe for the priests, even though they were not. Eli had countered with passages from Isaiah and Jeremiah in which the prophets had warned Israel about what would happen if they didn't turn from their evil ways.

A hush fell over the crowd when John stood before them on the back of the Jordan. An air of expectance, both positive and negative, hung heavy.

John raised his arms and spoke: "Repent of your sins and turn to Adonai, for the Kingdom of Heaven is near. Elohim is holy and cannot be where there is sin. Therefore, repent and give evidence of your repentance by being baptized. Let the old life, the sinful life, be washed away."

As he spoke, his tone and demeanor were earnest and compassionate. Suddenly, it changed. "You brood of snakes!" he exclaimed. Micah looked in the direction John was pointing. A group of Pharisees and Sadducees stood there, a frown on each face. "Who warned you to flee Elohay Mishpat's coming wrath? Prove by the way you live that you have repented of your sins and turned to HaShem. Do not simply say to each other, 'We are safe, for we are descendants of Abraham.' That means nothing, for I tell you, El Shaddai can create children of Abraham from these very stones. Even now the ax of Elohay Mishpat is poised, ready to sever the roots of the trees. Yes, every tree that does not produce good fruit will be chopped down and thrown into the fire."

The crowd was stunned. They had never heard anyone speak to the leaders in such a manor. A wave of murmuring rippled through the people. Could this be he? Could this rough man be the long-awaited Messiah?

"Are you the Christ? Are you the Messiah of Israel?" someone yelled. All eyes turned to find the one who had asked then turned back to John, breathless in their anxiousness to hear his answer.

"I baptize with water those who repent of their sins and turn to El-Elyon. But someone is coming soon who is greater than I—so much greater that I am not worthy even to stoop down to untie and carry his sandals. I baptize you with water, but He will baptize you with the Ruach HaKodesh and with fire. He is ready to separate the chaff from the wheat with his winnowing fork. Then he will clean up the threshing area, gathering the wheat into his barn but burning the chaff with never-ending fire."

John repeated his call for repentance and giving evidence of their forgiveness by how they lived.

Another in the mass of people called, "What should we do?"

John replied, "If you have two shirts, give one to the poor. If you have food, share it with those who are hungry."

A man everyone knew was a corrupt tax collector yelled out next. "Rabbi, what should I do?"

He replied, "Collect no more taxes than the government requires."

A group of soldiers surprised everyone by coming down the hill to the river's edge. "What should we do?"

John replied, "Do not extort money or make false accusations. And be content with your pay."

More and more people were rising and making their way to the water. John or several of his followers spoke with each man, woman, or child, then laid them back into the Jordan and lifted them out. The water streaming off each one reminded Micah of yesterday when he had felt his sins being forgiven and the desire for a new way of living and a new type of faith replacing the burden of his sin.

Dassa gripped his hand. Orli and Tabith were standing in line. Tabith was crying against his chest, and Orli's head rested on hers as he cried too. Micah looked around. Eli was gone, as was Perez's wife. He scanned the long line of people waiting to be baptized. They stood together, both visibly weeping. Eli had his arm around his sister-in-law's shoulder. Micah turned to look at his other son and daughter-in-law.

Perez said, "I need to think some more. It seems too simple."

Eli's wife, Geva, sat with a scowl on her face, elbows on her knees, fists on the side of her head. Micah said a silent prayer that her heart would be opened to John's message.

Micah felt Dassa shift beside him. He watched her get on her knees and bend down until her face was near the ground. He didn't disturb her. This was a position she often prayed in. Micah closed his eyes and prayed for his wife and each member of his family. He so wanted them to find the peace he had. He'd never felt closer to El Shamayim than he did now, and he had thought he was close before.

The noise of the crowd ebbed and flowed, but he heard the sobs Dassa let out. She was rocking back and forth just as she had with the deaths of each of their children. Grief poured off her in almost visible waves. He scooted closer and placed a hand gently on her back. Dassa collapsed toward him, and he pulled her onto her lap as she wept.

Seeing The Life

"Dassa," Micah said softly into her ear, "do you want to go and be baptized?"

"Y...yes. I need to have my sin washed away. I cannot stand the weight. I thought I was so devout, so obedient. But I am such a sinner. My heart is so foul."

"Come, I will help you." Gently Micah helped his weeping wife to her feet. The line was much shorter now. Eli was standing, soaking wet, while his brother's wife, Rachel, was being lowered into the water. He looked up the hill. Micah saw Perez look at his wife then search until he saw his parents. Eli smiled and waved before turning to help Rachel from the river.

When Micah and Dassa arrived in the river, John was the one who turned to them. All of his other disciples were with others.

"You were here yesterday," John said.

"Yes, this is my wife, Dassa. She wants to be baptized."

"Praise Elohim," John said. Then he looked at Micah. "Would you like to baptize her?"

Micah was shocked by the question. He looked at Dassa, whose eyes plead for an affirmative answer. Not wanting to hold up the line but unsure if he was qualified, Micah asked, "How can I? I am not a rabbi."

"Do you think HaShem cares who helps one of his children in repentance?"

Micah smiled. "No." He turned Dassa to face him. "Dassa, do you repent of your sin?"

"Yes."

"Do you want to be baptized to show you are washed clean and have a new closeness to Adonai Eloheikhem?"

"Oh yes, so very much." Tears were again streaming down her cheeks.

"Then I baptize you in the name of El Shaddai with the water of repentance." He felt tears on his own cheeks as he dipped her back into the Jordan and lifted her up into a tight embrace. When he loosened his arms, Dassa looked up at him with a bright smile.

John placed a hand on both of their shoulders and said, "May Adonai Elyon bless you as you bear the fruit of his forgiveness."

Micah gripped the hand on his shoulder and helped Dassa from the water.

📖 📖 📖

With the children all put to bed, the adults who lived in the house Micah had purchased years ago gathered in the courtyard. The fountain was silent, but the voices rose and fell as they spoke about John and his message.

"I am not so bad. I do not break the commandments." Geva's tone was defensive.

"What about sacrificing what you might simply want and seeing to the needs of another?" Eli asked.

Dassa knew what her son was referring to. Geva had been saving for a silk tunic. She embroidered beautifully on veils and shawls and sold them to a merchant in the city. When she had saved enough for the tunic, Eli and she had gone to the shop that carried them. On the way, a mother with three children all with the same color cloak stood on a corner. The woman had no cloak. The children were thin, as was the mother.

Seeing The Life

Eli had pointed them out to his wife. When he'd told Dassa of it later, Eli had been very disappointed with Geva. Instead of delaying her purchase of the silk dress and purchasing a cloak and some food for the family, she had brushed past them and spent all her money on the most expensive dress in the shop. That night Dassa had heard sharply spoken words from the room Eli and Geva occupied. Eli had given Dassa money and one of his wife's cloaks and asked her to find the mother and children. Eli wanted his mother to take them to the market and purchase food. Dassa had never been so proud of her son.

Geva sat, her mouth gaping, and looked at her husband. Her hand shook as she brought it to her lips. "Oh Eli, I never meant to be selfish. I had saved for so long." A sob broke out. She leaned onto Eli's lap. "How could I not see that their need should come before my want? Love your neighbor as yourself. We are trying to that to teach our children. What an awful mother I am? I am so guilty. Oh Eli, what am I going to do?"

Eli pulled her to him. "Tomorrow we will go listen to John again, and you can repent and be washed of your sin."

"I want to so badly but... I know I will be selfish again. I cannot live a perfect life. I will sin in so many ways."

"We all will, Geva," Micah said. He was sitting near, and he patted Geva's back gently. "I hope and pray I will realize when I sin, or even when I am tempted, so I can stop and ask for El Selich'ah's forgiveness and help in keeping me from sinning."

Dassa looked at each family member. "I would like to ask each of you to tell me when I am about to or have done something wrong and help me stop. I think it will take me a long time to learn to love my neighbor the way I should."

Geva replied, "Of course, but only if you will do the same for me. I know I will argue and try to justify what I want, but tell me anyway. Pleasing Adonai Elyon is so much more important even though at the time I will not think so."

Chuckles followed Geva's words, but everyone agreed to keep each other accountable.

Sabba Eli, Dassa's father, said, "Do you think this baptism needs to be in the Jordan for HaShem to accept it?"

"John didn't say to be washed in Jordan's water. He said to be washed in the water of repentance." This time it was Perez who spoke. He hadn't said much since they had left the river. He was the child who spent much time in thought, figuring out how to solve a problem and thinking about the passages of the Tanahk Micah had set the children to memorizing.

"Do you think the water of the fountain would work?"

"Do you want to be baptized, Abba?" Dassa asked. Her father couldn't walk much anymore. His joints hurt too badly.

Tears glistened in the lamp light. Eli tried to speak, but no sound came out. He nodded.

"I...I want to also." This time it was Miriam's quiet request.

Seeing The Life

Young Eli helped Sabba Eli rise, and he and Micah helped the old man into the fountain. Dassa held onto her mother's hands as they watched Micah ask the questions. Then the son-in-law and grandson lowered the frail man into the water and lifted him back up. Geva had gotten towels and blankets as well as another tunic. None wanted Sabba Eli to become ill. Once young Eli and Micah had helped dry and dress Sabba Eli, Dassa and Tabith helped Miriam into the fountain.

"We seem to all be crying," Tabith said. Dassa looked around and saw that even the men had tears in their eyes, if not on their cheeks. Her comment made them all chuckle, breaking the tension but not the mood.

Again Micah and Young Eli completed the baptism, and Geva was there, ready to help dry and change Miriam's tunic.

"Eli," Geva said, "would you baptize me? I cannot live with this guilt another moment."

"Of course, my love." Tenderly, Eli lifted Geva into the fountain and held her close while he asked if she repented of her sin and wanted to be baptized. Then he kissed her forehead and lowered her into the water as a repentant sinner and lifted her out as a forgiven daughter of El-Elyon.

All eyes turned to Perez, who was the only one who had not been washed clean of his sin. "Not tonight. I do not want any of you dipping me down into the fountain. You might not bring me back up." He grinned. "I will wait until tomorrow and go to the Jordan."

Chapter 14

The following day, Joseph joined Micah, Dassa, and Perez as they went to hear John the Baptist again. Benjamin, who was thirteen, and nine-year-old Abigail were also wanting to hear the teaching, so they tagged along. Soon they were sitting on the hillside. It seemed to Dassa that even more people were crowded there.

As John spoke, some people heckled, shouting that they believed the Pharisees and didn't need repentance. That the sacrifices and offerings kept them righteous. Some called out that John was the Messiah; others, Elijah.

When John called for those who were wanting to repent and be baptized, Perez jumped to his feet. Then he looked at Ben and Abby.

"Can I go, Ima?" Abby said. "I want to get right with El Selich'ah. I do not want to have my sin on me."

"Of course, sweetheart." Dassa saw the desperate look on her daughter's face. "Go with Perez." Ben, who had stood up, grabbed his sister's hand, and they ran to catch up with Perez as he made his way through the people sitting or standing on the hillside.

"What do you think, Joseph?" Micah asked. Dassa looked at her husband's employer and friend.

"What he says makes sense. Isaiah said the same thing. El Shaddai does not want our sacrifices. He is sick of them because they are accompanied by evil deeds."

A voice shouted, "Are you the one we wait for? Are you the Messiah? Tell us."

John finished the baptism he was performing and turned his attention to the crowd. "No, but someone is coming soon who is greater than I am—so much greater that I am not worthy even to stoop down to untie and carry his sandals. I baptize you with water, but He will baptize you with the Ruach HaKodesh and with fire. His kingdom draws near. Repent, for his judgment is holy and just."

"I am going down to be baptized, Micah. John's words burn in my heart." Joseph went to stand in line with the others.

Dassa leaned back against Micah. Tears choked her throat as they had the day before. This time they were not tears of repentance but rather tears of joy that so many in her family had listened as John preached and had repented of their sins. She would have to go see her married daughters and speak to them of this.

"Dassa, look. Is that not Yeshua Ben Joseph talking with John?" Micah asked.

"Yes, it is. I wonder if the rest of the family is with him." Dassa sat straighter and swung her head back and forth as she searched the crowd.

"Look, he is being baptized. Watch so we can tell Joseph and Mary at Pesach if they are not here."

They watched, eyes fixed on the two men. It was as if they could not look away. As John bent Yeshua back and submerged him beneath the flow, a white dove flew in a circle just above them. As Yeshua came back to standing, the dove landed on his shoulder. A gasp went up from those watching. Then it was drowned out by a voice that filled the heavens.

"You are my dearly loved Son, and you bring me great joy."

Silence reigned for several moments before arguments broke out amongst the people.

"It was the voice of El Shamayim."

"You are crazy. It was thunder."

"Could you not hear the words?"

"Words? I heard only thunder."

"Look around. The sun is shining. There are no clouds."

"Why do some people not hear the voice and understand the words, Micah?" Dassa asked.

"I do not know. Maybe the ones who heard were those who had been or want to be baptized."

"They are wanting a better relationship with El Shaddai. Maybe those who did not do not want that."

"*You are a stubborn and stiff-necked people,*" Micah quoted. "HaShem has been saying that since the time of Moses."

Dassa chuckled softly. "People never change, do we?"

"Not without Attiq Yomin's help."

"You are so right." Dassa pondered the meaning of the dove and Elohim's voice. She remembered the night Yeshua was born in the stable of her parents' inn in Bethlehem. Mary a virgin. The shepherds. Then later the wise men with their gifts. Joseph's dream and taking his family away in the night. Her first son, Perez. Now this.

"Abba, Ima," Abby's excited voice said, "I was baptized and my sins are washed away. And look who we found? Yeshua. He came to be baptized too."

Micah stood and helped Dassa up. She hugged Yeshua to her. He bent down and kissed her cheek.

"Doda, I am delighted to see you and Dod here. When Perez told me you had been baptized, as well as so many of your family, it cheered my heart. Then this little imp came to hug me, and I nearly got wet all over again." Yeshua smiled affectionately at the young girl who stood close at his side.

"Are your parents and siblings here?" Micah asked.

"No, they are in Nazareth. I have come from being with Rabbi Tzofar Ben Judah. I have finished my training and vetting, and now I am a rabbi. Also a carpenter, but more a rabbi." Yeshua smiled and, as always, it was bright and welcoming.

"Where are you staying?" Micah asked.

"I just came to the city today."

"Well, come home with us and stay as long as you want. You are family to us." Dassa patted him on the cheek.

"Thank you, I shall stay the night but I leave tomorrow. I have a need to be alone to pray."

"As much as I want you to stay longer, if Adonai Eloheikhem calls, you must go," Dassa said.

Joseph had come back to them by this time, and Micah introduced him to Yeshua.

"You certainly had a special baptism, young man. Seems Adonai Elyon favors you."

"Thank you, sir. I only hope to live up to his expectations."

After the evening meal, the family and Yeshua sat in the courtyard. Micah and Dassa's daughters and their families had joined them for the meal but left so as not to journey through the city after dark.

"Yeshua," Micah said. "What do you think the meaning of the dove and the words are?"

"You do not hesitate to ask questions do you, Dod?" Yeshua chuckled.

"You forget. We were there the night you were born."

"I help verify your ima's virginity," Dassa said as she blushed.

"Ah," Yeshua said. "Yes, Ima and Abba told me. It had slipped my mind."

"Dassa and I were witnesses to the miracle." This time it was Miriam who spoke.

Yeshua smiled but didn't respond. Rather, he covered a yawn with his hand and said, "I have walked a long way today. If you will not consider me rude, I ask that I may retire now. I have a long journey tomorrow."

"Of course. You know where to go to find the boys' sleeping room." Over the years, a second story had been added to the house—several sleeping rooms as well as a large room that spanned the front of the house and was used for meals when most of the family and friends were there.

"Yes, thank you for everything. Come on Ben, David, and you too, Perez, if you want to talk for a while. We can catch up as we get ready to sleep."

Those left in the courtyard watched them leave.

"How come he did not invite me?" Abby stuck out her lip in a pout.

"Because you are a girl, silly. Come on. We can do our own talking." Tabith jerked her little sister to her feet, and they went off laughing as they climbed the steps to their sleeping room.

The two couples who had been present at the birth of the young rabbi sat silently wondering, knowing something was special about him but not realizing how he would change the world.

In the morning, Dassa made Yeshua eat a good breakfast and packed him a satchel full of food. Then she waved as he went down the street. She didn't know that as he walked through the city, he handed every bit of food to beggars and poor children along the way.

Chapter 15

Yeshua returned for one night about six weeks later. He was quite thin but looked fit. Dassa fussed over him, urging him to eat more. She tried to get him to stay a few more days to regain his strength. He wouldn't tell them where he had gone, only that he spent the time praying and discerning how Elohay Elohim wanted him to proceed.

There was even more confidence in him than he'd had before. A new authority covered him like a cloak.

"Why do you not stay a few more days, Yeshua?" Dassa packed more food and another skin of watered wine into the satchel he had brought back with him.

"I am sorry, Doda. I need to return to Galilee and Nazareth. I do not want to worry my parents. We will come for Pasach and see you then."

Dassa frowned then grinned. "You are such a fine young man, Yeshua. Your love and caring for your family is a wonderful example for all. Give your ima and abba my love and tell your siblings I love them too. Also make sure they know they are welcome here during Pasach."

Yeshua kissed Dassa on the forehead. "May Adonai Eloheikhem bless you and yours today and always."

Dassa repeated the blessing and stood in the doorway to watch Yeshua walk away.

📖 📖 📖

"Ima, Sabba, Softa."

Dassa heard Ben's thirteen-year-old voice crack as he ran into the house yelling their names.

"Quiet, Ben," Sabba Eli scolded. "The babies are sleeping. What is so important that you have to scream it all over the city?"

They gathered in the kitchen along with Geva and Rachel. Each had given birth recently, and the babies were asleep in baskets in the shade of the courtyard.

"You should have seen it. Yeshua came into the Temple with a handful of ropes. He yelled at the merchants saying they were thieves and whipping them with the ropes. Then he lifted the moneychangers' tables. The ones made of the heavy iron. He just lifted them and threw them over. He kept hold of the ropes and whipped the moneychangers until they left the spilled coins and ran from the Court of the Gentiles out into the city. There were feathers flying everywhere, and the lambs got out and were running and baaing. The merchants were running around screaming for the Temple guards, slipping in the, well, you know."

Sabba Eli placed his hand on Ben's shoulder to stop the boy from bouncing up and down on his toes. "Did Yeshua say anything while he was doing this?"

"Yes, he said, 'Get these things out of here. Stop turning my Abba's house into a marketplace!' You should have seen him. You know what those moneychanger's tables are like. Iron strongboxes. He lifted them up and heaved them across the courtyard. Every last one of them. I did not know anyone could do that."

They all stared, amazed at Ben's tale. Just then, Micah came into the house. "Ben, I am glad and relieved to find you here. In the turmoil at the Temple I lost track of you.

As angry at you as I am for leaving without telling me, I am relieved you came to no harm."

"I came home after Yeshua finished throwing the strongboxes around." Ben grinned. "That whip he made from ropes helped me decide that I should get away from the Temple as fast as possible."

Dassa handed each of them drink and asked, "What happened after that?"

"The Temple guards finally stopped him, but Yeshua seemed to have completed his purpose." Micah sipped from his cup. "Then the Temple leaders asked him what he thought he was doing. Why he thought he had the authority to do such a thing. They told him to show them a miracle to prove it."

"Did he?" Miriam asked.

"He told them to destroy this Temple, and he would raise it up in three days."

"What?" There was a chorus of voices asking the question.

"That is what they asked. Then they said, 'It has taken forty-six years to build this Temple, and you can rebuild it in three days?' Then he turned his back to them and walked out of the Temple."

"And they let him?" Eli asked.

"I think they were so startled that they could not think of what to do or say."

"Micah." Dassa placed a hand on his arm. "You must go and find him. The Temple guards will probably be looking for him. We cannot let Yeshua be taken. It would break his mother's heart."

"I will go look, but it is getting close to sundown. Pesach is tonight. I will not miss celebrating it." Micah left and a short time later came home with Yeshua and four other men.

"Doda, it is good to see you. Thank you for inviting us to celebrate Pesach with you." Yeshua kissed Dassa on the cheek. "Let me introduce you to my friends. They are traveling with me." Yeshua introduced Dassa to Cephas, Andrew, Philip, and Nathanael.

📖 📖 📖

Joseph was waiting for Micah when he arrived at the warehouse the day after the Pesach Sabbath. It was evident by the expression on his face that he had heard about the incident at the Temple.

"So, Micah, I know he is a friend of your family and that you have known Yeshua Ben Joseph since his birth, but what was he thinking of, rampaging through the Court of the Gentiles and scattering the animals and overturning the moneychanger's tables? How could he manage to even lift them? It takes several men to move one of them."

"I must say, his anger surely gave him strength. It was stirring to watch. Passion for the Temple of Adonai Elyon seemed to consume him. What he saw, I think, was that the focus of the Temple had been changed from being the place where Elohim dwells and interacts with his people to a greed-filled marketplace."

Joseph looked as if he were confused. "Think about it. How is what goes on in the Temple court different from what happens in the marketplace in any city or town?

Animals and birds are sold at inflated prices. The exchange rate of regular coins for Temple coins is nowhere near equitable. Greed is rampant by the vendors and the Temple leaders who rent the spaces. But the animals need to be perfect and the coins cannot be ordinary currency. How else could these be purchased?"

"Joseph, where in the Tanakh does it say that the coins offered have to be special coins?"

Joseph thought for a few moments. "I do not remember anywhere."

"I have not found it either. What does that tell you? Why are special coins minted just to be sold to be offered in the Temple?"

Joseph nodded then in a discouraged tone said, "Only to make more money. They have little value in themselves. They cannot be used as legal tender. Only Roman and other foreign currency is legal. Their value is only to the Temple."

"Yes. They are sold to the moneychangers, who sell them to the people, who give them back to the Temple to be resold to the moneychangers. Do you see the cycle of greed?"

"I have never thought of it before. It is simply how it has been done for longer than I have been alive." After being deep in thought for a few minutes, Joseph looked at Micah. "And the animals come from farms and herds owned by Pharisees and other Sadducees. They are the only ones allowed to be used for sacrifice. Everyone must purchase the animal at the Temple. They cannot bring one from outside."

Micah nodded.

"I feel the same zeal Yeshua felt growing inside me. We have allowed the Temple to become a marketplace for greed and injustice." Joseph rubbed a hand down his face.

"I believe we have spoken before of the beginning words of Isaiah. *'What are the multitude of your sacrifices to me? says Yahweh.*
I have had enough of the burnt offerings of rams,
And the fat of fed animals.
I don't delight in the blood of bulls,
Or of lambs,
Or of male goats.
When you come to appear before me,
Who has required this at your hand, to trample my courts?
Bring no more vain offerings.
Incense is an abomination to me;
New moons, Sabbaths, and convocations:
I can't bear with evil assemblies.
My soul hates your New Moons and your appointed feasts;
They are a burden to me.
I am weary of bearing them."

Joseph nodded as Micah recited the passage. Sadness filled his eyes. "We have become a burden to Yahweh Yisrael. We have turned from righteousness to evil. From glorifying El Gadol Gibor Yare to making a mockery of his faithfulness."

That evening a knock was heard on the front door after dark. Young Eli answered it. Standing there was a man dressed in the robes of a Pharisee. He looked around nervously before he spoke.

"My name is Nicodemus. I would like to speak with Yeshua Ben Joseph. I hear he is staying here. May I come in?"

"Do you bring Temple guards with you?" Eli asked.

Nicodemus looked around again. "No. I come alone. I must speak with him."

"Come in then. We are in a room upstairs. Follow me."

They had gathered in the long room on the second story because of the drizzle wetting the courtyard. Young Eli, Micah, and Perez exchanged looks, all wondering if the door would be broken down at any moment with all of them being dragged away to be held for questioning. Only Yeshua seemed calm.

"Ah, Nicodemus. Ask your question."

The man seemed surprised that his name was known by Yeshua. "I have heard John preach that the Kingdom of Elohim is near and he has come to prepare the way. Rabbi, we all know HaShem has sent you to teach us. Your miraculous signs are evidence that Elohim is with you."

"I tell you the truth, unless you are born again, you cannot see the Kingdom of God."

"What? I am an old man. My ima has died. How can an old man go back into his ima's womb and be born again?"

They sat awed as Yeshua explained how people can only produce people, but the Ruach HaKodesh gives birth to spiritual life. It was not physical rebirth he was speaking of but spiritual rebirth.

Chapter 16

Micah sought out Joseph the next morning to tell him of the things Yeshua had spoken of. He had lain awake several hours thinking. What did he mean when he said the Son of Man must be lifted up like the bronze pole that Moses raised to stop the plague in the wilderness? Before he left the house he, Dassa, and her parents spoke and prayed about the teachings of Yeshua and what to reveal to Joseph of Arimethea.

"Joseph," Micah said when he found him standing with several of the other workers. "I would like to speak with you." They walked into Joseph's private office, and Micah closed the door.

"Is this very serious, Micah? You seem unsettled."

"I... Yes, I guess I am. Last night Nicodemus the Pharisee came to speak with Yeshua. He had questions, and I'm not sure the answers pleased him. Some of them I find easy to understand, others, well, more difficult. Also, there are things about him you do not know that we, I, Dassa, and my in-laws do.

"We have prayed about what to speak to you of and asked for a clear message from HaShem. My peace about it increased as I walked to work today. If you have important tasks for me to do, this can wait, but..."

"Nothing that needs done right away, Micah," Joseph interrupted. "Sit. I will pour some wine."

They settled on the rug, Micah swallowing some of the watered wine before he spoke. "You know Yeshua was born in the stable at Dassa's abba's inn."

Joseph nodded.

"There is much more to it you don't know. Mary, his ima, was a virgin. Dassa, Miriam, the midwife, and Dassa's cousin and several women guests all checked her." Micah blushed while Joseph's mouth dropped open. "Yes, I know. Astounding is it not?"

"*And a virgin with give birth to a son.* Oh, Bethlehem. You come from Bethlehem where the Messiah is to be born." Joseph stared.

"Yes. Other things happened that night. There was a strange star, brighter than ever before. Brighter than the moon. Shepherds came in the night saying an angel appeared to them and told them the Messiah had been born and where to find the babe. They said a heavenly army sang 'Glory to God in the highest and peace on earth to those with whom God is pleased.'

"Dassa and I were married shortly after. I had built the house where we lived when you came to us. Mary and Joseph took a small abandoned hut nearby. Dassa and

Mary became good friends. Our first son, Perez, was born while they were still in Bethlehem.

"When Yeshua was almost two, a group of men came. They were wealthy men, wise men of their country. They said they were looking for the infant king. They had seen his star. Myrrh, frankincense, and gold were given to the family. They worshipped Yeshua.

"A few days later, Joseph came in the night knocking at our door. He told me an angel came to tell him to take the boy and flee. He would not tell me where they were going."

Micah took another sip of wine and cleared his throat. "They left that night. I do not remember the number of days, but Roman soldiers came to Bethlehem and..." Micah's voice broke, and he took a deep breath before he continued. "They slaughtered all the boys two years of age and below."

"Your son among them," Joseph said. Micah nodded. "As you have been speaking, passages have been rising to the forefront of my mind. I want to ask... Do you know where Joseph took his family when they left?"

"Egypt."

Joseph gasped. *"I summoned my son out of Egypt."*

"Yes."

Silence reigned in the room for several minutes. Each man searching in their minds through the prophets' writings, looking for more instances where Yeshua fit with prophecy of the Messiah.

"So you think this Yeshua Ben Joseph might be the long-awaited Messiah?" Joseph looked Micah right in the eye.

"I think it is possible. Having my wife verify his virgin birth and then all that has followed makes me wonder. That is why I am speaking with you today. You have studied the Tanakh. You are very learned. If he is the long-awaited one then we need to listen to what he teaches."

"You are right. We need to listen and compare it with HaShem's words. That is the only way we can be sure."

"That is another reason I wanted to speak with you today. What Yeshua said last night is so very different from any teaching I have heard before.

"He told Nicodemus that we must be born again to see the Kingdom of God."

"What did he mean, born again?"

"We must be born of the Ruach HaKodesh, and it can't be explained how people are born of the Ruach HaKodesh."

"That is true," Joseph said. "At no time when the Ruach HaKodesh came upon a person has it been explained how it happened. It just did. Saul, David, Joshua, Gideon, the craftsmen who built the Tabernacle. I can think of many."

"As can I."

"I want to ask how." Joseph chuckled. "But your Yeshua said it cannot be explained?"

"Just as the wind blows and you cannot tell where it comes from or where it is going, you cannot explain how people are born of the Ruach HaKodesh."

"What else did he say?" Joseph had reclined on the rug, stretching out his legs.

"No one has gone to heaven and returned, but the Son of Man has come down from heaven. Then he said Elohim so loved the world that he gave his one and only Son, so that everyone who believes in him will not perish but have eternal life. God sent his Son into the world not to judge the world but to save the world through him."

"His son Yeshua?"

"Both Joseph and Mary, his parents, were told that Mary's son would be the son of Elohim."

Joseph nodded.

"He also said those who do not believe in him have already been judged. Light has come into the world, and evil will be revealed. People will reject the light because they want to keep their evil deeds hidden."

Joseph grinned slightly. "Well, that is certainly true. Those who do evil usually do it in the dark or at least out of the view of others."

"So how do we believe in him, Joseph? How will we know if he is the Messiah in truth?"

"The prophets were known to be real if what they said came true. If they did not, they were stoned."

"Yeshua said another thing I do not understand. Maybe you can explain it. It sounded like a prophecy to me. He said the Son of Man had to be lifted up like the bronze snake of Moshe so everyone who believes in him with have eternal life."

"It sounds as if something will happen that will make it so all of Israel will be able to see and know who he is, Micah."

"That is what I thought. Maybe he will overthrow the Romans. All of Israel would believe him then."

"Yes, I pray that is what he means. Here, have some more wine." Joseph poured more into each cup. "If I may be so bold, I would like to come to your house and meet with this Yeshua. I do not know if you realize, but his ima is a niece of mine. My brother was a proud man, and when Mary became pregnant before she and Joseph were wed, he cut her off from the rest of the family."

"I would gladly invite you, however, he has left and will be staying out amongst those who came from Nazareth for Pesach. He will travel back with them."

"Nazareth?"

"Yes, that is where he is from."

Joseph's jaw dropped. *"You will conceive a son and he will be called a Nazarene."*

Micah could only nod at the words from Judges.

[📖] [📖] [📖]

Joseph went to where his son Orli was weighing some silver. "When you are finished, would you please come and walk with me?"

"Of course, Abba."

Joseph left the warehouse and stood in the street. Soon Orli joined him. "Come, walk with me." They fell into step together and silently wove through the narrow streets.

"You were baptized by John, I know," Joseph said. When Orli looked sharply at his father, Joseph chucked. "Micah told me. Now for a greater shock. I was too."

That stopped Orli in his tracks, only to be bumped from behind. With hurried excuses, he apologized and

Seeing The Life

moved to the side, allowing the cart to be pushed past him.

"You are correct, Abba. I am surprised. It is a change from the teachings we held."

"Yes, not believing in God's judgment or punishment is a massive adjustment, but I know in my heart it is right. Also, I no longer think it is acceptable to use the Oral Torah as justification for the way I live. I know the Tanakh has been handed down through the generations without change. The scribes who do the copying take care that every jot and tittle are correct. Nothing is left out or changed. Spoken words can be altered too easily by the one who speaks them. It is too easy to modify to suit the circumstance in your favor."

"I agree."

"Have you listened to any of the teaching of the young rabbi, Yeshua Ben Joseph?"

"Yes, I find his words stirring. He teaches with such authority and straight from the Tanakh. He knows more than any other rabbi I've ever listened to."

They had arrived at the Temple. They went in the gate and walked across the Court of the Gentiles and into the Court of Israel. The outer court was curiously devoid of pens and cages of animals and tables with temple coins being sold. A crowd surrounded someone in the corner. For the number of people, there was little noise.

Orli spoke to a temple guard who stood near the entrance. "Who are they listening to?"

"It is that rabbi who caused all the trouble the other day. He comes every day and speaks. The crowds get larger every day. The only good thing is that he is leaving tomorrow. Maybe that will get things back to normal around here."

The crowd began to shift and separate, allowing passage through. Yeshua emerged, followed closely by several men.

"Those are some of his disciples. They have been with him most days. He teaches in that corner. People yell questions at him. He answers them. When he leaves, the people talk and sometimes argue about what he said. We have had to break up fights. The Pharisees are not pleased." The guard looked at Joseph then at Orli. "You are not going to make trouble, are you?" The guard lifted his spear just a bit.

"No, we were just curious."

By now Yeshua was walking through the gate followed by the crowd. Joseph and Orli went along. "Come, Orli. We have things to do and plans to make."

When they arrived back at the warehouse, Joseph sent Orli to find Micah, Eli, and Perez as well as his brother Ezra. Soon they were in his office, sitting in a circle on a rug with a pitcher of wine and loaf of bread.

"Micah, you told me Yeshua is leaving soon," Joseph said.

"Yes, he plans to travel with his family. The men with him are disciples. They have all been staying with us. He goes to Nazareth then plans to continue preaching in Galilee."

"Orli, Micah, I believe you have interest in his teachings just as I do. I am too busy here to follow along.

I know neither of you can leave your families or work too long. We have business in Galilee as well as other places he might decide to journey to. Here are my thoughts.

"Orli, you will follow him now and hear as much of his teaching that you can. There is business to be dealt with in Capernaum, as you know. There may be other opportunities as you travel with Yeshua, but that is not your main focus."

"But Abba..."

"Yes, I know. Tabith is here, as well as your children. She will not be available for you to marry for... How long until she is sixteen, Micah?"

"Three months." Micah grinned. "It might be best if Orli's gone for a majority of that time."

The disgruntled look on Orli's face caused the other men to laugh. Joseph clapped a hand on his shoulder and said, "My son, we will make sure you have returned long before that. I truly only want you to travel with him and be back not more than six weeks from now."

Orli sighed in resignation.

"You would not want to be sent on this mission soon after your wedding, would you?" Joseph teased.

"Oh no, Abba. I will go now."

"Micah, when Orli is returned, after the wedding we will plan a journey for you. That way the newlyweds can have some time to settle in. After that it will be Ezra, Eli, and Perez who follow and listen"

"Somehow I do not think settling in is what Orli has in mind." Micah playfully punched his future son-in-law in the arm. Eli and Perez teased the young man they worked with unmercifully as they went back to work.

Sophie Dawson

Chapter 17

Five weeks later

Micah opened the door and entered his house. It was chilly, so no one was in the courtyard. He looked back at his companion and signaled for him to be quiet and follow him. They silently moved through the rooms to the stairs leading to the second floor. They could hear the chatter of adults and children as they ascended. They stood waiting to be noticed. Finally a small boy looked toward them.

"Abba, Abba, Abba." The four-year-old ran over and was swept up in Orli's arms.

"Levi, how glad I am you are back in my arms." Orli kissed his son then nearly stumbled as Jude latched onto his leg. "Trade places with your little brother, Levi." Orli put him down and picked up his two-year-old, kissing his chubby cheeks and hugging him close. He looked over the boy's shoulder and saw the smiling face of Tabith.

"Here, let me take him," Micah said as he took the toddler to allow the young couple to greet each other.

Tabith had turned sixteen while Orli had been gone. Since Orli already had a room built onto his father's complex further up the hillside, there was no need to delay their wedding. All it would take was Orli coming for Tabith some evening for the festivities to start. Micah knew it wouldn't be very long.

Once supper was finished and the children put to bed, the adults sat near a brazer to listen to Orli tell about his travels, especially about what he'd seen and heard with Yeshua.

"Everything was much as we saw here in Jerusalem. Every town he preached in, and it was more like preaching than teaching, the crowds were large and listened eagerly. The disciples he had with him baptized, and Yeshua healed more than I could count. Yeshua was able to heal those who were sick or deformed. He also drove out demons. I've never seen anything like it."

"Did he preach all the way along the journey?" Young Eli asked.

"Yes, every day."

Sabba Eli spoke up then. "Even in Samaria?"

"Yes, I heard he was welcomed more in Samaria than in Judea. In Sychar, at Jacob's well, he even spoke to a woman of loose morals."

"You have got to be joking." Miriam gasped.

"I heard her tell about it in the village when I traveled through. She said he knew all about her and told her that he is the Messiah. He said rivers of living water flow from him that will bring eternal life to all who drink from it.

"He also said salvation comes from the Jews but that Yahweh Tzidkenu wants those who worship in spirit and truth."

"What does he mean by that?" Tabith was wrapped in Orli's arms with her back to his chest.

Micah rubbed his chin in thought. "It reminds me of when he spoke with Nicodemus. He said we must be born of the Ruach Ha-Melitz to understand spiritual truths. It makes sense that our spirits worshiping in truth would please HaShem."

"It was amazing in the two days he was in Sychar, how many Samaritans believed Yeshua is the Messiah. I know many people here in Jerusalem became believers, but it was Pesach, and lots more were here than usual. Sychar is much, much smaller, and so many believed I think it would be hard to find the few who didn't. I came through there on my way back just to see if the results of his preaching had a lasting effect."

"Was there?" Dassa asked.

"Yes, the woman... she left the man she was living with and was staying in a small hut and working at the vineyard. Several people told of how she was a totally different person. She was modest and kept away from men. Before, she revealed her body as often as possible. Some, of course, were skeptical as to how long it would last."

Micah accepted more wine from the pitcher Dassa held. She continued around the group before she sat down again at her husband's side. "Did you hear about John the Baptist?" Micah asked.

Orli's excitement dimmed some. "Of his arrest? Yes. It disturbed Yeshua. Did you know John is his cousin? Not a first cousin, but related."

Dassa thought back to when they lived in Bethlehem along with Mary and Joseph. Had she ever mentioned anything about a relative with a son about Yeshua's age? Elizabeth. She was some sort of relative who had a baby before Yeshua was born. Mary had gone to stay with her until the baby was born. Maybe that was John.

"Herod Antipas was enraged when John criticized him for marrying his brother's widow. It's said he spent hours yelling at his people about all John had said about his actions then ordered his arrest," Eli said.

"It sounds just like him. Herod doesn't care what he does, just as his father did, so long as it benefits himself no matter what the law says or how it hurts others," Orli commented. "It was then Yeshua went on to Galilee out of Herod's jurisdiction."

"Isaiah," said Micah.

"What?" Perez finally entered the conversation.

"There is a passage in Isaiah that says in *Galilee of the Gentiles who are in the darkness will see a great light.* I will have to look it up to find the exact passage."

"Why is Yeshua preaching to the Samaritans and the Gentiles?" Tabith asked then yawned. It was getting late.

"I am going to study Isaiah," Micah said. "There seems much there that pertains to Yeshua. I want to refresh my knowledge of it. Isaiah is the most important of the prophets. If his prophecies refer to the Messiah as well as his own time and what has already been fulfilled, I want to be able to recognize it."

"I think it would be wise for all of us, Abba," Perez said. "We need to pray for understanding his words also."

Everyone nodded. They broke up since it was late and they all needed to sleep. There was much teasing of Orli and Tabith as she walked him to the front door. Micah and Dassa waited until she finally climbed the steps to go her room several minutes later.

"Somehow I do not think it will be very many days before Orli comes to collect his bride." Micah wrapped an arm around Dassa's waist.

"If she is anything like her mother was, she hopes it is tomorrow."

[אΩ] [אΩ] [אΩ]

It wasn't the next evening, but it was only three more days until Orli and his friends came to "steal" Tabith away. Micah knew, since the groom had asked him, along with Eli and Perez, to be prepared to take over many of his duties for the next week. He clapped the young man on the back as he smiled. "You take good care of my daughter, son. I know you will, but I need to say it. I am her father, after all."

Orli had laughed and made the promise. He and Micah, as well as Joseph, Eli, and Perez, had spent many hours talking about the stir Yeshua was causing. Word had come that a well-known government official's son had been healed. The news of healings was becoming commonplace. Everywhere Yeshua went he preformed miracles, and they were talked of and spread from town to town.

This healing was different, however. Yeshua had not touched the boy. The official had come two days to find Yeshua before he requested the healing. Yeshua had told the father his son was well and to go home. The official had done as instructed. Word had come to him as he traveled that his son had been healed at the time Yeshua had declared it so. Now the event was spoken of the length and breadth of Israel.

Micah and members of his and Joseph's family all began studying Isaiah. Micah kept adding to the scroll he had started, recording all he heard about Yeshua. He began noting passages not only from Isaiah but from other books of the Tanakh when he thought of them, or the others did, and mentioned it to him. Being scribes themselves, Young Eli and Perez also started adding to the lambskin.

Joseph's sons, Abraham and James, who managed Joseph's holdings in Arimathea, either brought or sent what they heard with workers who came to Jerusalem.

Yeshua had chosen specific men as his close disciples. They were fishermen whom Yeshua had provided a huge haul of fish, more than enough to support their families while they traveled with him. Their names were Andrew, Simon, James, and John.

"Micah, have you heard Yeshua is traveling throughout Galilee?" Joseph asked one day.

"Yes, every day stories of his teaching and healings filter in the city."

"I do not want to separate Orli from his bride at this time." Joseph grinned. "Tabith has settled in as mother to his boys and into our house well. My Dinah and James's

Leah are glad to have her to help with the chores, and she is wonderful with the children. As you know, Leah is expecting James's fourth, and it's been harder on her than the others."

"All right, Joseph, what is it you want of me?" Micah asked with a grin. He had a clue as to what Joseph wanted and was amused by his roundabout way of getting there.

"Well, there is business in Capernaum that needs to be done. Orli would usually go. Eli and Perez are busy with the shipment from Britainia. Ezra I need here at the moment."

"I will go in their stead." Micah was really grinning now. "I would hate to take my daughter's new husband from her so soon after the wedding. They have only been married a couple of months. Besides, I would like to go and see what Yeshua is up to. Do you think he will welcome an old family friend nosing into his ministry?"

Joseph laughed. "If he does not, he should." Becoming serious, he continued, "I do not expect you to hurry back. There will be curriers you can summon to send any business that needs to come."

Micah nodded. "Would you mind if I took Dassa along? She is missing Tabith even though she brings Orli's boys, and often Ezra's children, at least twice a week."

"You may take whoever you want. I will only pay your and Dassa's travel expenses, though." Joseph patted Micah on the back as he began to leave the room.

"When do you want me to leave?"

"I will have everything ready on the first day of the week."

Chapter 18

Dassa was excited about the trip to Galilee. She had not been away from the city since her parents had moved to Jerusalem many years before. This time she would be traveling in more comfort. Micah had purchased a cart to be pulled by one of their donkeys.

Young Eli had always been interested in donkeys. He'd been given a mare as a child and bred her and its offspring over the years. He always had at least one mare, often two or three as well as any young he hadn't sold. His son Jonas was taking an interest in them as well.

They would travel the Roman roads, which would give them more safety as well as access to inns along the way. A contingent of Joseph's guards would travel with them, as what they were taking to Capernaum was quite valuable. They would still try to find another group to travel with for additional security.

Two days into the journey, the excitement had worn off and Dassa's body ached from hours sitting in the cart or walking alongside. She missed her family back in

Jerusalem. She hadn't realized how much she would miss her grandchildren. All of their offspring had come to see them off. It wasn't often that all eight sons and daughters were together.

"Just a few more miles, then we will be in the next town. We will find the inn and hopefully a bathhouse. That would be nice, would it not?" Micah was walking beside the cart.

"Do you think the town will be big enough to have one?"

"We can hope."

Their hope was realized; a garrison was posted near the town, so a Roman bathhouse had been built. After they had their room at the inn and a meal requested for when they returned, Micah escorted Dassa to the bathhouse, leaving her only when men and women were parted to proceed to their separate bathing areas.

Dassa relaxed in the tepidarium, soaking in the warm water. The soreness left her muscles as she lay in the pool with her eyes closed. The women around her gossiped as they bathed. She ignored their chatter until the name of Rabbi Yeshua and what he had been doing pricked her ears.

"She got right up and fixed them a meal. I am not sure I would if I had been so ill." One woman was saying.

"Maybe she felt so much better, it was her way of thanking him."

"I suppose so. What have you heard? Anything we have not talked of before."

"Have you heard of his control over demons?"

"What?"

"He can cast out demons. They try one last time to destroy the person as they leave. I heard it said the demons exclaim that he is the Son of Yahweh, and he prevents them from saying any more."

"The Son of Elohim? I have never heard such a thing. It sounds like blasphemy to me. I mean, how can anyone claim to be HaShem's son?"

"Then why would the demons say he is?"

"Who knows? Demons lie all the time. They are probably lying when they say that. After all, he is casting them out."

A girl came in and told Dassa that Micah would be ready to leave shortly, ending both her soaking time as well as hearing what the women were saying.

Later that evening as they lay in bed, Micah pulled her close and asked, "Would you mind a little detour? It would make our journey longer, but you might enjoy it."

"A detour to where?" Dassa wasn't all that interested in making the journey to Capernaum longer.

"Nazareth."

"Nazareth!" she squealed. "We can see Mary and Joseph. I love you. I will detour to Nazareth any time."

The next day they journeyed north then turned west. By the end of the day, they had arrived in the village. Micah arranged for rooms at the inn and inquired about Joseph Ben Jacob the carpenter. In the morning they would go and find their friends.

📖 📖 📖

"Dassa, Micah." Mary's squeal of delight caught Micah unaware as they walked past the well in the morning. "What are you doing here in Nazareth? I cannot believe you are here."

Micah chuckled as Dassa and Mary hugged and giggled like young girls, chattering at each other at the same time. Maybe it wouldn't be too long before Mary greeted him but he didn't care. He'd wait since his wife was so happy to see her friend. When Mary finally released his wife he was able to hug her, greeting her.

"Come, what brings you here? I cannot believe you are here."

They walked to the well and gathered the water bags Mary had filled, and Micah put the yoke over his shoulders to carry them to the house.

"Do you not have children to do this for you?" Micah teased. "Is that not why we have children? To fetch water?"

"My children are all grown and married. Well, except for Yeshua. He has never found a girl he was interested in. Now with all this wandering and preaching, I doubt he ever will." There was a bit of bitterness in her tone. "I enjoy getting out of the house and visiting with friends at the well. Believe me, I do not do all of the water hauling."

They exchanged news of their families as they walked through the town. Mary told them Joseph and the "boys" were working in the shop at home making chairs for a rich man in Sepphoris. Often they traveled the four miles to work in the capital city of Galilee.

After they left the water bags in the house and greeted the wives and children of Mary's sons, the trio went into the small courtyard to the corner room, which served as a carpentry shop.

Seeing The Life

"Look at what I brought home, Joseph." Mary stood aside and let her husband see Micah and Dassa standing in the sunlight of the courtyard. All the men stopped their work and greeted their visitors.

"What brings you to this backcountry town, Micah?" Joseph asked, slapping him on the back.

"Business in Capernaum. I thought a small detour was in order. Dassa agreed."

"Well, it is good to see you."

For a while the group visited; then Micah made an excuse so the men could get back to work. Joseph and his sons worked hard to make a living, and spending a day simply talking with friends wouldn't finish the projects. He and Dassa accepted the invitation to return for the evening meal and left the men to their work.

When they returned late in the day, Mary had invited the rest of the family as well, their daughters who were married along with the husbands and children. The small courtyard was filled with laughter and food. Micah and Dassa had purchased wine, fruit, and sweet cakes to add to what was cooked. Conversation turned to Yeshua and his activities.

"I think he should come home and work with us," said Ya'aqov. "He will inherit someday. He should be here, not traipsing all over the countryside telling people what he thinks HaShem wants them to know."

"Well, he did train as a rabbi." This was said by Elizabeth, only a year younger than twenty-eight-year-old Ya'aqov. "He just recently was vetted. I understand how he would want to share what he has learned."

"Why not do what most rabbis do and speak in the synagogue on Sabbath? He does not need to go all over showing off," Jude said. He was twenty-two but with a baby face that often had strangers thinking he was still a teenager.

"How is it showing off if it is truth? People are coming from miles around to hear him," Joseph asked, looking at his son. "Yeshua has always had an astounding understanding of HaShem's Word."

"I know. I just wish he had gotten in trouble once when he was growing up. I swear he never did anything wrong." Everyone laughed at Jude's disgruntled complaint.

"You were not born yet when Yeshua stayed behind in Jerusalem after Pesach when he was, how old was he, Joseph?" Mary asked.

"Twelve. We were so afraid he had been taken by the Romans. It took us three days to find him."

"Yes, I was expecting you then. Just what I needed was six extra days walking before getting home."

Everyone laughed, which broke the tension.

"Yeshua kept Samuel from bullying you, Jude," Joses said. "Shim'on, he helped you with your schoolwork all the time."

Elizabeth passed a tray filed with dates to Dassa, who was sitting beside her. "All my friends wanted to attract his interest. Several girls tried rather inappropriate actions to get his attention. Yeshua would ask me to go with him to speak to them. He would explain that he was not attracted and, even if he was, their behavior would have turned him away from them. He said he would want a woman to be modest and humble. Several were shocked when he said that."

"So," Micah said, wanting to turn the conversation to Yeshua's teaching and what his family thought of it. "Have you heard him preach?"

"He was here a while back. He taught at the synagogue. He caused an uproar," Joseph said. "What he preached made the people angry, and they tried to throw him off a cliff."

"But he walked away as if nothing had happened. I do not know how he got away from those men." Mary put a shaky hand to her forehead.

"I have heard people talk about him." Shim'on leaned forward and picked a date from the tray. "He certainly made a name for himself at the Temple during Pesach."

"The Pharisees and Sadducees are still quite upset with him," Dassa said.

"As are the moneychangers and livestock sellers," Micah said.

"I can understand," Joses said. "It made the sacrifices much more difficult. I cannot figure out why he became so angry."

Micah cleared his throat. "The Temple has become more of a marketplace than a house of Adonai Elyon. The selling of Temple coins and sacrifices brings in a lot of money. Isaiah the prophet talked of this." Micah went on to recite the passage and explain what he thought they meant and that Yeshua might have been fulfilling a prophecy.

Shim'on, at twenty years old the youngest of the boys, then said, "I have heard he can do miracles. It is said he can heal and cast out demons." Several others murmured either disbelief or agreement.

"Ima, did you not ask him to do something at the wedding festival of Adam Ben Daniel and Sarah?"

Micah saw Mary turn bright red.

"I just asked him to do whatever he could and told the servants to obey what he said. I did not expect him to do that."

At that moment a squabble broke out amongst the grandchildren. Everyone watched as the mothers separated the combatants, deciding it was time to settle them onto pallets on the roof so the children could sleep while the adults continued visiting. Micah and Dassa would be leaving in the morning, and no one wanted the evening to end quite so soon.

"That is what I mean," Jude said. "Yeshua never quarreled with any of us. We would get into fights, not him, but the rest of us, and we would get into trouble."

"Once, just once, you would think he would have gotten spanked for something, but it seemed as if he never did anything wrong." Ya'aqov growled, but his tone wasn't really serious.

"You just say that because you made most of the trouble and were punished the most." Elizabeth smacked him lightly on the back of the head as she passed her brother to go sit beside her husband.

"What happened at the wedding, Mary?" Dassa asked.

"They had run out of wine. I thought he would instruct the servants to go buy wine and we would pay for it. Instead suddenly there was the best wine any of us had ever tasted."

"We all heard he told the servant to fill the water jars. When they dipped out the water, it was wine," Ya'aqov said. "He had never done anything like that before."

"When was this?" Micah asked.

"It was before Pesach. We went to Cana for the wedding," Joseph said.

"He left soon after on his preaching journey. We saw him for a little bit in Jerusalem, but he was surrounded by so many people. We have not seen him since he turned the moneychangers from the Temple." Mary was worrying a cloth in her hands.

"He stayed with us that night. I found him and made sure he was all right. There was even a Pharisee who came to speak with him." Micah went on to tell of Nicodemus's visit and being born of the Spirit. "None of us really understood what he meant. He went on to say that God so loves us he sent his only son so whoever believes in him will not perish but have everlasting life." His gaze met Mary's and Joseph's as he spoke. Mary went pale. Joseph simply nodded.

[📖] [📖] [📖]

"This place smells worse than Jerusalem," Dassa said, wrinkling her nose as they entered Capernaum. The town sat on the edge of the Sea of Kinneret.

Micah laughed. "What do you expect? It is one of the largest fish-producing cities of Galilee. They also mill grain and press olives." He was walking beside the donkey Dassa rode. "Let us find the inn and get you settled. I need to go to Joseph's warehouse and make sure the workers who came with us arrived safely."

Dassa, having been on the donkey or walking beside it for more than two days, thought being in an inn would be most welcome. They had slept in a field the first night after leaving Nazareth and in an olive grove the next. She wanted a bath and something besides a bony donkey's back to sit on.

"Master Micah." A call came from off to the left. It was one of the workers who had traveled with them.

"Shalom, Ben, good to see you." Micah held out his hand, which Ben clasped with a smile. "You made the journey with no problems?"

"Yes. The others are at the warehouse. I was just going to get some food."

Dassa sat quietly, looking around as the men talked. Through the passageway streets she could see the gleam of the sun on the water of the lake. Micah clicked the donkey into motion with the sound and a pull on his rope. He and Ben kept talking as they walked. Dassa only wanted off the beast. When a lull in the conversation occurred, she cleared her throat rather loudly.

"Oh, sorry my dear," Micah said. "Ben, continue with your errand. I will get Dassa settled at the inn and meet you at the warehouse shortly."

Ben gave them directions to the inn, and soon Dassa was off the donkey and eating fish and fruit while getting directions to the bathhouse.

Micah's work kept them in Capernaum for several weeks. It seemed everyone was talking about the young rabbi. A week after they arrived, news came from

Nazareth that he had claimed to be the fulfillment of a prophecy in Isaiah. When the people in the synagogue heard, they rioted and nearly threw Yeshua over a cliff. No one could say how he had escaped. It seemed he simply walked away.

News spread that Yeshua was preaching along the Sea of Kinneret. He now had four men with him as constant disciples. Whatever town he went to the crowds were growing. They listened to his teaching and clamored for his healing and exorcizing of demons.

Then he came to Capernaum again. Micah had been trying to see Yeshua, hoping to be able to speak with him. He had no luck getting close until one day when he and Dassa were able to squeeze into the house where Yeshua was preaching. Micah figured there was no way he would ever get noticed with all those crowded around. He wanted very much to hear Yeshua, not only to report back to Joseph, but also for himself. Yeshua was preaching when Micah felt something fall onto his head. He looked up as clay and straw dusted down. He tucked Dassa close under his arm to shield her.

Soon there was a hole in the ceiling. The owner of the house pushed through the crowd, trying to get to the stairs as the hole got larger and larger. People backed into each other to stay out of the way of the debris falling from above.

Micah watched as a sleeping mat holding a man on a pallet was lowered to the floor in front of Yeshua. Everyone looked up and saw the four men who had torn the roof off holding the robes they had used to get their friend to Yeshua.

The young man's legs were atrophied and drawn up, bent kneed with his ankles crossed. His arms, elbows bent were against his chest. The wrists and fingers were turned in toward the forearms. The rigidity of his muscles and the look on his face told of the pain he suffered from his obvious paralysis.

Yeshua knelt beside the pallet. "Young man, my child, your sins are forgiven."

Stunned silence followed his statement. Yeshua looked at the frowning faces of the Pharisees and teachers. "Why do you question this in your hearts? Why do you have such evil thoughts in your hearts? Is it easier to say to the paralyzed man 'Your sins are forgiven,' or 'Stand up, pick up your mat, and walk'? So I will prove to you that the Son of Man has the authority on earth to forgive sins."

Everyone looked from Yeshua to the Pharisees and back.

Then Jesus turned to the paralyzed man and said, "Stand up, pick up your mat, and go home!"

All eyes turned to look at the paralyzed man. He jumped up and grabbed his mat and began shouting praises to the El Gadol Gibor Yare. He walked on straight, strong legs through the people, who parted before him. The men on the roof cheered and disappeared from the hole they had made.

The room emptied as people scattered to spread the word about what had happened and the authority with which Yeshua had preached. That Yeshua had forgiven the man's sins. His knowledge of what the Pharisees were thinking. The sight of a paralyzed man standing and walking.

Micah now had his chance. Guiding Dassa forward, Micah touched Yeshua on the shoulder. The young rabbi turned from specking to the men behind him and smiled.

"Dod, Doda. What are you doing here? You are far from Jerusalem." Yeshua hugged each of them, keeping his arm around Dassa's shoulder while Micah explained.

"It is good to see you. Let me introduce you to my disciples. Simon, Andrew, James, and John."

After the greetings were exchanged, Micah said, "You are doing truly amazing things. We hear of you and your teachings everywhere."

"Would that the people listen to the words rather than want the miracles. Not that I have no mercy and would refuse to heal them, but the truth of Adonai Elohai's words are eternal. The body is only temporary."

Chapter 19

"Orli, where is your father?"

Micah and Dassa had arrived back in Jerusalem that morning. Now Micah was wanting to speak with his boss as well as his sons and Joseph's.

"He and James are in the office. Welcome back. How did your journey go?" They visited about the travels as they went to meet with the other men. After the report of how the business went, they settled back to talk about the second reason for Micah's journey.

Micah told of all he and Dassa had seen and heard on their journey. Of the paralyzed man Yeshua had forgiven of his sins and then healed. The large following of people traveling with him. Of the men who Yeshua called his disciples and that one he had asked was a tax collector. Joseph and his sons gasped.

"How could he want a cheating tax collector as one of his disciples?" James asked. "They are almost more corrupt than the Romans they work for."

"I heard the tax collector is called Levi. The Pharisees and Sadducees condemn Yeshua for eating with him and other sinners." Joseph refilled their goblets. "He told them he had come for those who knew they are sinners, not those who thought they were righteous. The Pharisees do not like this Yeshua at all. They want him stopped."

"Why?" Micah asked.

"His teachings make them look arrogant and greedy."

"Do you think so, Abba?" Orli asked.

"I don't know. His words burn in my heart, but I was taught so differently."

"I know," James said. "With the Oral Torah, the Tanahk, the Pharisaical rules, as well as the teachings of the Sadducees and Essenes and now Yeshua Ben Joseph, how can we keep everything straight and yet still be faithful to El Shaddai? Everyone seems to twist and turn the Word to meet their own need."

"Or desire."

They all nodded.

"I am beginning to believe it is self desire, not faithful living, that drives many. Even those in leadership." Discouragement tinged Joseph's words.

"All I know is this man seems to be fulfilling many prophecies. My sons and I are keeping a record of what Yeshua does and the prophecies he seems to fit. If you have ones you would like to have us write out, simply let us know."

Joseph of Arimethea and his sons nodded.

Word spread through Jerusalem that Yeshua the prophet was again in Jerusalem. Everyone was talking about him. He was healing those who were blind, sick, lame, and paralyzed. Demons were being cast out. Micah and Joseph, as well as their sons, kept track of all Yeshua was doing. So did the Jewish leaders.

Joseph was at the temple one day and heard other Pharisees as well as some Sadducees discussing Yeshua.

"I say he is breaking the law. He heals on Shabbat. That is working. The Shabbat is a day of rest," one man was saying.

Another countered, "But he is doing miracles. Is that not of God?"

"Even Pharaoh's magicians could do such things. We cannot be fooled."

"What if the people start breaking Shabbat law because of him?"

"He told a man he healed on Shabbat to stop sinning or something worse could happen to him. I heard him. Then the man came saying Yeshua had healed him."

"I heard he claims Elohim is his father. Yeshua says that Elohay Mishpat has given him the authority to judge. He says his teaching and miracles are witness of this."

"Blasphemy. How can we let him keep preaching?"

"We should not."

"The man claims the Tanakh points to him."

Joseph stood listening. Rather than speak, he watched and took note of those who seemed to support the young rabbi and those who were critical. So much of what Yeshua taught was different from he had learned and believed all his life.

The conversation took a darker tone. Many of the leaders wanted Yeshua stopped. They were going to harass him for breaking Shabbat law. The plan was to keep a close eye on his teaching and find some way to trip him up so they could denounce him.

Joseph kept silent but vowed to watch and listen to Yeshua and what he said. He would ask his sons as well as Micah and his sons if they were willing to travel to hear the young rabbi teach. They should be able to have at least one of them following Yeshua at all times.

📖 📖 📖

A few weeks later, Joseph rushed from the Temple to his warehouse. When he arrived, he gathered Micah, James and Orli, and Eli and Perez in his office. "They are planning to kill Yeshua."

"What?" Explanations of horror mirrored the expressions on the faces of the other men.

"The leaders of the Pharisees and Herod's supporters are so angry they are almost insane with rage. They have been made to look foolish and without mercy. Yeshua healed this past Shabbat in the synagogue. The Pharisees asked him if the law permitted a man to work on Shabbat by healing someone. Yeshua countered by asking them if it was permitted that good deeds be done on the Shabbat or was it a day for doing evil. Seems they were unable to answer him."

"I suppose if you had the ability to heal someone and you did not, it could be said you were doing evil. Healing someone shows loving kindness, which is of HaShem," James said.

Micah nodded. "How cruel to allow suffering to go on for another day because a rule says you cannot on that day."

"That does not match with Elohim's character," Orli said.

"You are right, but now those Pharisees' pride has been damaged. They are looking for ways to kill Yeshua."

"What should we do?" Eli ran a hand through his hair.

"I am not sure there is anything we can do but warn Yeshua," Joseph said. "Micah, is he staying with you?"

"No, he has not stayed with us since Pesach when he threw out the moneychangers. He has not sent any word to us either. Dassa is worried and has been pressuring me to contact him."

"Have you?"

"No, there are always so many crowding around him. I guess I am trusting El Shaddai to keep him safe. I'm sure word of this would surely reach him. If I think he does not know in a few days, I will press through the crowds and at least try to talk with the disciples I have been introduced to."

The men looked at each other. Jerusalem didn't need those who were against Yeshua to begin publicly calling for him to stop his teaching. The Romans were never slow to cut down those who caused problems. Innocent bystanders could easily fall victim to the Roman sword as well.

Within a few days, there was news saying Yeshua had left Jerusalem.

Chapter 20

Micah found Dassa on the roof, where she had set up her looms and was weaving. Dassa had become a skilled spinner and weaver, making tunics and robes for the more wealthy citizens of Jerusalem.

"So who has ordered a tunic from you, my love?" Micah asked as he bent to kiss the top of her head.

"No one. I am making this as a gift."

Micah didn't quiet understand how Dassa did it, but she wove tunics with no seams. Several of the priests and more wealthy Pharisees and Sadducees had purchased them from her. The front and back were woven at the same time, with the shuttle moving from the front of the loom through the back then to the front again. It became even more complicated when she was working on the sleeves. Dassa had explained it to him, but he had gotten lost somewhere in the middle and hadn't asked again. He simply loved the tunic she had made for him.

"A gift, huh? Is it for someone in the family?" Micah couldn't keep the longing out of his voice.

"No. You all have one. This I am making for Yeshua. He deserves the best we can give him, and this is what I do best. His teachings have changed my life, so I want to give him a tunic fit for the High Priest."

Micah sat down beside her and watched her work for a while. The talk in the city was all about Yeshua and his teachings. Daily news was brought back with those who traveled to Galilee either on business, to see family, or to see and listen to the young rabbi.

"Did you know he has picked twelve men as close disciples?"

Dassa looked at him for a moment then went back to her weaving. "I know of Peter, Andrew, and James and John. We met them on our journey to Capernaum."

"He now has eight more. Orli returned today and told us about them. He, Tabith, and the children will be here for supper tonight. I told Geva and Rachel. I'm sure Tabith will bring something to contribute."

"Did Orli tell any more about Yeshua than he picked eight men?"

"He said he would tell us all tonight. Joseph, James, and Orli went home so he could talk with his family before they come here. I think there is much Yeshua taught this time. Orli seemed full of excitement. He did say there were crowds everywhere Yeshua spoke. People from all over Judea, Jerusalem, and Galilee follow him wanting to hear what he says."

Dassa slipped the shuttle through the loom again then beat down the linen thread. "I cannot wait to hear what Orli heard."

Seeing The Life

There was a large group seated around the mats on the roof that evening. The weather was warm and the moon was full. Dassa loved having her children and grandchildren sharing a meal. Not all were there, but most.

The littlest grandchildren had been put to sleep, and the older ones either played together in a corner or sat with the adults. Orli was the focus with the news from his travels. He sat with his arm around Tabith, who was showing signs of her pregnancy.

"It is amazing," Orli was saying. "No matter where he goes, there are huge crowds. He cannot really stay in the villages since so many want to see him. He and his disciples try to find secluded places where they can camp for the night. Often people find them."

"Why do they not let Yeshua alone?" Abigail asked. At ten, she was inquisitive about anything, and the fact that Yeshua was a friend of the family made her even more curious about him.

"Yeshua is not only teaching, but he is healing many people of their diseases. He casts demons out too. I saw him heal a leper. It was just after the most amazing sermon I have ever heard. I know I can't remember all he talked about. I wished I was a scribe so I could write it all down. He spoke with more authority than I have ever heard before.

"He started with a list of those whom El-Elyon blesses; those who realize their need for HaShem, those who weep and mourn, the humble, those who are starved for justice, the ones who show mercy to others, the ones who are pure of heart, peacemakers, and those who are persecuted."

"The persecuted could be all of Israel," Perez muttered.

"He said Elohim blesses people who are hated and cursed because they are followers of him and great rewards await them in heaven. Yeshua compared that sort of persecution to that which the prophets had."

"Many of them were killed for their words. Killed by their own people," thirteen-year-old Benjamin said. "Will the same thing happen to us since we know Yeshua?"

Micah poured more wine into several cups. "No one knows the future, but I have a feeling Yeshua may be persecuted. Joseph says the Pharisees and some Sadducees think Yeshua is trying to overthrown the hierarchy of the Temple. They are afraid he will turn the people away from them as the leaders."

Orli spoke up again. "Yeshua says he is not trying to abolish any of the laws of Moses or what the prophets said. He said he has come to fulfill their purpose. What astounded me most was when he said our righteousness had to be better than that of the Sadducees and Pharisees."

Geva, Eli's wife, gasped. "How can we be more righteous? They are the most righteous people there are, aren't they?"

Silence hung for a few moments before Micah said, "Maybe some are. Many twist the commandments to suit their desires. I've heard of some who leave their mother or father to starve because they claim what they have is set aside for Yahweh Yisrael. Then they have nothing to provide for their parents in their need. How is that righteous? We are told to seek justice and mercy. Where is the justice and mercy Elohay Mishpat wants?"

Geva nodded. She was obviously thinking hard about what she'd heard from Orli and her father-in-law.

"Yeshua spoke of the Oral Torah too. He basically condemned them, mentioning several in particular. He said being angry at someone and not reconciling with them makes your sacrifice at the altar worth nothing. You must go and be reconciled before you offer your sacrifice."

"It makes sense," Eli said. "Why would El Selich'ah accept an offering if you are not forgiving or forgiven?"

"He said a husband who divorces his wife, unless she has been unfaithful, causes her to commit adultery if she remarries."

"What is adultery?" Joses, Eli's eight-year-old asked.

Some hemming and hawing passed among the adults. Then Geva said it was time for bed for most of the remaining children. She led them down the steps to settle them for the night.

"Here is a hard lesson he taught," Orli continued. "We are to love our enemies. To bless those who curse you. Do what you can for them. Pray for them. By doing so, we are acting just as HaShem wants us to."

"That is what it says in Proverbs. You will be heaping coals of fire on your enemy's head." The gleam in fourteen-year-old Benjamin's eye said he liked the idea of heaping fiery coals on those he didn't like.

"That is not what he meant, Ben," Orli said. "Yeshua said we must be compassionate to everyone, whether they are your friend or enemy. HaShem sends rain and sunlight to both the evil and the good, so we should too."

"Humph." Ben's shoulders dropped. "I would rather heap on the burning coals."

The chuckling from around the room gave evidence of understanding Ben's comment. It was much easier to want bad to happen to those who did you wrong than to be compassionate and help them.

"If we only are giving to those we love, we are not any better than the pagans. They also give to those they love. How does that show we and Elohay Elohim are better than them or their god?" Micah asked. Ben was sitting next to his father, who gave him a quick squeeze around the shoulders.

"I understand, but I still want to heap burning coals on Nathaniel's head. He tripped me the other day, and I skinned up my leg when I fell."

"What do you suppose he would think if you shared some food while you were together? You know his family does not have much." Dassa looked intently at her son.

"I do not know."

"Maybe he would feel bad about what he had done. That might feel like burning coals on his head, you doing something nice for him after he was mean to you. What do you think HaShem would think about you then?"

"Oh, I understand. He would see that I was being merciful, giving him good for evil. In Proverbs it says not to feel good when your enemy stumbles, or Elohay Mishpat might look at you in wrath instead of your enemy."

"You have been studying well, my son," Micah said. "Knowing the Tanakh is good, very good. Obeying it is even better."

"Sometimes understanding it is hard." Ben's comment brought nods of agreement from the others on the roof.

Orli nodded. "Not only did he give instruction on how we should live, he also spoke in stories. They were hard to understand, and we needed to listen and think about them. There was much talk after Yeshua finished preaching and came down the mountain," Orli said. "Some people understood the stories and tried to explain them. Others said they were just ramblings set to confuse people so they would think Yeshua was a prophet. If I were a scribe, I would have written the stories down so I could remember them fully."

Since it was late, they ended the discussion for the night, and Orli invited them to his and Tabith's home for supper and talk in a couple of days. Orli knew his father would welcome the entire family and the opportunity to talk about the teachings of Yeshua.

Every day in the markets, at the wells, the Temple, and across the rooftops, tales of what Yeshua was saying and the miracles he was performing was the focus of many conversations. Who was this man who could heal everyone who touched him? Was he a prophet or the long-awaited Messiah?

Uria, Dassa's friend, and Dassa met every couple of weeks at one home or the other. This week, Dassa had traveled back to her old neighborhood. She'd gone to the seller, who purchased her linen for his booth. She used some of her proceeds to buy fruit and nuts for sharing with her friend.

Uria welcomed Dassa, and they went up to the roof. "Remember the first time we met?" Uria asked.

Dassa smiled. "Yes, I was so lonely, just having moved to Jerusalem. Having to stay in the house so much because of turmoil of the eagle on the Temple roof."

"I was lonely too, having been confined inside, not even being able to come onto the roof. It's hard to believe Nadav is a mother herself now. I do enjoy being a softa, though. When the babies are wet or messy, I can hand them to their mother." Uria grinned.

Dassa smiled back and nodded. "Where are your daughters-in-law and their children?"

"They went to the river to gather more reeds. It's hot today, so the intent is to let the children play in the water."

"And you get some peace and quiet." Dassa laughed as she pulled her spindle from the bag of flax she'd brought.

"That is true." Uria poured water into the trough that held the reeds she would weave into beautiful baskets. Soaked and wet, the reeds bent without breaking as she worked. "There is more talk of that rabbi, Yeshua. It seems as if no one talks about anything else. I get tried of hearing about him."

Dassa glanced up from her spinning. "Have you heard what he is teaching?"

"I heard the Pharisees don't like what he is doing. They are mostly worried about losing their power and money."

Seeing The Life

"He is teaching about how El Shaddai wants us to live. He tells us to seek Yahweh's kingdom first. To set him above everything else. To treat others in the same way we want to be treated."

"I've heard it all. Seems to be just another rabbi to me."

"What of the healings and casting out demons?" Dassa wondered if her friend even cared about HaShem.

"He can do miracles, but I heard those men who travel with him can do them also. So I guess that makes him not so special after all."

Chapter 21

Micah and Dassa journeyed again to Capernaum. Both wanted the chance to hear Yeshua teach again. It gave the younger men the chance to stay home with their families. Yeshua was not in Capernaum, however. He was traveling from town to town teaching and healing. Dassa hoped to be able to give him the tunic she had made. While there, they heard that Yeshua was preaching in the towns west, away from the Sea of Kinneret. They decided to go home by way of Nazareth hoping to find Yeshua along the way and to see Mary and Joseph.

News of Yeshua was everywhere. It grieved Micah and Dassa to hear that his family members were calling him crazy. It seemed he was making enemies of the Pharisees and Sadducees. They accused him of being a prince of demons. Yeshua had scoffed and refuted their logic. How could Satan's kingdom stand if Yeshua was part of it and casting out demons?

"Micah, Dassa," a man called. It was Ya'aqov, Mary and Joseph's second son. "I cannot believe you are here. How did you know?"

"Know what?"

Joses, Shim'on, and Yehuda joined them as well as their mother, Mary. She looked terrible. Dassa rushed to her. "What is wrong?"

"Joseph is dead. He died two days ago." Mary began weeping, and Dassa wrapped her arms around her.

"We are looking for Yeshua," Joses said. "We heard he is preaching in the nearby towns. He needs to come home and take over the business."

"It is time he stopped this..." Ya'aqov waved his hand in the air sharply at a loss for words. "It is time he grows up and takes responsibility instead of traipsing all over the countryside stirring up trouble."

"You do not think he should be preaching and healing?" Micah asked.

Shim'on slashed an angry hand in front of his chest. "He could do that from Nazareth. The people flock to hear him. They would come to listen and to get healed. He should come home."

"All they want is the healing anyway," Yehuda said, stepping up to stand by his mother. "His stories are too hard to understand. It is as if he talks in riddles."

"Stop this instant." Mary's tone was harsh. "We will find him and speak with him. He will want to know about..." She paused. "Your abba."

It wasn't hard to learn Yeshua's whereabouts. A question to others on the road yielded where he had last been and where he was headed. They joined the many people heading there.

The town was crowded and all talk was of Yeshua. What was the sign of Jonah? Had he really and why had he healed a centurion's slave? Should not a Jew only heal Jews? Have you seen the leper who said Yeshua had healed him? Only someone stupid would build a house on sand. What did he mean?

Finally, they were able to get near to where Yeshua was. Unable to enter, Micah and Dassa kept Mary from being shoved aside as Ya'aqov passed a message saying Yeshua was needed to speak with his mother and brothers.

They waited, the group of grieving brothers, mother, and friends. A man came up to them, his expression grim. "He said, 'Who is my ima? Who are my ach? Look, these are my ima and achi. Anyone who hears Elohim's word and obediently does the will of my Abba in heaven is my achi and achowth and ima.' Um, I don't think he is coming."

Mary collapsed onto the ground. "Why will he not come and at least speak with us?" Her sons knelt around her, trying to give her comfort.

"You see." Ya'aqov spat. "What kind of prophet or rabbi or decent son will not even come out to speak with his ima?"

"Come, Ima. Let us go home. Yeshua does not want to see us. He must think we do not love him." The anguish in Yeduha's voice tore at Micah's heart.

"No, I am sure he does not think that," Dassa said, but Micah stopped her from continuing by placing his hand on her arm and shaking his head. He looked around, seeing many people looking at them.

"Take your ima home. She needs her daughters and you now. Get her home as quickly as possible. You do not want her to become of interest to the crowd," Micah said. "Do you want me to hire a donkey and cart for you?"

Ya'aqov shook his head. "We have a donkey. We will leave immediately."

"If you need anything, contact me or Joseph of Arimethea in Jerusalem. He is your ima's uncle, am I correct?"

Ya'aqov nodded as he and Joses helped Mary to stand. Micah's heart grieved for Mary and her family as they walked through the crowd. Her sons were shielding her from any who came close. He would miss Joseph. The talented carpenter had been a good friend.

"Why, Micah? Why would Yeshua not come and see them? I do not understand." Dassa looked up at him with tear-filled eyes.

"I do not know. The words he said, 'Anyone who hears Elohim's Word and obediently does the will of my Abba in heaven is my achi and achowth and ima.' Does he not think his family obeys Yahweh?"

A man standing near said, "A while back his family tried to take him away from the crowds. They said he was out of his mind. Crazy. I know I would be angry if my family said that about me."

"Do you think Yeshua is crazy?" Micah asked.

"If he is crazy, I want that kind of crazy. He heals all types of illness and affliction. He can cast out demons. His teachings are full of wisdom. I believe he is, at the very least, a prophet. He could be the Messiah. I am waiting judgment to see if he can overthrow the Romans and get the Promised Land all back under Jewish control."

Micah nodded, discouraged by the events of the day. "Let us go, Dassa. We will not see Yeshua today."

"I am not sure I want to see him," Dassa said. "Maybe I will just give the tunic to someone else. Someone who will not deny their family."

Chapter 22

"I do not believe it. How could he do such an awful thing?" Micah heard Orli's voice. It was filled with shock, disgust, and grief. He went into the other room of the warehouse and saw his son-in-law Joseph, and Timothy, men who traveled for Joseph.

"What?" Micah asked.

"He has killed John the Baptist. Antipas, that son of the monster Herod, has killed the prophet," Timothy said. "Beheaded him because that Jezebel of a wife asked him to at a party!" He shouted the words. Everyone in the warehouse was still and silent. Shocked by the callousness of the people who ruled over them.

"*Certainly Yahweh does not forsake his people; he does not abandon the nation that belongs to him. For justice will prevail, and all the morally upright will be vindicated. Who will rise up to defend me against the wicked? Who will stand up for me against the evildoers?*" Joseph quoted the passage from Psalms.

No one said anything for long moments. All was stillness in the busy warehouse. Each man knew the evil of the Herod family. The wickedness had passed from father to son. The wickedness of those who ruled in Rome did nothing to stop. For little or no reason, men, women, and children could be taken into slavery and just as easily discarded. This was especially the case if the heavy burden of taxes were not paid.

"*Do not fear, for I am with you; do not be afraid, for I am your God. I will strengthen you; I will help you; I will hold on to you with My righteous right hand.*" Micah quoted Isaiah.

"*Blessed are those who mourn for they will be comforted.* Remember, Orli. Yeshua said that when we heard him preach on the mountain." Timothy looked at Orli.

"If there is a time to mourn, this is it. We must count on El Shaddai to be our comfort." Orli placed a hand on Timothy's shoulder. "We can trust in Yahweh Yireh's help and that he will meet out justice in his time."

"Let us hope his time is near." Joseph turned away after saying these words, walked into his office, and drew the curtain over the doorway closed. No one would disturb him. The others went back to work. The normally noisy, cheerful workers were silent.

[📖] [📖] [📖]

"Has everything been washed?" Dassa asked Rachel, Perez's wife.

"Yes, Geva and I made sure everything is clean while you were at the market." Rachel grinned. "Since the children are not in school today, they helped. It was a good lesson in working together and doing what was needing to be done. We set the little ones to searching out yeast. They looked in everything and everywhere."

"They enjoyed that I am sure." Dassa was taking the foods she had gotten to make the Pesach meal from her basket. "I need to purchase a new basket from Uria. See?" Dassa put her finger through the hole worn through the curved corner. Her grandchildren made a game of trying to grab it.

"Did you hear if Yeshua is coming to Pesach?" Geva came in from the courtyard.

"No word as to whether he is here yet, but I am sure he will come. It is commanded all of Israel attend," Dassa said.

"Do you think he will beat the moneychangers again?" Joses, Geva's eight-year-old son, asked. "I hope so. I would like to see him do it. Abba said I could go with him when he takes our lamb." The mischievousness of a boy lit his face like a signal fire.

"Well, I hope he does not. I think the Romans might cancel Pesach if it happened again. I heard the Pharisees have plans for if he does it again," Rachel said. The women were beginning to prepare the evening meal. Each child had a piece of fruit for a snack.

"They do not like Yeshua very much. What he teaches helps me understand what El Shamayim wants of me, but some of what he teaches is hard to understand," Geva said, cutting mutton into thin strips.

"What do you not understand? I know some of his stories are difficult. He says that if we want to understand, the meaning will be given." Rachel finished cleaning rice in water.

"I heard Yeshua said he is the bread of life. That anyone who eats his flesh will have eternal life. Also that his blood is true drink. That we must eat his flesh and drink his blood and we will not die."

"Yuck," three-year-old Julia said. "I do not wanna drink blood."

"Me neither," said six-year-old Samuel. Samuel was Geva's son and Julia, Rachel's daughter.

"Do you think he was using symbolism?" Dassa asked. She was making unleaven bread since Pesach was in two days time and all yeast had been cleansed from the house. "It is hard to think he meant to literally eat his flesh and drink his blood."

Geva added fuel to the fire and poured water into the pot over it. The mutton strips, onions, rice, hyssop, marjoram, and salt were added. "I suppose that's what he meant. Maybe like the unleaven Pesach bread and wines. They all have symbolic meaning. I hope Yeshua teaches more about this and explains it better."

📖 📖 📖

Micah and Dassa followed Phillip, one of the twelve disciples closest to Yeshua, up the side of the Mount of Olives. Micah had seen the young man earlier in the day. He had agreed to take them to see Yeshua. It was two days after Pesach, during the seven days of celebration. Dusk was falling. The crowds that daily surrounded Yeshua had thinned as people went to their homes and campsites.

Dassa's stomach twisted when she saw him. There were still people around to him. She saw him reach out and touch a baby in its mother's arms. A man stood next to her; fear and hope fought for primacy on his face. Then he fell to his knees, crying. He kissed Yeshua's feet over and over.

"Yeshua must have healed the child," Micah said.

"Yes," said Phillip. "I cannot tell you the number of people he has healed. I used to try to keep count each day, but it is impossible. He never turns anyone away."

They had reached the edge of those near Yeshua. They stopped, waiting for their chance to speak with him. Dassa had a bag hanging from her shoulder.

When the couple with the baby left, Yeshua looked toward them. "Doda Dassa, Dod Micah, welcome. It is good to see you." He came to them and gave each a hug. "You are not ill, so you do not need healing."

"We need nothing from you, Rabbi, but your blessing," Micah said. "We have heard much of what you teach. Your words come back to Jerusalem with everyone who comes from the north."

"So you have ears to hear?"

"We try, but some things are difficult."

"All will be revealed in time."

Yeshua looked as Dassa. "You are troubled."

"We were with your ima and achi when they came to tell you of your abba's death."

"Ah. You're troubled by my response."

"How could you reject your family so?" Dassa's eyes filled, her tone accusing.

"Though I love them all, I cannot leave what I do and become what they want. I must do what my abba in heaven tells me to do. If I love my family more than Adonai Elohai, I am not worthy of his favor. I must obey him above all things."

Dassa nodded as a tear slipped down her cheek.

Yeshua wiped the tear away with a gentle finger. "I do love them. They will come to understand but do not now. I have seen them. I went to Nazareth. We spoke and made some reconciliation. Ya'aqov is beginning to understand. His ears are still weak but becoming stronger."

Dassa held Yeshua's hand. "I'm so glad. Your ima was devastated by Joseph's death."

"She has El Shaddai's comfort surrounding her. I ask you both," he included at Micah in his gaze. "Please do what you can for my ima. She will need your strength and love."

"What? Why"? Dassa began.

"In time you will understand."

"We will do whatever it takes, Yeshua. You can depend on us," Micah said. The people on the hillside slowly moved away and down the mountain, leaving Yeshua, the disciples, Micah, and Dassa alone.

"I know." There was sadness in Yeshua's eyes. He looked off into the distance for a moment. "Now, you have come all this way. May we offer you some wine and something to eat?"

"No, thank you. We've eaten." Dassa took the bag from her shoulder. "I have made you something." She held the bag out to him.

"Oh?" Yeshua accepted the bag and reached inside. He brought out the tunic Dassa had woven for him. The linen thread had been bleached as white as she could get it. Some of the thread she had dyed red. There was a wide band of red near the hem, and around the sleeves she had embroidered red bands near the cuff. Yeshua shook the garment out, holding it by the shoulders. "This is wonderful. Thank you. Look, John. It has no seams."

The disciple came near and looked the garment over. "Very nice."

"Doda, I thank you. I shall wear it gladly. I know you wove much love into it." Yeshua bent and kissed Dassa on the cheek. "Will you please stay for a while? It is not often someone does not want something from me. I would like to hear of your family."

Shortly, the couple who had been witness to Yeshua's birth were seated around the fire, speaking with and listening to the man he had become.

Chapter 23

During the week of Sukkot, Yeshua went to the Temple. The Jewish leaders had been trying to find him. There was much grumbling among the crowds. Some were supportive. Some thought he was a fraud. No one was courageous enough to speak up publicly for Yeshua, because the Jewish leaders were against him, and the people feared both their leaders and the Romans.

When Yeshua began teaching in the Temple, his knowledge and authority astounded the crowds. How could a carpenter who had not had the best schooling know so much? When he stated there were those who wanted to kill him, many in the crowd did not believe him. They said he was demon possessed. Others had heard of the Pharisees' plans to have Yeshua killed. Rumors flew all over the city, dividing the populous into those who were for him being the Messiah and those against.

The priests and Pharisees sent Temple guards to arrest him, even though they had no reason. Rather than arresting Yeshua, the guards stood and listened, awed by his words. When they returned to the Pharisees and priests, they were mocked by those who had sent them.

Nicodemus stood listening to the other Pharisees. They were condemning Yeshua, not on what he said but on how his teaching was a threat to their position and leadership. "Money and power," mumbled Nicodemus. "They do not want their high standing in the Temple or their income from the animals they sell for sacrifice to suffer. Now they want to kill him when he only speaks the truth." He listened a while longer before he spoke loudly to be heard throughout the room. "Match what he preaches to the Tanakh. Then look at your lives. You may see that Yeshua speaks the truth."

Many hostile eyes turned toward him. "Are you from Galilee too?" someone called out. "Search the Tanakh and see for yourself—no prophet ever comes from Galilee!"

Others joined in mocking Nicodemus, who left the gathering. He went to the Upper City, to Joseph of Arimethea's house.

"Come in, Nicodemus," Ezra, Joseph's oldest son, greeted and ushered him into the luxurious home. "What brings you here this evening?"

"I would like to speak with you, your brother, and father."

Ezra led Nicodemus to the courtyard, where the men had been discussing business plans.

"Abba, Orli, Pharisee Nicodemus is here."

Both men rose and shook hands. "Welcome to my home," Joseph said. "What can we do for you?"

"Did you know the priests and Pharisees are wanting to stop Yeshua from teaching? They tried to have him arrested today. The guards they sent to get him listened to him instead. They mocked them for listening and me for speaking up for him. I fear for his life."

"Surely they would not try to kill him, would they?" Joseph asked.

"I'm not sure. The other Pharisees do not like what he is saying, how he criticizes them. They are following Yeshua wherever he goes and ask questions trying to force him to make mistakes. They want to discredit him."

"People are starting to wonder if he is the Messiah," Ezra said. "What do you think?"

"He certainly knows Tanakh better than anyone I know." Orli poured wine into cups Tabith had brought to the men. "His life seems to fulfill many of the prophecies. Micah told me of his birth. He and Dassa were there. His mother was a virgin. Dassa, her mother, the midwife, and several women guests checked her before... Well, you know."

Joseph, Ezra, and Nicodemus all stared at him with mouths open.

Nicodemus's hand shook so that his wine spilled. "What? *He shall be born of a virgin. Isaiah,*" Nicodemus said, his voice shaky.

"You can ask him yourself. Micah and his sons have been writing down everything they hear and matching it to Tanakh."

"What else do you know?" Joseph asked.

"Yeshua was born in Bethlehem. His parents had gone there since Joseph was of the tribe of Judah."

"The Prophet Micah and Numbers both speak of this," Ezra said.

"A number of shepherds came and worshipped the night of his birth. Then some rich men, he didn't know if they were rulers or wise men, came a couple of years later."

"Psalms," Nicodemus said.

"Jeremiah," said Ezra.

"Isaiah has many prophecies that Yeshua is fulfilling. Micah told me what you are saying, Orli," Joseph said.

"Micah said Joseph came in the night saying they were fleeing. That an angel came to him in a dream telling him Herod wanted to kill Yeshua. He wouldn't tell Micah where they were going. Micah and Dassa's first son was killed when the Romans came and slaughtered all the boys under two years old."

Nicodemus and Ezra gasped.

"Where did they go? Joseph and Mary?" Nicodemus's voice was low.

"Egypt."

"*Out of Egypt I called my son.* The first words of Hosea." Erza wiped a hand down his face. "He was born the year Daniel prophesied."

The men looked at each other. They all knew the prophecies. Just the first years of Yeshua's life had fulfilled more than any of them had thought.

"Orli, why did you not say anything about this?" Joseph asked. "Micah never mentioned that he told you."

"I guess I never really put it all together. Micah and Dassa do not really talk about it. It has all come out over a course of years. A bit here and there."

Seeing The Life

"You say they have more things written down?" Nicodemus asked.

"Yes, a number of scrolls. Micah, Eli, and Perez all write on them."

Nicodemus looked intently at Orli. "Do you think he would let me see them?"

"I do not know. They do not talk about them much. I think only when someone adds something or when they discuss what prophecy they think he has fulfilled."

"I do not think we should ask Micah. Not at this time anyway," Joseph said. "We need to keep our thoughts to ourselves just as they have. We know the Pharisees are against him. Yeshua speaks out against the Sadducees also. We do not need to tell all that we know."

"Yes," said Nicodemus. "We need to keep this quiet. If he is the Messiah, he will free us."

"He certainly has enough of a following to gather an army to expel the Romans." Ezra's expression told of his determination to join that army when called.

📖 📖 📖

The last day of Sukkot found all of Joseph's and Micah's families listening with thousands of others as Yeshua spoke. He shouted to be heard while standing in the Treasury of the Temple. "I am the light of the world. If you follow me, you will not walk in darkness, because you will have the light that leads to life."

"You are making those claims about yourself! Such testimony is not valid," a Pharisee yelled back.

Yeshua said, "These claims are valid even though I make them about myself. For I know where I came from and where I am going, but you do not know this about me. You judge me by human standards, but I do not judge anyone. And if I did, my judgment would be correct in every respect because I am not alone. The Abba who sent me is with me. Your own law says that if two people agree about something, their witness is accepted as fact. I am one witness, and my Abba who sent me is the other."

"Where is your abba?"

"Since you don't know who I am, you don't know who my Abba is. If you knew me, you would also know my Abba."

People jostled each other. Some were Pharisees, who gathered together speaking to each other.

"I am going away. You will search for me but will die in your sin. You cannot come where I am going," Jesus said.

Questions broke out amongst the crowd. "Is he planning to commit suicide?"

"What does he mean, 'You cannot come where I am going'?"

"You are from below; I am from above. You belong to this world; I do not. That is why I said that you will die in your sins. For unless you believe that Ehyeh asher Ehyeh, you will die in your sins."

"Who are you?" The shouted question came from different parts of the crowd.

"The one I have always claimed to be. I have much to say about you and much to condemn, but I will not. For I say only what I have heard from the one who sent me, and he is completely truthful. When you have lifted up the Son of Man on the cross, then you will understand that Ehyeh asher Ehyeh. I do nothing on my own but say only what the Abba taught me. And the one who sent me is with me, he has not deserted me. For I always do what pleases him."

A cheer went up from the crowd as many of the people proclaimed their belief in Yeshua.

Micah leaned close to Eli's ear. "What do you think? Do they really believe?"

"I do not know. You know how crowds are. They can cheer and praise one moment and jeer the next."

Yeshua looked over the people listening to him and cheering him. "You are truly my disciples if you remain faithful to my teachings. And you will know the truth, and the truth will set you free."

"But we are descendants of Abraham," many voices cried. "We have never been slaves to anyone. What do you mean, 'You will be set free'?"

Jesus scanned the crowd. "I tell you the truth, everyone who sins is a slave of sin. A slave is not a permanent member of the family, but a son is part of the family forever. So if the Son sets you free, you are truly free. Yes, I realize you are descendants of Abraham. And yet some of you are trying to kill me because there is no room in your hearts for my message. I am telling you what I saw when I was with my Abba. But you are following the advice of your abba."

"Our father is Abraham!" they declared.

"No," Jesus replied, "for if you were really the children of Abraham, you would follow his example. Instead, you are trying to kill me because I told you the truth, which I heard from Elohim. Abraham never did such a thing. No, you are imitating your real father."

They replied, "We aren't illegitimate children! Elohim himself is our true Abba."

Jesus said, "If Elohim were your Abba, you would love me, because I have come to you from Elah Shemaya. I am not here on my own, but he sent me. Why can you not understand what I am saying? It is because you cannot even hear me! For you are the children of your abba the devil, and you love to do the evil things he does. He was a murderer from the beginning. He has always hated the truth, because there is no truth in him. When he lies, it is consistent with his character; for he is a liar and the father of lies. So when I tell the truth, you just naturally do not believe me! Which of you can truthfully accuse me of sin? And since I am telling you the truth, why do you not believe me? Anyone who belongs to El Shaddai listens gladly to the words of Elohim. But you don't listen because you don't belong to El Shaddai."

"You Samaritan devil! Did we not say all along that you were possessed by a demon?" a voiced accused.

"No," Jesus said, "I have no demon in me. For I honor my Abba, and you dishonor me. And though I have no wish to glorify myself, Melek Kabodh is going to glorify me. He is the true judge. I tell you the truth, anyone who obeys my teaching will never die!"

Someone yelled, "Now we know you are possessed by a demon. Even Abraham and the prophets died, but you say, 'Anyone who obeys my teaching will never die!' Are you greater than our abba Abraham? He died, and so did the prophets. Who do you think you are?"

"If I want glory for myself, it does not count. But it is my Abba who will glorify me. You say, 'Adonai Eloheikhem,' but you don't even know him. I know him. If I said otherwise, I would be as great a liar as you! But I do know him and obey him. Your abba Abraham rejoiced as he looked forward to my coming. He saw it and was glad."

Shouts were heard. "You are not even fifty years old. How can you say you have seen Abraham?"

"I tell you the truth, before Abraham was even born, Ehyeh asher Ehyeh!"

A roar went up through the people. Many began picking up stones and casting them at Yeshua. Others scattered, as the stones didn't reach where he was standing, falling instead on the heads of the people in the crowd.

Joseph sent his sons to find Micah and sons after they escorted their families home. He wanted the men to gather at his warehouse. He felt a strong need to speak with them and plan. The quick switch from cheering Yeshua to wanting him stoned worried Joseph.

Someone grabbed Joseph's arm. It was Nicodemus. "He is claimed to be Adonai Elyon. We need to see those scrolls of Micah's. We must know more about him. We must study them."

"You are right." Joseph told of his plans to meet at the warehouse, asking Nicodemus to come and bring any whom he was positive was in agreement with them that Yeshua was the Messiah, the true son of Yahweh.

Chapter 24

Micah entered the warehouse of Joseph with his sons Eli, Perez, and young Benjamin. They were met by Orli, who instructed them to go to Joseph's office. He would wait until all those expected had come.

It was late afternoon, the final day of the last fall festival. Jerusalem was still filled with those who had traveled there from all over Israel and Galilee. In the streets, people argued over what Yeshua had said about himself. Was he the Messiah, the Son of El-Elyon, Yahweh Yisrael himself? Was he a fraud? Should he be worshiped or stoned for blasphemy?

With Joseph were Ezra, Abraham, and James, Joseph's sons who managed the business in Arimethea, and Nicodemus.

"Nicodemus, these are Micah and his sons, Eli and Perez. Benjamin, I had forgotten you were now a man." Joseph patted the youth who had turned fifteen recently on the shoulder. "This is the Pharisee Nicodemus. He is a believer and is trustworthy. We wait for another."

Micah shook hands with the Pharisee. "It is good to see you again, Nicodemus. Also good to know you have kept your belief."

"You know each other?" Ezra asked.

"Nicodemus came to my home at the time of the Pesach when Yeshua whipped the moneychangers and herds of animals in the Temple. Yeshua was staying with us and answered some questions Nicodemus had." Micah smiled at the older man.

"Yes, I have kept my faith. I hear you've been following his ministry too. That you have written much of it down."

Micah shot a glance at his sons. Benjamin stood with his mouth open in shock. "How did you know?"

"It is still kept quiet. Orli spoke to us about it. We have not told anyone else, nor will we. We will not say anything to the others who are coming. What you've recorded is too important to have revealed at this time," Joseph reassured the others.

Orli and two others entered then. "I have locked the warehouse door. No one else should come in."

"Good," Joseph said.

Nicodemus introduced everyone to the men who had come in as Lazarus of Bethany and Shaanan Ben Yagil. Once they were all settled on the rug and wine was poured, Nicodemus looked at each man. "First and foremost, nothing said here should be spoken of to anyone else. Not family, friends, anyone. If what we believe is truth then no word must find its way to the Romans. We already know most if not all other Pharisees are against Yeshua. Also, the Sadducees and priests are not trustworthy. What Yeshua preaches shows their pride and greed.

"The people are fickle. If they like what he says they cheer and believe. When he says something they do not like, they turn on him like jackals.

"Yeshua himself said those who believe in him will be set free. This is something we can work with. If Yeshua is the Messiah, we must help him raise the army to fight the Romans and take our land back."

"I am ready to fight," Ezra said. "Rome is a blight on our land. With the way Yeshua can stir the crowd, many will follow him when he calls for war against Rome."

"I agree, but I wonder about his words, 'I am going away.' That we will not be able to follow or find him. What did he mean?" Perez asked.

Lazarus said, "He often says things which are difficult to understand. Then we are challenged to have ears to hear. It is no wonder many are confused. The prophets also spoke in this way."

"Do you think he will come for Hanukkah? We could prepare between now and then. If he comes, we could possibly speak with him, telling about our plans to aid him," Abraham said.

"Yes, we can gather and stockpile arms in Arimethea. That would help to hide the weapons," James added.

"It will all have to be done very carefully to keep the Romans from finding out," Joseph said.

"And the Pharisees as well. At this time, if they found out," said Nicodemus, "they might turn him over to the Romans. That would get him stopped and crucified."

"Yes, we must keep this secret. When Hanukkah arrives, we can approach Yeshua and offer him our support." Eli held his hand out in front of him, palm down. The others, one by one, placed their hands on top of his.

※ ※ ※

"Abba," Benjamin said as they walked home, "I'm confused. Not about our talk." Micah's eyes had shot a warning to his son. "The people at the Temple said we had never been slaves. Is not Pesach all about remembering HaShem taking us out of slavery in Egypt? How can they say we've never been slaves?"

"A very good question. It seems we are a people who forget what Adonai Elyon has done for us. How many times in the Tanakh does HaShem remind us that he brought us out of slavery?"

"A lot."

"The people choose to forget all that HaShem has done for us." Micah placed his hand on Benjamin's shoulder.

"El De'a even told the people that they were going to be overthrown and carried away to Babylon. No one believed Jeremiah when he predicted it. They were held for seventy years."

"I know," said Ben. "So why did they say we had never been slaves?"

"They don't want to think about how we have been conquered when we turned from HaShem and did what was evil in his sight. Do you remember Yeshua's next words?" Micah asked.

"That we are all slaves to sin?"

"Yes, and he spoke the truth. We all sin. Remember John the Baptist's message. Repent of your sins and be baptized to show you are dedicated to not sinning and being righteous instead."

"But I know I still sin even though I was baptized." Ben's confusion was evident.

"We all do. Yeshua was telling us that believing in him sets us free. Then we are not slaves to sin anymore but are accepted by El Selich'ah."

"That is truly a great hope," said Perez. "It is not something any Pharisee or priest has ever said before."

They walked along in silence for a while. "What should we do about the scrolls?" Eli asked. "I do not want them out where someone could find them."

"I agree," Micah said. "If Joseph or Nicodemus want to look at them, they can come to our house and see them there. I do not want them leaving the premises."

"That is wise," said Eli.

At the meeting it had also been decided that they would take turns following Yeshua as he traveled. Each fortnight the younger men would change who went. They would report what they had heard by coming to the warehouse and reporting to Joseph and Micah. Micah and his sons would then add it to the scrolls.

Joseph, Nicodemus, and Lazarus would begin purchasing weapons a few at a time from various dealers so as not to alert the Romans garrison or the Pharisees, Temple leaders, and Sadducees. The men discussed the guilt they felt. It seemed as if they were betraying friends and colleagues. Obeying and following El Shaddai, it was decided, was more important. They remembered when Moshe came down from the mountain only to find the golden calf. He called for those who were for El-Elyon to strap on a sword and kill their brothers, friends, and neighbors. The men chose to follow Adonai Adonim.

Orli was the first to travel with Yeshua as he preached in Judea. Seventy-two of his disciples were sent out in pairs to the towns and villages Yeshua planned to go. Orli stayed with him, hearing him preach and seeing the miracles of healing and exorcism.

"Yeshua is declaring that anyone who rejects him is rejecting HaShem, since it is he who sent Yeshua." Orli told of the seventy-two who came back rejoicing that even the demons obeyed when Yeshua's name was invoked.

"*Love the Adonai Eloheikhem with all your heart, all your soul, all your strength, and all your mind.* And, *Love your neighbor as yourself.* He said this was how to inherit eternal life." Perez reported when he returned to Jerusalem. "Then he said loving your neighbor is not just those like youself or your friends. Your neighbors can also be people you do not know and are in need. Having mercy for anyone is what makes you a neighbor."

"That is certainly not what the priests and Pharisees do. The Sadducees either," Joseph said.

Perez chuckled. "Those were the very people he used in his story to illustrate not loving your neighbor. I am writing the entire story on a scroll. Then you can all know precisely what he said."

Seeing The Life

"You can remember it that clearly?" Lazarus asked. He had come into Jerusalem to tell them about Yeshua staying with him and his sisters.

"It is surprising. I can recall what he said exactly. It is as if I hear him speaking again when I think of it."

"So, Lazarus, when was Yeshua at your house?" Micah asked. Seven men were again seated on the rug in Joseph's office. Micah, Eli and Perez, Joseph, Ezra and Orli, as well as Lazarus.

"He and his disciples came a few days ago. He was speaking, and the room was filled with people. Mary was sitting right by him. My sister Martha, she is always bustling about, was in a dither about the huge meal she was making. She came right up to Yeshua and placed her hands on her hips and said, 'Lord, does it not seem unfair to you that my sister just sits here while I do all the work? Tell her to come and help me.' Do you now what Yeshua said?" Lazarus paused. "He told her to relax. Mary had chosen the correct thing to do in listening to him, and he was not going to make her help with the cooking. You should have seen the look on Martha's face. She went all red and her jaw bobbed up and down." Lazarus was laughing. "Then she wiped her hand on the cloth she held and sat down too."

📖 📖 📖

"Micah," Dassa murmured, "what is going on?" They were on their pallet in the small room they used for sleeping. It was barely more than a nook but gave them privacy in the household of four couples and their families.

Miriam, Dassa's mother, still lived with them. She were very frail, and Dassa worried she would not live much longer. Dassa's father Eli had died after Sukkot. The house was crowded, but the love they had for each other brought joy to everyone. Eli's wife Geva, was expecting their forth child. Perez and Rachel had two. Rachel had just announced another child was on the way that evening. Benjamin, Abigail, and David were Dassa and Micah's youngest. When daughters Sarah and Miriam brought their families for visits and Tabith, Orli, and their three came, the children made enough noise to scare all the chickens, goats, and donkeys in the neighborhood.

"What do you mean?" Micah pulled her closer and nuzzled her neck.

"I know you all are wanting to know everything Yeshua is teaching. It is why one of the sons are gone all the time, to follow and hear him. But what about the rest?"

"I still do not know what you are asking about."

"Micah, I know you all are buying weapons. Why?"

Micah turned onto his back with a sigh. "How did you find out?"

"I'm not stupid. I hear you and our sons talking."

"Dassa, we think Yeshua is the Messiah."

"Yes, I do too."

"We think, with his popularity, he could amass a great army. He said he will set us free. We want to be ready when Yeshua calls for an uprising against Rome."

"Do you really think Yeshua means to lead a rebellion?"

"He said he will set us free. Even John spoke of the Kingdom of Elohim. Yeshua speaks of it so very often. We are his chosen people. Yeshua implies he is to be king. What king doesn't fight for his kingdom? Israel is the Promised Land. It makes sense that Yeshua would be king of Israel. King of the Jews."

"Micah, do you remember when he said to seek first Elohim's kingdom and righteousness? What if he means HaShem's kingdom in heaven?"

"No king is a king unless he has land to rule over." Micah sighed. "I do not know if Yeshua will lead a rebellion and free us from Rome, but we plan to be ready and able to arm those who go to fight."

Dassa didn't say anything else. She lay on her side, her back against his front, and pulled his arm around her. As she drifted into sleep, she prayed that if Yeshua led a rebellion, the men of her family would not go and fight.

Chapter 25

Joseph and Micah were examining a shipment in the warehouse when Nicodemus rushed in. The Pharisee's face was flushed, his breathing labored. He raised a hand and waved them toward the office as he headed there himself. Joseph had installed a wooden door to insure privacy when they spoke. There was a pitcher of wine on a low stool. Nicodemus poured a cup and took a large swallow.

"What has happened?" Joseph asked. Micah had called Orli and Ezra, as well as Eli and Perez, who had been in another part of the warehouse. Wine had been poured by the time everyone was in the room with the door tightly shut.

"I was invited to Pharisee Zebediah's for a meal yesterday. I just returned. Several others as well as some Sadducees were there. Imagine my surprise when Yeshua arrived and was given a place of honor."

"What happened?" Joseph asked.

"It started when Yeshua sat down without doing the hand-washing ceremony. Zebediah noticed and made an issue of it. You would not believe what Yeshua said. The Pharisees, he said, wash the outside of a cup so well but are filthy inside. Then he called them, I guess I should say *us*, fools. Don't we know that HaShem made both the inside and outside? He said for us to clean our insides by giving to the poor. Yeshua said sorrow awaits the Pharisees who ignore justice but tithe the tiniest of income. He basically called them prideful, wanting praise and respect but they are corrupt."

"I am sure they responded to that insult," Micah said.

"That is just what one of the Sadducees there said. Yeshua then turned his focus to them. He told them they were crushing people with unbearable religious demands. That the same sorrow awaits them as for the Pharisees. Yeshua said the Sadducees of today agree with those of the past who murdered the prophets, and this generation will be held responsible for the murders from Abel to Zechariah. Not only do they not enter the Kingdom but keep others from entering."

"How did they all react?" Ezra asked.

"Yeshua got up to leave, and the Sadducees and Pharisees started asking questions. It was so they could trap him by his answers so they can discredit him."

"Were they successful?" Joseph asked.

"No, every answer he gave was correct. It actually made the questioners look even worse since it showed what he had said of them was true. I had to stay in the town inn last night. It was too late to journey back to

Jerusalem. As soon as I arrived, I came straight here. I fear Yeshua is making many enemies."

📖 📖 📖

All around Judea, Yeshua preached as the crowds grew into the thousands. Daily he taught and answered questions the people put to him.

Yeshua always taught by using stories. His meanings were understandable to those who wanted to learn. Those who didn't want to change didn't understand and derided the teachings. They only came to be seen in the crowd since Yeshua was so popular.

Ezra, Orli, Eli, or Perez was always following in the crowd. Sometimes Benjamin accompanied one of his brothers. More scrolls were added to the chest Micah had bought to store them. It was kept locked. Joseph, his sons, and Nicodemus came separately to read the scrolls. Sometimes the men would gather and discuss what had been recorded. When he could come to the city, Lazarus came and read the scrolls also. Each man added what he learned from and about Yeshua. Micah and his sons wrote what the others told them.

One day, news spread that Pontius Pilate, the prefect of Rome in Judea, had murdered some Galileans at the Temple as they offered sacrifices. When Yeshua heard, he turned to the people and asked, "Do you think those Galileans were worse sinners than all the other people from Galilee? Is that why they suffered? Not at all! And you will perish too unless you repent of your sins and turn to God. And what about the eighteen people who died when the tower in Siloam fell on them? Were they the worst sinners in Jerusalem? No, and I tell you again that unless you repent, you will perish."

"Yeshua's continuing theme is repentance of sin. Don't our Days of Repentance between Yom Kipper and Yom HaZikkaron take care of that? We spend ten days thinking about the sins we committed the previous year and repent of them," Eli said. All the men were gathered in Joseph's office except Nicodemus and Lazarus.

"How do you show your repentance is true?" Micah asked his son.

"John said it was by how you lived your life," Eli responded.

"I have heard Yeshua say for people to go and sin no more," Orli said. They sat on the rug in their accustomed places.

"I do not think I can never sin." Benjamin sat between Orli and Perez.

"*The law of Elohim controls their thinking; their feet do not slip.*" Joseph quoted the psalmist.

"*In my heart I store up your words, so I might not sin against you.*" Perez did the same.

"*You despise all who stray from your statutes, for they are deceptive and unreliable.*" This time Ezra spoke.

Ben looked discouraged. Then his face brightened. "*I want to do what pleases you, Elohai. Your law dominates my thoughts.* That's from Psalms too."

"Very good, my son," Micah said, smiling. "If you keep that in the forefront of all you do, you will find it easier not to sin."

Quietly spoken amens came from the other men.

Eli waited for the people to leave as night fell. It was the fifth day of Hanukkah. He stood under an olive tree on the Mount of Olives. He wanted to speak with Yeshua. As the closest in age to Yeshua, Eli had played with him whenever the family had visited during the festivals. He felt they were friends. Eli hoped and prayed Yeshua was the long-awaited Messiah. Now he waited to speak privately with him.

After speaking with his disciples, Yeshua turned and walked to where Eli waited. "Eli, my old friend, it is good to see you." The men hugged, patting each other on the back. "You have questions. Come, let's sit."

Once they were seated on the ground, Eli said, "We have been following your teachings. We, my family, believe you are the Messiah. Your words fill our hearts with hope."

"I have seen you, your brothers Perez and Benjamin, my he's grown. He's all arms and legs right now."

Eli chuckled. "His face turns very red when his voice cracks."

Yeshua laughed. "I remember feeling the same way."

"You used to trip over your feet when you were his age."

"You were not so graceful yourself."

They laughed, remembering running, wrestling, and swimming in the Jordan together as they grew up.

"Yeshua, you said you have come to set us free. There are those of us who know this is true. You fulfill so many prophecies of the long-awaited one. We, my family, a few leaders within the Pharisees and Sadducees, and others have begun preparing to support you when you become king. Slowly, cautiously, we are gathering what we will need when the time comes." Eli looked around, wanting to be sure no one heard what he was saying. "You understand, do you not?"

"Eli, my kingdom is not as you imagine. As John said, the Kingdom of Heaven is near."

"Yes, we are seeking Elah Shemaya's kingdom as you instructed. We are living righteous lives, attempting to stop falling into sin through what tempts us."

"Then you do well. I do not want you to be discouraged when my time comes. It will not be as you think. I ask you to believe and have faith. Trust in El-Elyon's plan. Nothing he sets forth can be stopped."

Confused, Eli nodded. "You are right. El Shaddai created all things. What power is greater than his? I will keep my faith in HaShem and you."

"Does Perez still breed donkeys?" Yeshua asked.

"Yes." They spent a few minutes talking and laughing about their youthful adventures involving those donkeys.

"There will come a time when I will need a donkey for a while. Do you think he would allow me to borrow one? A young one who has not been ridden," Yeshua asked.

Eli thought Yeshua looked pleased and sad at the same time and wondered. "I'm positive he will. There is a yearling still with his dam. Do you know when you will need it?"

"Near Pesach but before." Yeshua gave the instructions as to where and how the colt should be for his disciples to find it for him. They talked on for a while; then Yeshua stood. "You must get back to the city. Tell everyone I love them and am very glad their hearts are turned to El Shaddai."

꧁ ꧁ ꧁

"Did you heard what that man, Yeshua, said?" Uria asked. She was visiting Dassa. They were seated inside the house near a brazier since the winter day was cold and windy.

Dassa laughed. "He says many remarkable things. Which one are you referring to?"

"That we have to hate our family to be his disciple. He said we need to hate even ourselves. I don't understand. Why do I have to hate my family? And he says we must love our neighbor as we love ourselves. I do not understand how we can do both."

"Micah and I had a discussion about this same topic." She didn't say they had understood what he meant by each. They were two different concepts. "Yeshua says we must love our neighbor by doing for them as we would do for ourselves."

"Why would I want to do that?" Uria's tone was negative.

"If you were hungry and had no food, would you not want someone to care enough to give you food so you do not starve?"

"Of course."

"What if someone you did not know was starving, would you give them food if you found out?"

"Um... Why would I? I do not know them."

Dassa looked sadly at Uria. "But you want someone to give you food. Would you not take it from a stranger if they offered it?"

"I see. Give to those who are in need. He calls that loving others as you love yourself. Why did he not just say to be charitable? I can do that." Pride laced Uria's words.

"What if the starving person was a leper?"

"Eeou. I don't want to be near those people."

"What if you were the leper?"

"I do not see you heading out to the leper colony giving out food."

"Actually, we do and have been for years. Micah and I went until we hired Moshe and Nissa. They go now, taking food I purchase. We give clothing too."

"Why did you hire those two anyway? I've always wanted to ask you. Moshe only has one hand, and Nissa, yuck, that scarred face is awful."

"Moshe had lost his hand in an accident, and Nissa had fallen into a fire as a child." Dassa looked up from her spinning defending her choice of servants.

"I would not have them around me."

"It took some getting use to, I have to admit, but it illustrates Yeshua's point. If I, or one of my children or grandchildren, had those problems, I would want someone to hire me. I would rather work than beg. Both are hard workers and very grateful we hired them. They are like family now. They have been with us for a number of years."

"Now you have to hate them as well as your family in order to be one of Yeshua's disciples," Uria stated bluntly.

Seeing The Life

"In comparison to my love for HaShem, yes. My love for HaShem must make it seem as if my love for my family is hate. You know how much you and I love our families. Think of how much we need to love HaShem to make it seem like we hate our families."

"He certainly wants us to love him a lot."

"*You must love the Adonai Eloheikhem with your whole mind, your whole being, and all your strength.*"

Chapter 26

Hanukkah was four months past and spring was coming. Lambs were being born. The barley harvest had begun. Pesach would bring people to Jerusalem from all over Judea, Galilee and the far reaches of the Roman Empire. Yeshua had spent the winter traveling Judea and Galilee preaching to larger and larger crowds. The things he said continued to anger the Pharisees, Sadducees, and priests.

Lazarus had come to Jerusalem on a regular basis and met with Pharisee Joseph, Micah, and their sons as well as Pharisee Nicodemus. Several Sadducees had secretly expressed belief that Yeshua was the Messiah to Nicodemus but were not taken into the confidence of the group that met at the warehouse.

Since they were members of the group Yeshua was criticizing so heavily, Joseph and Nicodemus kept quiet during meetings of the Pharisees. It was easy to see those who opposed Yeshua. The ones who might agree kept silent. Those who said anything in support of Yeshua's teachings were immediately condemned by their peers.

Between all their travels, the men in Joseph's and Micah's group had witnessed almost everything Yeshua had taught. The number of scrolls in the trunk in Micah's house increased with all the things he and his sons recorded.

This day, news came of a different sort. Lazarus had died. Micah, Joseph, and their families hurried to Bethany when they heard the news. Both Lazarus's sisters were distraught.

"We contacted Yeshua when he became so ill. We asked him to come quickly but have heard no word from him," Mary said as she wept. Dinah, Joseph's wife, held the grieving woman in her arms. Martha stood silently, tears coursing down her cheeks.

The number of people who had come from Jerusalem to help console Mary and Martha was large since the siblings were well known and liked. Bethany was a village in mourning.

Dassa helped with the preparation of the body. She had brought linen to wrap the body in, as had several others. The journey to the grave had a fleet of mourners. Everyone wept and wailed their grief over the loss of Lazarus.

"If only Yeshua had come, our brother would still be alive. I know he would have healed him," Martha said as they rolled the stone over the opening to the grave. "Now it is too late."

Concerned not only for the sisters, Joseph and Micah decided to remain in Bethany for a few days. The cache of weapons there would need to be moved. Martha and Mary were vulnerable as unmarried women. The chance discovery of the weapons put them in even more danger. Dassa and Dinah stayed even though the rest of their families returned to Jerusalem.

The couples, as well as other friends, were in the house when, after speaking to a youth who had come in, Martha rushed out of the house. After a short while, she returned and took Mary away from those she was with. Martha spoke a few words then they both rushed from the house.

"What do you think is going on?" Dassa asked Micah.

"I know not. Maybe they are going to the grave."

"Let us go with them. I do not want them to mourn by themselves," Joseph said. Those in the house followed. Mary and Martha were not going to the grave but a different way. Wondering where they were headed, the people kept up with the sisters. In a field near town, they saw Yeshua. Mary fell at his feet weeping.

"Lord, if only you had been here, my brother would not have died." Mary's words brought wails from the people with her.

Yeshua looked over the people then asked, "Where have you put him?"

"Come, Lord, and see."

Yeshua wept as they walked to the grave. Micah heard people saying, "See how much he loved him." Also, "This man healed a blind man. Could he not have kept Lazarus from dying?"

Micah watched Yeshua. He was grieving as evidenced by his tears, but there was some other emotions as well. Anger, though Micah didn't know why, was evident in his bearing. There was also a sadness that wasn't connected to the death of Lazarus. Micah wondered if Yeshua was bearing a burden he carried alone. One he could not share with any other.

When he arrived at the grave, Yeshua stood beside it looking at the cave with the stone over the entrance. "Roll the stone away."

"Lord, he has been dead for four days. The smell will be terrible," Martha said.

Yeshua looked at her. "Did I not tell you that you would see God's glory if you believe?"

Martha signaled for the grave to be opened. Several men moved to do as instructed.

Yeshua turned his gaze heavenward. "Abba, thank you for hearing me. You always hear me, but I said it out loud for the sake of all these people standing here, so that they will believe you sent me." Loudly Yeshua yelled, "Lazarus, come out!"

Gasps of disbelief rose from the crowd when Lazarus, stumbling with his hands and feet wrapped in linen and his face covered by a head cloth, came into the light from the darkness of the cave.

"Unwrap him and let him go," Yeshua said.

Mary and Martha were hugging their brother and helping release him from the wrappings. Now their tears were for joy and thanksgiving. Those who had been mourning were now cheering. A few men kept silent and simply watched.

Seeing The Life

"I saw it with my own eyes. Lazarus had been dead four days and in the tomb. Even his sister said the body would be stinking. Yeshua just told them to roll away the stone. They did, and Lazarus came out, alive."

Caiaphas, the high priest, looked at the man who had brought the news and then at the Pharisees and leading priests he had called together. He waved the man away then listened to what was being said by the men around him.

"What are we going to do?"

Caiaphas had called most of the high council together. There were a few who had not been contacted — any who had ever spoken in support of Yeshua's teachings. Something had to be done about this Yeshua from Nazareth.

"This man certainly performs many miraculous signs. If we allow him to go on like this, soon everyone will believe in him. Then the Roman army will come and destroy both our Temple and our nation."

Others talked about Yeshua's criticism of them.

"You do not know what you are talking about!" Caiaphas said. "Do you not realize it is better for you that one man should die for the people than for the whole nation to be destroyed." Caiaphas sat back, watched, and listened as the Pharisees and priests began plotting Yeshua's death.

"Do you think Yeshua will come for Pesach?" Tabith asked. She, Orli, and their children had come for Shabbat as they did every once in a while. Now that the ceremony was finished, they were eating.

"That is the question that seems to be on everyone's mind," Dassa said. "It seemed to be the only thing we heard when we went to market today, was it not, Rachel?"

"Yes, but that is not all. I heard the Pharisees have ordered that anyone who sees Yeshua must report it to them so he can be arrested," Rachel replied.

"For what?" Perez looked at his wife. "He has done nothing wrong."

"I do not know. It is simply what I heard."

Eight-year-old David moved next to Dassa and looked at his mother, his face full of heartbreak. "I miss Softa."

Dassa pulled him into her lap. "I miss her too. You and she were best buddies." Miriam had died a week ago, leaving a little boy missing the grandmother he had spent so much time with. David was the youngest of Micah and Dassa's children. He had nieces and nephews older than he.

David's words had reminded the other children of the loss. Tears rolled down little cheeks, and sleeves were used to wipe noses. Miriam and her husband Eli had moved to Jerusalem when they sold the inn in Bethlehem. That was over twenty years ago. Eli had died in the fall. Now Miriam was gone.

"In Ecclesiastes it says there is a time to be born and a time to die. Even though we miss her, Softa is now in

Seeing The Life

Paradise. We will see her some day." Dassa gave her son a hug.

"Yeshua says we will be resurrected on the last day. I am not sure what he means, but I believe him." Benjamin spread honey on his bread then stuffed it in his mouth.

📖 📖 📖

"I hope he does not come," Dassa said later that evening when she and Micah were snuggled under their blankets. "The Pharisees do not like what he says about them, so they want to arrest him."

"I do not see how they can. He has done nothing wrong. It is not against the law to tell someone they are wrong."

"Humph."

"I think he will come. He has never missed any that I know of since we saw the family so many years ago. Besides, Yeshua always obeys what the Tanakh says," Micah said then kissed her ear.

"Yes, I know. I just fear for him. There is a long history of prophets being murdered. I do not want him to be added to the list."

"If he is the Messiah, they will not be able to kill him."

"I do not know. I just fear for him." Dassa lay awake a long time after Micah fell asleep.

📖 📖 📖

Perez tied the colt to post beside its dam. He'd brought them each day for three days and waited at the edge of the small village outside of Jerusalem. Eli had told him of Yeshua's request. Joseph had allowed him to miss work and would until someone came for the animals.

He thought of the passage in Zechariah: *Tell the people of Israel, Don't be afraid, people of Jerusalem. Look, your King is coming to you. He is humble, riding on a donkey—riding on a donkey's colt.* Ezra had quoted it when Eli had told them about his visit with Yeshua at Hanukkah.

Perez watched as two men walked toward town. He was standing under an olive tree nearby. There were others talking and laughing in a group. The men walked up to the donkeys and began untying the ropes.

"Hey, what do you think you are doing?" someone in the group asked.

Perez's hands shook as he went to the men. He hid them in the folds of his cloak. "Why are you untying the colt?" He understood the significance of Yeshua's request. He planned to ride into Jerusalem, fulfilling the prophecy from long ago.

"HaShem needs it," one of the men said.

"Take it with my blessing," Perez said. Once the men and colt were leaving, with shaking hands Perez untied the mare and headed back to Jerusalem.

📖 📖 📖

"He is coming to Pesach. Two men came for the colt. I came back just as they left," Perez said as he entered the warehouse. Joseph put a hand to his forehead. Micah, who was walking toward him, stopped in his tracks. Ezra stood off to the side.

Orli came in behind Perez. "Yeshua is coming. The news is spreading like wildfire. He is riding a donkey.

People are cutting palm branches and cloaks and laying them on the road. He is coming from the Mount of Olives and will enter through the Shushan Gate"

They looked at each other and as one started running to the door. Joseph shouted to his warehouse manager to send everyone home and to lock the door.

They ran toward the Temple. The Shushan Gate was in the eastern wall. It was directly in line with the Temple and the Holy of Holies. They could hear shouts of hosannah. The streets were crowded. Thousands of pilgrims were arriving daily for Pesach. People called out, asking whom they were cheering for. "It is Yeshua, the prophet from Nazareth in Galilee."

They couldn't get close to the Temple but could hear a chant rising from the masses. "Praise Elohim for the Son of David! Hail to the King of Israel! Blessings on the King who comes in the name of HaShem! Blessings on the coming Kingdom of our ancestor David! Peace in heaven, and glory in highest heaven! Praise Elohim in highest heaven!"

Each day that week Yeshua went to the Temple and taught. Each day the Pharisees, leading priests, and Sadducees heard more stories that angered them. A few Pharisees came to Joseph saying they believed Yeshua was the Messiah. Although Joseph had kept his viewpoint to himself, the others of like mind had figured it out.

Micah, Eli, and Perez spent the days before Pesach listening to Yeshua teach in the Temple and filling lambskin scrolls. They discussed the questions put to Yeshua and his answers by the priest, Pharisees, and

Sadducees. His ability to answer each one, confounding the questioners, amazed them but also caused them to worry. Yeshua was making enemies of the most powerful men in Jerusalem.

"Can you believe it?" Eli said. "Again he nearly causes a riot in the Temple by knocking over the moneychanging tables and releasing doves and livestock."

"Well, just as he said, it has been turned into a den of thieves." Micah laid down his pen, lifted his arms over his head, and stretched. The bones of his spine popped loudly enough that his sons could hear.

"You are getting old, Abba." Perez chuckled. "You sound like Sabba used to."

Moshe entered the room with a paper he handed to Micah. He opened the folded missive and read silently then said, "Thank you, Moshe. Please ask Dassa to join us."

"What, Abba?" Benjamin asked. He was copying practice lines in training to follow the family scribing tradition.

"Wait until your ima gets here."

Dassa entered then. "Do you want something?"

"Just to inform you that I sent a message to Yeshua offering our upper room for him to use for an evening meal on Preparation Day. I know it will make more work for you and the wives." Micah looked at Eli and Perez. "But I wanted to let them have a good, filling meal this week. I do not know how often they get them."

"It is fine of you to offer, and we will be please to have them, but I know they have been staying with Lazarus, so they are getting very good meals." Dassa smiled and kissed Micah on the head. "You are generous to offer. Now I must go tell my daughter-in-laws so we can plan."

Dassa left, and Perez looked open-mouthed at his father. "You asked Yeshua before you mentioned it to Ima?" He laughed. "You are braver than I. Rachel would have my head if I did that."

"Ah, my son, there is a difference between you and me. Your ima is the matriarch of the family. Rachel would have to ask for her help. Dassa can tell. Besides, I knew she would not object. Any time she can see Yeshua, even for a few minutes, she will jump at the chance. She has always doted on him," Micah said.

Preparation Day came, and the ladies of Micah's house were busy. They had gone to the market early and brought back baskets full of food. Fixing meals for thirteen men in addition to the family was a major undertaking.

"I wish it were later in the year. There is no fresh fruit, only dried," Dassa said as she stood among the baskets on the floor. Geva and Rachel were unpacking and sorting the purchases. Dassa had sent the servant Nissa, along with eleven-year-old daughter Abby, son David, and grandsons Joses and Samuel to draw water. Normally the boys would not be carrying water, but sending them along fulfilled two purposes. The water jars would be filled more quickly, and it got the boys out from underfoot.

The women divided the cooking between them and began their tasks. Nissa was sent to sweep the upper room even though it and the entire house had been cleaned from top to bottom to make sure every bit of yeast was removed. By evening the house was filled with flavorful aromas that made everyone's mouth water.

Yeshua arrived with his disciples before sundown. He sent them up the stairs to the room prepared for them then turned to Dassa and Micah. "I appreciate your offer. We have stayed the last nights on the Mount of Olives. This meal is welcome."

"You are always welcome in our home," Micah said. "I am pleased to be able to offer it to you."

Yeshua looked at Dassa. She saw love and grief in Yeshua's eyes. She hurried to him and wrapped her arms around his neck. "Son of my heart. You will always have a place here."

Yeshua leaned down and kissed her cheek. "May Adonai Elyon bless this house and those who live here, always." He looked at them both once more then turned and walked up the steps to his disciples.

"Something is wrong," Dassa said. "I can feel it. Yeshua is grieved. I feel like he just told us good-bye. That we will not see him again." Tears streamed down Dassa's face.

"I am sure he is simply tired." Micah pulled her close, giving what comfort he could. "He teaches every day at the Temple and is questioned continually by the Pharisees and priests. It must be exhausting."

Seeing The Life

Later in the evening, Dassa heard footsteps on the stairs. She hurried over. "Do you need something? More food or wine?"

"No. I have an errand," the man said then turned and left the house.

Dassa didn't know many of the disciple's names. She knew of Cephas, Andrew, Nathaniel, Phillip, James, and John. This man was not any of them.

"Do they need anything?" Geva asked, coming to stand by Dassa.

"No, one man was just leaving." Dassa placed her arm around Geva's waist, and they went to join the rest of the family.

Chapter 27

A banging on the front door woke Joseph and Dinah. Joseph got up and pulled on a tunic. "I will go see. Jacob will have answered it by now."

"Who is it, Jacob?" Joseph asked his servant as he entered the foyer.

Micah pushed past the servant as he entered the house. He rushed to where Joseph stood near the hallway to the private rooms. "They are crucifying him. They arrested him and had a sham of a trial overnight. The High Council met and proclaimed him guilty."

"What?" Joseph yelled. "That is illegal. I was not there, and as a member I have to be there to vote."

"They voted by acclamation."

"Another illegality. What was the charge?"

"From what I was told, there was not one they could prove. Pilate declared him innocent."

"But he is being crucified? Why?"

Micah slumped against a wall. "Because the crowd cried for Yeshua to be crucified and Barabas released."

"That murderer?" Joseph was shaking with rage. To free a convicted murderer and crucify Yeshua. "You, Israel, are a stubborn and stiff-necked people."

"Joseph, I'm going to the Praetorian. I was told Yeshua was being beaten there." Micah sounded sick with grief.

"I will meet you there or at Golgotha." Joseph rubbed his face. "How can it have come to this? I knew a number of Pharisees and Sadducees, as well as many of the priests of Jerusalem, did not like Yeshua's teachings, but to murder him." Joseph fell to his knees. "I am ashamed to be connected with them. El Selich'ah, forgive me for not speaking in his defense. I should have told them how wrong they are." He swallowed. The lump in his throat hurt as it loosened.

"Amen, Joseph, amen." Micah turned away and left.

"Sir," Jacob said. He had stood off to the side. His face was white and covered with tears. "Is there anything I can do?"

"Arrange for burial clothes. Purchase the best. Wait... Go to Micah's. His wife, Dassa, weaves beautiful linens. Get them from her."

Joseph turned around to head to his room. His sons stood there. Ezra, Orli, and Abraham and James who worked in Arimethea. The emotion on their faces mirrored his. Grief, disbelief, anger, sorrow. "Go tell your families. Those of you who want to join me are welcome. Know now that I am going to be asking Pilate to release the body to me. Ezra, you will lead the Shabbat ceremony tonight. I will be defiled." Joseph's eldest son nodded. "Today will change our lives forever."

Seeing The Life

"Micah, I'm going with you. I need to find Mary." Dassa's eyes were red, her face blotchy from weeping.

"Dassa, crucifixion is the worst way to die. The Romans are masters of torture. He has been beaten and will be nailed to the cross naked. It will be painful to watch."

"I was at his birth. I will be at his death. He is the son of Adonai Elyon. I will watch Yahweh Yisrael's chosen people murder him." Steel will filled each of Dassa's words.

"All right, but I do not like it. If it gets too much for you, I will make you come home. Come then. I told Joseph I was going to the Praetorian. We will go there first." He looked at the others in the room. It tore his heart to see the anguish in every face, from the youngest child to the oldest, Eli. "Are any of you coming?"

Eli stepped forward. "Perez and I are going to see if we can find his disciples. I heard they scattered when he was arrested. We hope to hide them here if that is all right with you."

"I want to go," Ben said.

"No, it is no place for a youth like you. You stay here. With the rest of us occupied with these awful chores, it will be up to you to take the Shabbat lamb to the Temple."

"But you always to that, Abba. It is for you to do," Ben protested.

"It is an awesome responsibility. You can do this." Micah laid a hand on Ben's shoulder. He could tell his son was confused by the events of the day. Micah knew there would be many questions Ben would ask later. Questions Micah did not have answers for.

Someone knocked at the door. Geva went to answer it and brought Jacob to the courtyard where they stood.

"Master Micah, Master Joseph has asked that he purchase linen from your wife as burial clothing." The servant bowed as he spoke.

"He cannot purchase my linen," Dassa said. "I will give it to you. It is the last thing I can do for my Adonai Elohai." She left and came back with a length of finely woven, pure, white linen and a small rectangle. "High Priest Caiaphas ordered this for his wife. I will not sell it to him for all his wealth." The bitterness in her voice concerned Micah. If she held it within, her soul would suffer.

As they headed to the Praetorian, a procession was winding its way through Jerusalem. Dassa and Micah found a place along the narrow street and watched. A Centurion led the way holding a sign as a standard. It was wooden and in Latin, Greek, and Hebrew it read: King of the Jews.

Behind came a soldier; then, beaten and bloody from a scourging, came Yeshua. Bent under the weigh of the wooden beam across his shoulders, he stumbled along. On his head was a woven crown, still green from the freshly cut branches used to create it. Thorns on the branches pressed into his flesh. Rivulets of blood traced their way down his forehead into his eyes.

Dassa collapsed against Micah, her hands clutched at her mouth. "Oh my, oh my. How could they do that to

Seeing The Life

him? You can barely tell he is a man." She began weeping, her sobs tearing at Micah's heart and control.

Micah's stomach turned as he saw the ribs of Yeshua's back. The flesh was torn away, hanging in small ribbons. A piece fell away as the skin holding it to the muscle broke. He swallowed down the bile that rose in his throat.

People along the street jeered and spit. Others were weeping. One young man vomited. Micah knew just how he felt.

"Let me take you home," Micah said.

"No... I have... to... be there... for Mary." Dassa struggled to get the words out as she sobbed. They stepped into the street once the group moved past.

Three more soldiers kept the crowd from touching the condemned man. When Yeshua stumbled several times causing delays, a man on the street was hauled from the onlookers, and the wooden beam was placed on his shoulders. Yeshua walked bent over, panting. Blood and sweat dripped off his body, splashing softly on the cobbled stone of the street.

Most of those who lined the streets faded away once the spectacle passed them by. Others followed until they reached the city gate. Few went through and on to the small hill where three poles were permanently placed.

Dassa looked at the other women who had come this far. There were few. Miriam was holding another woman. Dassa hurried over.

"Mary." Dassa took her friend in her arms. The baby Mary had labored to give birth to was now being laid on the beam, his arms stretched out to either side.

One of the soldiers knelt on his arm. Another placed a six-inch spike at Yeshua's wrist. A third lifted a hammer and swung.

A cry of pain came from two people: Yeshua and Mary. With swing after swing, the soldier drove the nail into the wood and Mary to her knees as Dassa and Miriam dropped with her, their arms wrapping the grieving mother in a tight embrace.

The strident call of hammer upon spike stopped. Dassa, holding Mary's head to her breast, looked up. The soldiers were positioning Yeshua's other arm. Soon the pounding resumed. She tried not to count the strokes, but in the absence of any other sound each one imprinted itself in her mind.

Mary pulled away when the hammering quit. She leaned against Dassa and Miriam, watching as the soldiers lifted her son's crossbeam to the pole and slid it in place. Yeshua hung limp, then forced his shoulders to tighten and took a deep breath.

Dassa closed her eyes and covered her ears when the hammering began again. Yeshua's feet had been crossed over, and a spike was being driven through and into the pole he hung against.

When the metal meeting metal sound, ended Dassa looked. Yeshua, stripped of all clothing, hung dying on a Roman cross. Blood dripped from his hands and feet. She couldn't believe he still had blood to spill.

Micah laid a hand on her shoulder and Mary's. "Do you want to stay here?"

Mary nodded. She was biting her knuckle so hard blood was beginning to flow. Micah took her hand in his and held on tightly.

Two other criminals were being crucified with Yeshua. When they were hanging from their crosses, the signs listing their crimes were hung above their heads. Two signs listed the capital crimes each had committed. One sign read 'King of the Jews.'

It was the middle of the morning. The deaths would take a long time. Crucifixion was considered the most cruel execution method anyone could devise.

Those who had come to watch, peasants and leading priests, shouted insults and taunts.

"Ha! Look at you now!"

"You said you were going to destroy the Temple and rebuild it in three days. Well then, if you are the Son of God, save yourself and come down from the cross!"

A major highway passed Golgotha, so many people carrying their sacrificial lambs to the Temple looked at the men hanging on the hill. Some called mockingly, others averted their eyes or covered their children's. A few stopped and picked up stones, casting them at the one who hung in the center.

Several other women came. Dassa backed away, relinquishing her hold on Mary. She knew one was Mary's sister, Joanna; another was Mary, the wife of Cleopas. Dassa recognized few of the men. The disciple John was there. He went to Mary and said a few words to her. Then he approached Dassa and Micah.

"It is a sorry day for Israel," John said. "We did not want to believe him. I think we just ignored it because it was so terrible to hear Yeshua say it. He predicted his death. Many times he said he would be turned over to the priests and murdered. If I did not believe in him before, this would make me." He walked away to stand off to the side.

"He saved others," Saul, a young Pharisee shouted, "but he cannot save himself! So he is the King of Israel, is he? Let this Messiah, this Chosen One, this King of Israel, come down from the cross so we can see it and believe him! He trusted HaShem, so let El Shaddai rescue him now if he wants him! For he said, 'I am the Son of Elohim.'"

The soldiers mocked him too by offering him a drink of sour wine. They called out to him, "If you are the King of the Jews, save yourself!" Then they took the clothing they had stripped from Yeshua and began dividing it between them. Dassa saw the tunic she had given to Yeshua. It was stained with blood and sweat.

"This is a fine garment. Someone must have given it to him. He certainly could not afford it." One of the soldiers held it up with dirty hands. "Let us cast lots for it."

Dassa turned away, not wanting to see who won the garment she put so much love and labor into. She saw Micah speaking with Nicodemus. Dassa walked to where they stood.

"I am glad he at least refused to do that," Nicodemus said.

"What?" Dassa asked.

"When I was at the Praetorian hoping to stop this"— Nicodemus wave an impatient had toward the crosses

—"a number of the priests who forced this came to Pilate and demanded he change what it says on the sign. He refused." A sad smile pulled at Nicodemus' lips.

Mary had gone to stand below her son's cross. She gently kissed his toes then stood back, looking up at him. Blood and tears stained her face. John was standing next to her.

"Dear woman, here is your son." Yeshua then looked at John. "Here is your mother."

"You honor me, Adonai. I will care for her always," John said.

Just then one of the men hanging to Yeshua's side sneered, "So you are the Messiah, are you? Prove it by saving yourself...and us, too, while you are at it!"

The voice of the other man replied. "Do you not fear God even when you have been sentenced to die? We deserve to die for our crimes, but this man has done nothing wrong." Then he said, "Yeshua, remember me when you come into your Kingdom."

"I assure you, today you will be with me in paradise."

As noon came, the sky darkened. It wasn't cloudy, but the entire sky turned blacker than night. Joseph had arrived along with Ezra. Some of those watching became frightened and left. The Roman Centurion ordered the small fire they were cooking on be enlarged. The fire seemed dim, unable to give off its normal glow.

"What is this darkness?" Dassa asked.

"I would say Adonai Elyon is displeased, would you not?" Joseph said.

Time passed slowly. The darkness masked the passing hours. Dassa and the other women huddled around Mary giving what comfort they could as they grieved as well. The soldiers continued their games of dice in the fire light. The men wandered from where the women were to the crosses and back. Murmured words were spoken sporadically. Occasional moans came from the men on the crosses as they pressed against the pole with their feet to allow air to flow into their lungs more easily.

Yeshua cleared his throat. Everyone looked at him. The light of the Roman's fire danced along his body.

"Eloi, Eloi, why have you abandoned me?" Although called out with strength and volume, Yeshua's voice was achingly despondent.

"He is calling for Elijah," someone said.

"I thirst," Yeshua said.

A soldier picked up a stick with a sponge tied to it and soaked it in wine. He reached up and held it to Yeshua's lips.

"Wait," another man said. "Let us see whether Elijah comes to take him down!"

In the dim light, those standing nearby could see Yeshua sip wine from the sponge. With a cry of unbelievable strength, Yeshua shouted, "It is finished! Abba, I entrust my spirit into your hands!" He inhaled, then exhaled. No inhale followed.

The earth began to shake. People screamed in fear. On and on the shaking went. Cracks appeared in the rocks and ground. Stones fell from the wall behind them. Dassa clung to Micah. Everyone had gathered around Yeshua's cross when he had begun speaking. The sky began to lighten.

Seeing The Life

The Centurion was standing looking up at Yeshua's body hanging on the cross. "This man truly was the Son of GoElohim! Praise Elohay Elohim, the one true Elohay Elohim. Surely this man was innocent."

A soldier came walking up the hill a short time later. "The Pharisees who want the prophet dead asked Pilate to break the legs of the criminals. It starts Shabbat tonight. They want them dead before sundown. Pilate has ordered their legs be broken."

The soldiers who had crucified the men broke the legs of the men on either side of Yeshua.

"This one is already dead," said the Centurion.

"How can that be? He's not hung on the cross long enough."

"See for yourself."

"I will." He took his spear and stabbed it into Yeshua's side. There was no jerk of pain, not sound; only blood and water flowed down the spear then out onto the ground when the weapon was pulled from the body's side.

Joseph came to stand beside Micah and Dassa. John came over too. "I must go speak to Pilate. I will ask for the release of his body."

"You are a relative of his mother?" John asked.

"Yes."

"Joseph, will you take Dassa home? I will wait for you here and help. John, you can bring Mary to our home too." Micah lowered his voice and leaned close to John. "My sons are looking for the other disciples. It might be dangerous for you all to be out and around the city now."

"Thank you. I will see what she wants to do. Her sister and Miriam are with her."

"We have plenty of room. Mary is familiar with the family and house," Dassa said. "We will prepare food and places to sleep."

John spoke with Mary. The other women came with her and John to where Dassa stood. "They want to stay and see where the tomb is."

"Joseph, I will stay with Micah. Our servants should be here shortly with the myrrh and aloe ointments," Nicodemus said.

"Jacob has the linen."

"I will see you all at home later," Micah said to Dassa. "Do not wait Shabbat for me. I will be defiled. It is the last I can do for him."

"The last any of us can," Nicodemus said. He turned and looked once more at the cross. In a quite voice he read, "King of the Jews."

Chapter 28

Dassa walked beside Joseph. There was evidence of the earthquake everywhere. Collapsed houses, roofs, pillars. People were moving in all directions, shouting, crying, pushing. As they went deeper into the city, Joseph wrapped an arm around her.

"I will make sure you get home safely. Do you have enough food and water? If Eli and Perez have found any of the disciples, you may end up with many. Some have families. They may come as well."

"Before we left, my sons' wives and children were going to fetch water and food. Our servants, Nissa and Moshe, too. I will see how well stocked they are. We can start making bread. At least it came be made quickly. No yeast, so no rising time."

"If you do not have enough, send Moshe to my home. We will send supplies to you."

"Thank you, Joseph." They stopped as people and animals came from the opposite direction, filling the street. Dassa and Joseph pressed back against the wall, allowing them to pass. When they began walking again, Dassa asked, "Joseph, I know he was the Son of Elohim. I know Mary was a virgin when she gave birth. I know he was the Messiah. How could El-Elyon allow him to be killed?"

"I do not know. The prophecies say the Messiah will free his people. He cannot do that if he is dead. Someday soon I would like to come and study the scrolls Micah has kept more. Maybe between those and the Tanakh we can figure it out."

They arrived at the house, and Joseph left on his grim errand. Dassa entered and found Geva and Rachel wide-eyed with fear. Ben ran to his mother.

"Ima, it tore. I saw it. From the top down all the way to the bottom."

"What tore?"

"The veil hiding the Holy of Holies. When the earthquake happened, I was nearly to the altar with the lamb. It was so dark. They had lit torches throughout the Temple. Then the light came back. When the earth shook, people started running. They were screaming. I could not move. I was facing the Holy of Holies. Suddenly the veil began to tear apart. I could not take my eyes from it. It seemed as if hands just pulled it apart. Like you do when you tear your linen. You know how thick that veil is. How could it do that?"

"I... I do not know. What happened then?" Dassa was stunned. She had never been close to the veil or the Holy of Holies. Only the men were allowed in the courtyard with the altar. She knew fabric and embroidery, though.

Seeing The Life

No human hand or hands could tear that heavy, thick fabric.

"The wind was blowing, and each half of the veil waved into the Holy of Holies, allowing us to see in. One side caught on something and stayed open. Several priests ran in to try and pull it closed, but whatever it was caught on was too high for them to reach."

Only the High Priest on Yom Kippur could pass the veil into the Holy of Holies offering the sacrifice for the sins of the people. If it was accepted, the High Priest would emerge. If not, HaShem would strike him dead.

Dassa understood now why her daughters-in-law were wide-eyed.

Joseph made his way to Pilate and requested an audience. He waited for a while in an anteroom. When he was led to Pilate, Joseph bowed. "Prefect, I come to request the body of Yeshua the Nazarene. He has died. With the Shabbat tonight, he needs to be buried before sundown."

"It has not been long enough for him to have died," Pilate said.

"The man you sent to break the legs of the men can confirm. Yeshua was dead before he arrived."

"Oh yes, those Jewish leaders of yours hounded me to hasten their deaths because of your festival," Pilate complained then turned and shouted, "Marcus!" When a soldier appeared in the doorway, Pilate addressed him. "Go and confirm whether those crucified have died. Be quick about it."

"Thank you, Prefect."

"I just want this entire episode behind me. The Sanhedrin kept me awake last night. Then they nearly caused a riot when I said the man was innocent. Now they want him dead before nightfall. What will they want next?" Pilate looked at Joseph, who was at a loss for words. "Were you with them last night?" Pilate eyed Joseph suspiciously.

"No, Prefect, I did not hear about any of it until the morning."

"How are you related to that man? Only a relative can claim a body."

"I'm an uncle of his mother. I have her permission to receive him."

"Good. You can claim him and be on your way." Pilate called a scribe and dictated. When the scribe had finished writing, Pilate signed the papyrus and pressed his seal into melted wax.

"Sir." Marcus had returned. "The Centurion and the soldier you sent to break the legs both confirm Yeshua of Nazareth is dead. So are the other two. Their legs were broken, but the King of the Jews's were not."

Joseph then remembered a passage in Psalms. *He protects all his bones; not one of them is broken.* Was this another prophecy fulfilled?

"Here is your release. I hope this is the last I hear of this King of the Jews." Pilate handed the papyrus to Joseph and turned away.

Joseph followed Marcus out of the Pretorian on his way back to Golgotha.

Seeing The Life

Micah watched the guards move around, taking the bodies of the two criminals down. They would be burned with the refuse. A cart was pulled up the hill. Micah recognized Joseph's servant Jacob.

"Master Micah, I have taken the linen and spices to the tomb. Master Joseph wants the body placed in the cart to be moved."

"He is not back yet. We cannot take him until Pilate gives the release."

Jacob nodded.

John was standing with Mary, Joanna, and Miriam of Magdala. Another Mary, whom Micah didn't know, also stood with them. A shout was heard, and they all looked to see Joseph coming up the hill. He lifted his arm with the paper, showing he had the permission to release Yeshua's body.

John went to the Centurion. "Joseph comes. He has the release. May we take down the body now?"

"Yes. This is a crucifixion that will long be remembered. I do not understand, but I know he is the Messiah." The Centurion signaled to his soldiers, who set a ladder against the pole and began lowering the crossbar after the spike in Yeshua's feet had been removed.

John nodded and went back to stand with the women. Micah saw him place his arm around Mary's shoulder, giving what comfort he could.

The body of the man they had worshiped was gently laid in the cart. Micah picked up the handles. He would push it to the tomb. He knew the tomb was unused. Joseph had commissioned it to be carved from the soft limestone that lay beneath the firmer type that was the foundation of the city.

Jacob had brought a torch he had lit on the fire the soldiers had built on Golgotha. He led the way into the tomb. Micah, Nicodemus, and Joseph carried Yeshua in. Linen strips were waiting with the jars of ointment nearby. Joseph had asked John to keep the women out. They could come another day to anoint the body again.

Yeshua was laid upon the platform. They carefully washed the blood away. Jacob had brought a brush. Joseph rinsed then brushed Yeshua's hair and beard. Micah helped Jacob bring the jars of myrrh and aloe over, and the men dipped their hands in and anointed the body. Then they began wrapping Yeshua in the linen, placing spices within the layers. No one spoke. No one paid attention to the tears on the other men's faces. Now was a time for grief.

Chapter 29

On Shabbat, no cooking was to be done, but Dassa, Geva, and Rachel broke the law. They had not prepared food for the number of people who now needed to eat. Dassa's life at her parent's inn served her well. She knew how to cook for a large crowd. The meals were simple — porridge and lentil stew with dried fruit and bread.

Along with John, Mary, and the other women, Eli and Perez had been able to locate Cephas; James, John's brother; Thomas; Andrew; Phillip; and Bartholomew. They would search for others in the evening when Shabbat was over.

"Cephas is very troubled," Micah said to Dassa. He had taken food up to the disciples, who were staying in the upstairs room. "It is more than grief. It is guilt over something. I do not know what the cause is, but guilt is there. He sits rocking, holding his knees close to his chest. John said he only mumbles as he weeps."

"Do you think he is going mad? Will he do something to hurt himself?" Dassa asked.

"I do not know. I will wander in and out checking on various things and watching him. John and the others are concerned also."

When evening came and Shabbat was over, Mary and Miriam, escorted by James, went out and came back with spices so they could go and anoint Yeshua's body again. Eli and Perez went out too. They were searching for the other disciples. As night fell, there was intermittent knocking as those who had followed Yeshua so closely for nearly three years arrived at Micah's door.

Eli and Perez came home. They had news. Judas, the disciple who had betrayed Yeshua, had hanged himself. They heard he had thrown the thirty pieces of silver he had received into the Temple and run away before any could stop him.

It was three days since Yeshua had been crucified. Joseph was keeping the warehouse closed for several days. Business could wait. Micah and Dassa stayed in bed later than usual. No one for either household wanted to face the day. Pounding on the house door woke them. By the time they were dressed, the commotion had moved into the house.

Miriam was breathing heavily. Her voice was shaking as she said over and over, "I have seen Adonia. He has risen." She described how they had found the tomb unsealed and the huge stone rolled away.

"But there was a crevasse we rolled it into. It would have taken many men to move it." Micah was stunned by what he was hearing.

Mary, James's mother, was saying the same thing. "He has risen. He told us to tell you, and we are not to be afraid. He said to tell his brothers, including Cephas, to go to Galilee and wait for him there."

While the men were declaring their disbelief, Cephas and John ran from the house.

"How can this be?" James asked. The disciples dismissed their news as the wishful ravings of weak-minded women.

"Do you not remember?" Miriam said. "He told us he would be betrayed and turned over to sinful men, crucified, and rise again on the third day. The angels we saw in the tomb reminded us of it." Her words did not convince them. Dassa could understand the women's frustration.

John returned later saying the tomb was indeed empty. He and Cephas had gone into the tomb. The linen wrappings were there. The cloth used on his face was folded and lying away from the platform. "Cephas said for me to come back and tell you. He stayed behind." John's excitement now mirrored that of Miriam and James's mother, Mary.

Yeshua's mother, Mary, began weeping. Dassa took her into the bedroom. "Mary, do you think this is true?"

"I do not know. I do not believe they would lie or mistake the tomb where they laid him."

"Are your other sons here for Pesach?"

"Yes"

"Do you know where they are?" Dassa felt the need to find and tell them. If it was true, they needed to know.

"They camped in our usual place. I do not know if they are still there."

Micah came in. "Mary, I need to go find Ya'aqov and your other sons. They need to know what has happened."

"We were just speaking of that," Dassa said. "They camped in their usual spot."

"I will go. Eli is going to tell Joseph. Perez is going to find out what the Chief Priests and Pharisees are saying. They cannot be pleased with this news."

"Do you think they know about it?" Dassa asked.

"If they do not yet, they will soon. I know they had Pilate post guards around the tomb. If they let someone steal the body, their lives would be forfeit."

"Micah, please, go find my sons." Mary gripped him on the arm. "I fear they will be taken since they are his brothers."

Micah pulled Mary into a hug. "I will find them and bring them. You can prepare to go back to Nazareth from here. You will be safe there."

Mary turned to Dassa and lifted her hand to her chest. "I know Yeshua has risen. I feel it in my heart. I will see him soon. I lost my faith that he was the son of Elohim when I saw him die. Now I know he told the truth when he said he and the Abba are one."

Dassa saw the change that had taken place in her friend. The weeping woman who had grieved so over her son's death was replaced by one with joy and peace shining from her countenance. Dassa prayed Mary was right. She hoped with her entire being. Those who had gone to the tomb had all come back saying it was empty. The women claimed to have seen him, spoken to him.

What did all this mean? Was the resurrected Yeshua going to free Israel from Roman occupation like Micah

Seeing The Life

and Joseph thought? If he could rise from death, Yeshua was powerful enough to slay every Roman in the world.

Mary went to speak with the others. Dassa stayed in her room. There was a small window, just large enough to let a little light in. She stood by it and gazed out, sorting through her memories of what Yeshua had said. Never had he spoken about overthrowing Rome.

His kingdom was not of this world. His kingdom was HaShem's. The kingdom of Elohim is what he said to seek. Then they would receive his righteousness.

Believe in the son and receive the gift of eternal life. Forgive as you have been forgiven.

They had been weeping and mourning over Yeshua's death, the cruel beatings, the betrayal. Now they had hope. Dassa had seen the change in Mary. In an instant when she believed Yeshua had risen from the grave, her grief had been turned to joy. The words Yeshua had spoken were true.

Yeshua had not come with news of overthrowing the oppressive government. He had come telling of the need for repentance from sin. John the Baptist had declared the coming of the Lamb of Elohim, who would take away the sins of the world.

The Lamb of Elohim. The lamb sacrificed at Pesach. *Everyone rejects God; they are all morally corrupt. None of them does what is right, not even one!* One after another, verses of the Tanakh she and Micah had read and discussed over the years rushed through Dassa's mind.

Elohim had created man for a relationship, for someone to lavish his love on. Adam and Eve had broken the bond, bringing sin. He had sent prophet after prophet telling of Adonai's desire that people turn from their sin. He had set up the sacrifices as a payment for the sin. A blood sacrifice.

"The life is in the blood." Yeshua's innocent blood had been spilled just like the lamb's on the altar. A blood sacrifice to cover sin. Dassa fell to her knees, her head in her hands. Her sin. Yeshua had taken on her sins and received the punishment that should have been hers. That is why he had died. Not only her sin, but that of anyone who believed in him.

Now Yeshua's body was gone. The women who had gone to the tomb said they had seen him. John said the tomb was empty. Yeshua had said he would rise on the third day. The sign of Jonah.

Joy, starting in her heart, surged into every part of her body. Now Dassa knew Yeshua had risen from death. His death had been the final sacrifice. The last barrier between Elohay Elohim and his creation. That was why the veil had torn.

Voices raised in excitement caused Dassa to rise and leave her room. When she reached the bottom of the stairs, she saw Cephas. Micah was standing beside him. Both were smiling.

"I have see him. He lives," Cephas was saying over and over. "Yeshua has forgiven my denial. Any who ask that his blood be the covering for their sin will be forgiven and are part of Yeshua's kingdom."

📖 📖 📖

The rest of the day was a mix of jubilation and activity. Micah had not found Yeshua's brothers. Those he spoke to said they had left Jerusalem, heading north once they heard the news about the empty tomb. They were afraid the Sanhedrin would come after them next. Their mother, they knew, was safe with John, who could garner help from Micah and possibly Joseph. They would return to Galilee and wait for John to either bring Mary home or another disciple come to them.

The news was spreading through the city and surrounding countryside. Micah locked the front door and had the eleven men go to the upper room and bar the door. Today was not the day any of them should be seen outside. Once evening came, Thomas left, sent on an errand for the group. Meals were delivered to the disciples upstairs and eaten by the family and others in the courtyard.

When the rest of the household and guests had been settled for the night, Dassa, Micah, and Mary sat in the kitchen near the fading fire. They had been talking about the day, trying to figure out what to do next. Mary would be going with John and the rest of the disciples to Galilee; Miriam also.

Micah wanted to travel with them, hoping to for a chance to see the risen Lord. Dassa also wanted to go. They both knew others of the family would also want the chance. The desire to be able to speak to Yeshua and ask his forgiveness for their sin, to worship, and possibly touch, again, that much-loved face burned in their hearts.

"Peace be with you."

The voice startled them from their revery. Gasps burst from all three sets of lips. Standing in the doorway to the courtyard stood Yeshua.

"Yeshua, my son." Mary jumped up and ran to embrace him. "I knew I would see you again when I heard the tomb was empty."

Yeshua wrapped her in his arms. Micah and Dassa stood and watched as Mary wept on his shoulder.

"Dod, Doda, you have been a faithful presence my entire life. I am pleased to have you as part of my kingdom." Yeshua looked at each individually. "Thank you for your service to my mother and my disciples."

"How could we do other? You are Adonia and our Salvation." Micah's voice shook as he spoke.

"Do not cry, Doda. I know your heart. You are forgiven and accepted." Yeshua held out his arm to Dassa. She ran to him and wept. Then she knelt before him, bending down to kiss his feet.

"Oh, Yeshua, your feet. The scars." Dassa looked up.

"My hands, feet, and side show the payment is complete for the sins of mankind." Yeshua opened his hands to show the scars where the spikes had pierced through.

Dassa stroked the scar on his foot softly. It was circular with a jagged edge. The center was blood red. Then she straightened and taking his hands, kissed each scar.

"Adonai," Micah said, "what would you have us do now? Anything you ask we will do."

"Allow my disciples to stay until I come to them again. They will then go to Galilee. Mary, my ima, will go with them. They will take word to my brothers." Yeshua paused and looked at his mother. "They are safely on their way to Nazareth."

Seeing The Life

"Anything else, Adonai? It seems so little," Micah said.

"When the eleven return to Jerusalem, welcome them and listen to them. When the Ruach Ha-Melitz comes, you will know what to do."

"Yes, Adonai Elohai. We will."

Yeshua handed Mary and Dassa over to Micah. Then he said, "Bless you," and faded until he was gone.

Chapter 30

Life seemed to go on the same and yet was entirely different. When the Pesach week was over, people began leaving Jerusalem. The streets became less crowded. The Temple guards quit scouring the city when they didn't find any of the disciples or Yeshua's brothers. Since no one caused any trouble, the Chief Priests had begun to fear Pilate would object to the continued search.

Conflicting tales flew through the city. Cleopas had come back from Emmaus saying he and his friend, Daniel, had spoken and eaten with the risen Messiah the same day he had risen. Yeshua had explained the Tanakh and how everything written had been about him. They hadn't realized it until they were at a meal and he blessed and broke the bread. Then he had disappeared. Others claimed it was all lies.

The Eleven stayed in the upper room, spending most of their time in prayer. Other than the disciples, the only guests remaining in the house were Mary mother of Yeshua and Miriam. Joseph had opened the warehouse, so Micah, Eli, and Perez had gone back to work. Ben had gone also to continue to train as a scribe.

"What shall we do with the weapons we have?" Orli asked one day. "Our view of Yeshua's plan was vastly in error."

"You are right," Joseph said. "They may be needed someday though. Those who believe in the Messiah may have problems with those Jews who reject him. They have been saying his body was stolen."

"I have heard the Sanhedrin bribed the guards at the tomb to lie and say that," Perez said.

"Are not those set to guard something and fail put to death by the Romans? These guards failed to keep Yeshua in the tomb." This time it was Eli who spoke.

"Money can be used to put someone to death or keep them from it," Ezra commented.

"True. Sad, but true."

"Can you believe it? His disciples had to have stolen the body. What else could have happened?" Uria laid more reeds into the trough of water.

"Yeshua had predicted he would die and rise back to life on the third day." Dassa had arrived at her friend's house in the early afternoon. It was actually Uria's week to come to Dassa's, but not wanting the Eleven to be compromised, she had come to her old neighborhood instead.

"Just how can anyone rise from the dead? I tend to believe with those Sadducees. There is nothing after we die."

"Oh Uria, the Tanakh has many passages which speak of it."

"Name one," Uria challenged.

"David talked about going to the child of Bathsheba who had died."

"Well, yes. But I still do not think someone can be raised from the dead."

"What about Yeshua raising Lazarus? He was dead and in the grave. He is now living."

"I heard about it. Some people are saying they are lying." Uria dismissed Dassa with a wave of her hand.

"You are calling me a liar?"

"What? No, of course not."

"I was there. I saw it happen. Lazarus was dead. Then he walked out of the grave, and Yeshua did it." Dassa spoke seriously; then a grin broke out on her face. "Actually, it was funny how he was walking all wrapped up in the linen strips. We didn't laugh, though. Everyone was so startled when he came out. Then we were so delighted and thankful. The men wrapped a cloak around him and hustled him to the house for clothes."

Both women giggled. Uria fell silent.

"Dassa, how can it happen? I just do not understand. They killed him and now his body is gone. The leaders of the Temple and the Sanhedrin said he was calling himself Adonai and king."

"I do not understand it either, how it all happened. I do know Yeshua was innocent of any wrong doing his entire life. He certainly did nothing that warranted him being crucified. He fulfilled what the prophets said in so many ways. Micah has studied and told me of so many."

Dassa looked her friend directly in the eyes. "Uria, do you really need to understand the how and why? Isaiah says, *'For as heaven is higher than earth, so My ways are higher than your ways, and My thoughts than your thoughts.'* HaShem says in Job, *'Where were you when I laid the foundation of the earth?'* We answer to El Shaddai. He does not answer to us."

"You are right. I know you are, but... I am so confused. What should I do?"

"Pray for understanding. Yeshua said to repent and be saved. To seek his kingdom first and all righteousness will be given."

"You believe Yeshua is the Messiah, don't you?"

"Yes, Uria, with all my heart."

Micah and his sons had just returned home from work when the door to the upper room opened and Cephas and John came running down the steps.

"We have seen him again."

"Yeshua was just here."

"Thomas now believes."

"We are to go to Galilee and wait for him there."

They were talking over each other in their excitement. The other disciples came down more slowly, laughing at the pair.

Micah clasped John by the arm. The tall man had tripped over his feet and nearly fallen. "Do you have everything you need for your journey?"

"Yes, you have been most generous," Cephas said.

"Not just us. Joseph and his family as well as Nicodemus and Lazarus have contributed greatly."

Seeing The Life

"Would it be an imposition for Ben and I to travel with you?" Eli asked. "I need to go to Capernaum on business for Joseph and Ben, well, he just needs to get out from underfoot."

Everyone laughed.

"Of course," Cephas said.

"He just wants a chance to see the risen Messiah, Cephas," Ben said. Then he blushed. "Me too."

They set out early the next morning in twos and threes. There was no need to attract attention by leaving in a large group. They would meet up in the evening to camp by the road then travel on together.

Dassa hugged each of the Eleven, the Marys, and then her sons. "El Shaddai go with you and bless your every step."

When the last small group left, Micah laid his hand on his wife's shoulder. "They will be back. All of them."

"I know. I will miss them all. Seeing Yeshua that night... Since then I have had a special feeling for those eleven men. I liked them before, but now... There is a love. I think it is what loving a brother, or a bunch of brothers, would be like. With all their faults, and although we do not share blood ties, they are my brothers."

"I know. I feel the same, and I know what having and loving brothers feels like. But this is more. I think it is the bond through Yeshua that makes the difference."

[Aω] [Aω] [Aω]

Almost daily over the next few weeks news came from Galilee. People other than the Eleven had seen

Yeshua. It was said more than five hundred had seen him with his disciples on a mountain. Many were believing in Galilee, Judea, and Jerusalem that Yeshua was the Messiah. Others commented with scorn, saying only fools believed.

One day Dassa answered the door and stepped back in shock. Then she gave a small chuckle and said, "Ya'aqov, you look so much like your brother. I thought you were Yeshua come again to see me. Come in."

"You have seen him?" Ya'aqov asked.

"Yes, while the Eleven and your ima were still here."

"He came to me, Doda. He asked me if I believed. Doda, I could do nothing but weep. He is my brother, and I did not believe in what he was doing. I did not see. Yeshua asked again if I now believed. I confessed that I did and always would. I told him I was not a brother to him but a slave." Ya'aqov was weeping as he told Dassa about his encounter. She led him into the courtyard, brought him wine, and washed his feet while he composed himself.

"What did he say then?" Dassa asked when she sat next to him on a bench.

"Yeshua told me my sins were forgiven and that he had plans for my service for him. He said to come to Jerusalem and stay. All would be revealed, and I would understand when the time was right." Ya'aqov's eyes cleared, and he looked at Dassa. "Then he whispered in my ear to give Doda my love."

Dassa gasped then slapped Ya'aqov on the shoulder. "You always were a great storyteller. I should never believe what you say."

Ya'aqov laughed. "You are right. He did not say that, but I know he does. He did say to come to you and Dod, that I would be welcome here."

Dassa gave him a hug. "Of course you are, always."

The Eleven came back to Jerusalem, either alone or in small groups. Each stopped at Micah and Dassa's, but not all stayed with them.

It forty days since Yeshua resurrected. It was bright and sunny. The air was warm. A light breeze kept it from becoming too hot. It had been forty days since the day the tomb was found empty. Dassa, Micah, and their family, and Joseph and his family were following the crowd going to Mount Olivet. Yeshua had told the Eleven to come to him there.

Yeshua stood on the top of the mountain. His robe was pure white. It ruffled in the breeze. When he began to speak, the breeze died down. Everyone was silent, listening to the Messiah's words. White clouds fluttered across the sky.

Yeshua raised his hands and looked at his Eleven. "Do not leave Jerusalem until Adonai Eloheikhem sends you what he promised. When the Ruach Ha-Melitz has come upon you, you will receive power. You will tell people about me everywhere—in Jerusalem, throughout Judea, in Samaria, and to the ends of the earth."

He looked over the entire crowd. Later all said he had looked them straight in the eye.

"All authority in heaven and on earth has been given to me. Therefore go and make disciples of all nations, baptizing them in the name of the Abba and the Son and the Ruach Ha-Melitz, teaching them to obey everything I have commanded you. And remember, I am with you always, to the end of the age."

The white of his robe became whiter still. The breeze blew softly. The people held their breath as Yeshua, his arms outstretched as if to hold the entire world, rose into the sky and disappeared into a cloud.

Epilogue

Approximately Three Years Later

Pesach was over. Since Yeshua's death and resurrection, appreciation of the meanings of each element and each cup of wine grew within the hearts of the members of Micah and Dassa's household. Joys and sorrows had filed the years. Persecution of believers of Yeshua as the Messiah, disagreements over ways to worship and with the Jews who rejected Yeshua. More and more people, both Jews and Gentiles, became believers.

Micah, Dassa, their sons and wives, and grandchildren, were gathered in the courtyard. The family was praying for direction. Should they stay? Should they go?

Joseph and family had moved to Britannia, leaving Micah in charge of the business in Jerusalem. The business sites around Israel had slowly been closed or sold. A letter had come recently asking Micah and his family to sell off what was left and move his family to Britain. There was little Roman persecution of Christians there. Joseph had expressed his fears for the safety of Jerusalem.

With tensions growing between the Jews and Christians as well as with the Roman occupiers, Jerusalem was set to erupt at any moment. Now was the time to decide. Ben had brought the letter from the warehouse. Micah was titular head of the business, but the majority of the work was done by his sons and grandsons.

"Ruach Ha-Melitz, we await your guidance. We will gladly obey what El-Elyon wills for us. We will worship you as we have since the death and resurrection of our Adonai Yeshua. We only want to know your plan for us. Make it clear, we ask you, in the name of our Adonai Yeshua. Amen."

A chorus of murmured "amens" followed. They sat in silence, some in prayer, others thinking of leaving the Promised Land forever. Dassa squeezed Micah's hand. The young women picked up the small children and infants and carried them away to settle for the night.

Knocking on the front door caused all those in the courtyard to turn their heads.

"Who comes now?" Dassa asked as Benjamin went to find out.

He was soon back, guiding a man into the courtyard. The stranger was dressed in physicians robes.

Seeing The Life

"Pardon my coming so late in the evening. My name is Luke. I have been told you have scrolls containing much of what Yeshua the Messiah did while he lived."

If you enjoyed Seeing The Life please take a moment to review it on Amazon. As an independently publishing author having readers post reviews is extremely valuable. You few words can help me gain credibility as an author. Thank you.

CPSIA information can be obtained at www.ICGtesting.com
Printed in the USA
LVOW01s2342200514

386633LV00008B/14/P